NED

David Sgalambro

Edited by: J. Ellington Ashton Staff
Cover Art by: Michael Fisher

J. Ellington Ashton Press

http://jellingtonashton.com/
Copyright.

David Sgalambro

This book is dedicated to my mother Grace. Thank you for your endless support and especially your love.

Chapter 1

Deep within the gritty district known as downtown, the slow moving wheels of a rusty old shopping cart discharge a faint squeaking sound, as it trenches across a snow covered sidewalk. The force behind the forward motion is a heartbroken homeless man, who pushes and guards what's left of his life's possessions within the steel apparatus. He once was a successful man of great pride and dignity; a series of unfortunate and life-altering tragedies has changed his life forever. He is now just a minor part of human existence.

Hopelessly, he slowly walks around the city, his hunched over appearance conceals the fact that he actually stands over six feet tall. His long gray hair matches a beard that falls far below his chin. The clothing he has is a collection of dumpster finds. A thick gray tweed overcoat and black woolen hat is his lone protection against the harsh cold of the winter months.

The years spent as a vagrant, mindlessly roaming New York City's streets and avenues have left him with a tormented soul. He has been challenged with a slew of detriment, never knowing what type of danger lies ahead as he now lives in an underworld of urban contamination. He has become wary of humanity and survival has become his sole purpose.

A corner in Greenwich Village has, over the passing months, become an oasis of salvation to him. He has experienced peaceful solitude here, and the people he has encountered have treated him with kindness. Nobody has threatened to evict him or call the police. He now travels to this spot every day, seeking out the non-threatening environment, and if somehow possible, a sense of normalcy.

***

With both hands still tightly gripped on the shopping cart's horizontal bar, he continued pushing his belongings along today's journey. The turning wheels rang out their usual squeaky sound while forming a path along the slushy snow. He was within a few blocks of his beloved corner, when he stopped upon the sight of a desolate city park. The concrete foundation was still covered with several inches of untouched snow. The flawless purity of the park was a beautiful sight to the man's eyes. The absence of people over the last few days had allowed the snow to remain unblemished, clean and pristine.

As he stared at the immaculate vision, his mind wandered back to the summer months, when he spent hour's just watching young people playing and laughing in their recreation. He recalled a small group of teenagers playing an enthusiastic and rigorous game of baseball. Both teams were playing as if it was the final inning of the World Series. There were several people hanging on the outside of the fence, cheering their own team on as the score pivoted back and forth. The memory of that day made the homeless man smile beneath his long gray beard. His memories continued as he recalled the winning hit; a long soaring fly ball over the centerfielders head. The team erupted in joy and bedlam. His smile lingered on for a moment. He glanced down and his eyes began to follow along the bottom of the chain link fence. He was suddenly surprised when he noticed on the other side a round object, protruding out from under the snow. He took a few steps forward and then bent down to get a closer look. His eyes grew wide as he identified it as a baseball. He pushed his fingers through the fence, trying to grab the round object, but the trapped ball kept spinning within the ice. Determined, he then used both hands, lifted up the bottom of the flexible steel, and nabbed it. As he brought the ball close to his face, he noted that the once white leather was extremely soiled and some of the lacings were broken.

He held the ball in his hands and began to reminisce back to his childhood. His mind went through a procession of thoughts. His first remembrance was throwing a baseball back and forth with his dad, a young boy having a great time with his father. He recounted both of them exchanging smiles and laughter. His talents had gradually progressed, leading to his next memory of playing on the neighborhood Little League team, where he was chosen to be the pitcher. Next came his high school years, where he dominated the district and won MVP, which led to a college scholarship that paved the way for his higher education.

He gripped the dirty ball tighter as his mind raced forward, where he saw himself as an adult reliving the same completive cycle once again. He pictured himself in a park throwing a baseball back and forth with his...

"Hey man, get the fuck out of our way," said a young man in a loud threatening voice that suddenly broke the homeless man's

2

concentration.

The homeless man was immediately brought back to reality when he saw three young men standing in front of him. He stared silently with confusion, not knowing what the individuals wanted, but based on what was just said, it was quite obvious they were foes not friends. His eyes quickly bounced between the three strangers as he began to size them up, guessing the three of them were somewhere in their early twenties.

The young man who spoken the threatening line was taller than the others, and seemed to be the one in control. He had long blonde hair that was pulled back in a ponytail, along with a mean and serious look on his face. The next man, slightly smaller with a black crew cut, was holding a large stick. Last was a short but stocky individual with a shaved head, and by the look in his eyes, he seemed to be the craziest out of the three. The man also noticed they all had one thing in common; they were all wearing black leather motorcycle jackets, as if they might be affiliated with some gang.

"This is our neighborhood and we don't like people like you polluting it," said the tall blonde leader.

The man remained still and silent as his eyes continued to pivot back and forth between the three young men.

"What the fuck are you looking at? The short bald thug said, trying to immediately prove his masculinity.

"Yeah, are you looking for trouble old man? Because if you are, you've come to the right place," said the dark haired one, as he took his stick and began gently tapping it against the shopping cart.

The homeless man tossed the baseball into the cart, quickly grabbed the horizontal bar with both hands, and tried to make an attempt to leave. He pushed the shopping cart just a few inches, when the short bald guy reached out and quickly grabbed a hold of it.

"Not so fast, motherfucker," he said, with an evil grin.

"Yeah, where the fuck do you think you're going?" The dark haired one said, as he started to drag his stick back and forth against the side of the cart, causing a thumping sound.

"We would like a word with you, if you don't mind," said the blonde leader in a faux polite manner.

The homeless man remained silent as he kept both hands wrapped tightly around the shopping cart's bar and made another attempt to flee the situation. The bald thug quickly terminated his advances by forcefully grabbing hold of the rusty metal cart. Shaved head shook the cart wildly, causing all the contents within the steel metal cage to topple upon each other. The homeless man looked down and then back up,

3

staring into the young man's crazy eyes with a newly reformed hatred.

"Listen, I don't like you," said the tall blonde leader, trying to return the man's attention to him.

He continued by saying, "I don't like the sight of you, I don't like the smell of you and I definitely don't like the thought of you wandering around my neighborhood. In my eyes, you're a worthless piece of shit that doesn't deserve to breathe, let alone live."

The leaders' final words gathered the homeless man's full attention upon him. He looked him directly in the eyes and suddenly felt a deep feeling of anger. He let go of the shopping carts handle and began to mentally prepare himself for what was about to happen. His resentful eyes continued to pivot back and forth among the three threatening individuals.

He was now waiting for one of them to actually make a move. He stood before them as his once hunched over body began to slowly rise, causing all three of the young men a feeling of surprised intimidation. As the homeless man was now standing in a straight vertical position, they suddenly realized how tall he was, causing the blonde leader to think fast, realizing the shoe might now be on the other foot.

"Listen, you don't scare me, I'll cut your fucking ass right down to my size," said the now desperate leader, as he began to reach into his back pocket for his weapon.

The homeless man had to make a quick decision to save himself from the current conflict. In one last attempt, his hand disappeared from everyone's sight as it began to dig into his coat's inner pocket. His fingers fumbled at first, but eventually grabbed the top of the solid object that lay hidden within. Upon his grasp, he immediately heard the imaginary and familiar voice that he relies on, when any pretentious situations arise.

"Look out! He's reaching for something!" The dark haired one shouted.

The leader stopped and looked back into the homeless man's now angry eyes, while the short, bald thug quickly released his grip on the cart and took a few steps back in fright. The dark-haired individual tightened his grip on his stick but remained at a safe distance, as he too became very cautious not to make any sudden advances. All three men realized that the homeless man wasn't going to back down as his hidden hand continued reaching for something the gang of thugs assumed he would defend himself with.

The leader stood his ground and remained staring into the homeless man's eyes, but the other two turned and looked at each other.

4

They both quickly identified the fear they felt within themselves, but tried desperately to hide it. The blonde leader, using some common sense for the safety of his comrades, changed his mind and brought forth an empty hand but a pointing finger.

The leader shouted out trying desperately to hold onto his dictatorship: "Listen, you've got sixty seconds to get the fuck out of here or there will be trouble! It's not just the three of us that patrol this neighborhood; there are many of us that want filth like you gone. I'm not fucking around; I want your fucking ass out of here now!"

The homeless man continued to keep his grip tightly on the hidden object deep within his coat. He watched as the three young men suddenly turned and began to walk away from him. As they continued strutting side by side, he once again took notice of their black leather jackets. When the three were about half way up the block, the blonde leader stopped, turned and motioned with his arm for him to leave.

He stood there with his feet planted deep within the snow as he watched the three hoodlums trek through the icy slush until they finally reached the far corner. Two of the individuals turned and disappeared from his sight, but the blonde leader stopped, looked back and repeated the same arm gesture telling him to leave the neighborhood.

The homeless man continued his long and defiant stare up the block with his grip remaining relentless upon the hidden object. The leader stood and stared back at the man for just a few more seconds before he turned and also disappeared from his sight. The man finally felt relief as he slowly and calmly released his tension.

He took a deep breath of the ice cold air and then slowly exhaled. His warm breath colliding with winter's chill, formed a cloud of stream that surrounded his long gray beard. He noticed that his hand was still shaking deep within his coat. He pulled it out slowly and shook it a few times, trying to bring some circulation back.

He turned his head and looked at the serene, desolate park one more time. For a slight moment, the sun appeared through the dark gray clouds that hovered over the day. The sun's warm and bright reflection made the icy park glisten like a sea of diamonds. He stared at the beautiful sparkle which brought about another smile to his face. He then turned his eyes back to the baseball he had previously thrown into the shopping cart. He picked it up and tossed the ball ever so lightly into the air. The wet soiled leather of the ball caught the reflecting rays of the sun. The ball momentarily lost its grimy appearance and transformed into a shining star. He reached out and caught the descending ball with one hand and placed it gently back into the rusty steel compound of the cart.

As quickly as the sun had appeared, with equal suddenness, it migrated back behind the gray clouds. A brief moment of sadness fell upon the man before he slowly bent down and placed his hands back on the cart's cold steel handle. Step by step, he began to push his shopping cart back up the block along the snow covered sidewalk. The squeaking sounds of the wheels returned, as they once again trenched their way through the white slush.

As the man approached the corner, he cautiously stopped, not knowing what might be lying around the bend, especially after his encounter with the gang of thugs. His hand instinctively disappeared back into his coat grabbing the top of the object, once again seeking its protection. As he slowly peeked past the building's concrete structure, his eyes began looking specifically for people wearing black leather jackets. He quickly scanned the avenue and was relieved to see only a few scattered pedestrians walking along the quiet sidewalk.

He pushed his shopping cart past the building and up to the corners curb, where he felt a cold gust of wind barreling down the avenue. His hair and beard began to blow freely within the icy breeze. The man tucked his head into his coat, trying to avoid the chill that rode on the back of the sudden winter blast.

He peeked out from under his collar and looked both ways, as he slowly dropped the two front wheels of the shopping cart onto the icy black surface. He quickly pushed it across the avenue until he arrived at the other side. Due to the amount of items within his cart, the weight prohibited him from lifting up the front wheels, so he had to turn it around. He stepped up and then backwards onto the slippery curb, while he forcefully dragged the back end of the cart onto the sidewalk. Now back on level ground, he turned around and once again began pushing the rusty cart forward.

Within just another block was the place he was destined for. It was the quiet corner in front of the grocery store and across from the friendly pizzeria. It was a place where he can sit and mind his own business, a place where people occasionally stop and would give him money, a place that feels comfortable enough to call home amongst the cruel city streets.

As he arrived, he once again looked around to see if anyone on the street was wearing a black leather jacket. He knew deep inside he wasn't afraid of the young men who'd approached him earlier, but at this point, he just didn't want to deal with any more trouble. Relieved after seeing that the area was clear of any threats, he proceeded to cross the street, repeating the same routine he did at every corner.

6

With both feet, and all four wheels of the shopping cart, now safely standing in front of the grocery store, he slowly moved towards the side of the corner building. He parked the old shopping cart against the wall in its usual spot and then slowly reached inside the rusty steel bin to gather his daily items.

Another gust of cold wind soared up the avenue, stinging his face and causing him to suddenly shake. He leaned over and quickly pulled a large gray blanket from out of the cart. He wrapped it tightly around himself and proceeded to gather the rest of his belongings. He then pulled out a large torn plastic garbage bag, and laid it upon the snow. Next, he pulled out an old shoe box he used to collect money, and finally, he removed an old, hand-written cardboard sign that stated his status and his dire situation.

As he sat down in his usual comfortable spot, he placed the open shoe box in front of him. He rewrapped the large blanket tightly around himself and then leaned back against the wall. He closed his eyes momentarily, as a small feeling of security rushed upon him and warmed his inner soul. It was a positive feeling that relaxed his troubled mind and gave him sudden sense of relief. As he slowly reopened his eyes, he grabbed his cardboard sign and propped it up onto his lap for all to see.

It's a handmade sign that he made many years ago, when he first began living on the streets. It's a sign that has basically kept him alive from the generosity of others. It's a sign that simply says …**HOMELESS** – **N**eed **E**very **D**ollar.

Chapter 2

Trent placed his fingers in a G chord formation and strummed his guitar once again. A brief smile appeared on his face as he heard the bright brilliant sound of his instrument ringing forth. He was down in his basement, rehearsing the songs that he and his band were playing tonight at a club in The Village and his nerves were a little on edge. He wrestled with doubts that maybe the band was a little premature, but a great opportunity arose that he couldn't pass up. He continued strumming his way through the songs, until a sharp feeling of hunger hit his stomach. A vision of warm pizza entered into his mind, followed by an immediate thought of running around the block and grabbing a bite to eat, before the guys showed up for today's band practice. Trent bent down and carefully placed the guitar back into its' case, then stood back up to turn off his amplifier and the rest of his equipment.

He grabbed his black leather jacket and his keys off the table, then proceeded to walk across the large room towards the front basement door. He slipped his arms through his jacket, adjusted his long black hair and then reached over to flick off the basement lights. He pulled the door open and stepped outside into the mid-afternoon daylight and into the brisk cold winter air. The below-freezing chill factor stung his face as he turned and quickly shut the door. He inserted the basement key into the lock safeguarding his bands practice space, then zipped up his jacket. He grabbed hold of the ice cold handrail and cautiously climbed the steps that led up to the snow covered alleyway. He then tucked his hands into his jacket pockets and began hiking towards the entrance. As he exited the narrow space, he turned and began making his way up the block towards the neighborhood pizzeria.

He got about halfway there, when he suddenly stopped and glanced at his car. It was parked on the other side of the street and just like earlier in the day, the '99 Ford Mustang was still blanketed under an inch or two of snow. He shook his head with uncertainty as he crossed the slushy street to approach the automobile. He began swiftly brushing the loose snow off the roof and then the hood. As he started to clear the windshield, he was disturbed to discover that a layer of ice had securely fastened itself to the large glass. He tapped on the hard frozen film, but the impeccable solid mass was unbreakable.

"Fuck, how the hell am I going to get that off?" he asked himself, knowing the heater wasn't working in the old car.

Hoping to somehow crack the ice, he hit the windshield harder with a closed fist, but his sudden, forceful gesture had no prevail and the slick, icy sheet remained unscathed.

"Son of a bitch!" he yelled out loud.

Again, the abrupt growling in his stomach returned, reminding him why he originally left the basement in the first place. He looked at his car one last time and shook his head in utter disbelief.

"I'll fucking deal with it later," he said to himself as he tucked his cold wet hands back into his jacket, then turned and walked back across the street towards the restaurant. Upon reaching the corner, he immediately felt another gust of cold wind rushing throughout the intersection. He lowered his head, as he turned and briskly walked towards his destination that was located on the far opposite corner.

As he hurried along the sidewalk, he looked up and noticed the homeless man sitting in his usual spot on the corner. The man was huddled under a heavy woolen blanket and was leaning against the wall of the grocery store. As Trent approached the man, he stopped for a moment, reached into his pants pocket and pulled out a dollar bill. He then crouched down and dropped it into the open box the man had placed in front of him. Out of his own curiosity, he leaned over and took a quick peek into the shoe box and noticed there wasn't much inside. He looked up and stared at the homeless man and like he always did, felt a twinge of deep inner sympathy.

Then Trent's eyes wandered over towards the man's rusty old shopping cart parked against the wall, and like before, he wondered what all of the items were that lay within the steel basket. It appeared to be filled with years of possessions that he'd gathered along the way of his long, homeless journey. His eyes then traveled back to the man, as they focused on the cardboard sign that he had sitting upon his lap.

"**HOMELESS** - **N**eed **E**very **D**ollar," he re-read to himself quietly.

It was quite obvious the homeless man had made the sign many years ago based on its condition. It looked old, crinkled and slowly deteriorating. Trent had also noticed that the word **HOMELESS** and the first letters of **N**eed **E**very **D**ollar were written in bold black capital letters. Many people in the neighborhood claimed that the sequence of the all the bold lettering is how his nickname, Homeless NED was derived.

"Hey man, how's it going?" Trent asked politely.

The man sat silently with his head down within his blanket until he heard Trent's voice. He slowly raised his head, looked up and upon noticing the familiar boys' face, he nodded graciously. Trent smiled at the man and said "It's really cold today, are you gonna be alright sitting out here?" The man once again nodded and then began to slowly lower his head back into the blanket.

Trent watched with concern as the man's face descended from his sight. He continued staring at the bowing homeless man, when suddenly the man quickly lifted his head and instantly gave him a deep and deadly stare. Trent was startled by the man's sudden reaction and instantaneously felt a rush of fear. He looked back at the man with a frightful expression and stuttered the words, "Are …you …okay?" Unknown to Trent, the man's triggered reaction came upon the realization that he was wearing a black leather jacket.

The homeless man's mind quickly raced back to the brief altercation he had earlier in the day. He began to wonder if the young man in front of him was affiliated with the gang of leather jacket punks. He remembered the leader telling him that there were more of them patrolling the neighborhood and maybe Trent was just another one of his henchmen.

Underneath the blanket, the man began to slowly reach into his coat. His fingers once again located and touched the top of the object that lay within the inner pocket. He didn't know what motives, or intentions, the young man had, but he wasn't about to take any chances. As he stared at Trent, he knew he had seen his face before, but seeing him wearing a black leather jacket gave him a whole new meaning, which caused his blood to race.

"Are…you …okay?" Trent repeated his stuttering question again.

Trent didn't know why the man was now staring at him with such hateful eyes. Just a moment ago, he had given him some money and the man had thanked him, but then something instantly changed his whole demeanor. Trent felt another jolt of fear and immediately stood up.

"Take care," Trent said, as he turned and quickly walked away.

He put his hands back into his jacket as he stood there waiting on the corner. He slowly turned his head and looked back at the homeless man and noticed that the man's relentless eyes were still fixated on him.

"What the fuck is wrong with that guy today?" He muttered to

11

himself.

Trent nervously turned his head away and waited for the light to change. Trying to get his mind off he man, he suddenly looked down and noticed a stream of melting snow flowing along the gutter. He watched as small bits of ice and slush slowly arrived at the corner, and then fell deep into the darkness beyond the sewers grate. He smiled for a moment as he recalled a childhood memory, in which he would watch twigs do the exact same thing after a spring rainfall. His memory was soon interrupted when he slowly turned his head, looked back and witnessed the homeless man's piercing gaze still directly upon him.

The deadly stare sent a chill down his spine, but sudden movements from the other waiting pedestrians forced Trent to refocus his attention. He looked up and noticed the light had turned green and everybody, including himself, quickly rushed across the avenue. As he stepped back up onto the opposite sidewalk, he stopped and looked back across the street, and once again saw that the homeless man's eyes were still locked on him.

"God damn, what the fuck is wrong with that guy today?" He confusedly asked himself once again.

He turned, took a few steps, then grabbed the handle of the restaurant's door and entered Lorenzo's pizzeria. The restaurant immediately felt warm to Trent's face. He removed his other hand from his jacket pocket and began rubbing the two of them together, trying to absorb some of the restaurant's heat. He then reached up and ran his fingers through his hair as he approached the counter.

"Hey Lorenzo, how's it going?" Trent asked the owner.

"Fine Trent, how are you?" Lorenzo replied.

"Fucking freezing man but it feels nice in here."

"Yeah, the hot pizza ovens always keep us warm on a cold day like today," said Lorenzo as he pointed over to his employee Tony, who was busy making a fresh pizza.

"What's up, Tony?" Trent said as he waved.

"Same old shit man, same old shit." Tony said as he looked up, nodded his head and smiled.

"What can I get you?" Lorenzo said.

"The usual, two slices and a Coke."

"Here, let me toss two in the oven for you. I'll make them nice and hot," said Lorenzo, as he pulled the two slices off a large pizza pie and then placed them into the oven.

"That'll be great, I'm going to grab a seat," said Trent, as he reached up and unzipped his jacket.

12

"That's fine. I'll let you know when they're ready," replied Lorenzo.

"Here, let me pay for them now, how much?" Trent asked, as he glanced up at the sign that said Today's Special Two Slices and a Small Drink for $6.00.

"For you my friend, the usual, four bucks," said the owner grinning.

"Thanks Lorenzo, you always take good care of me," said Trent, as he dug into his pocket and pulled out his money.

"Here you go man, thanks again." Trent said politely.

"You're always welcome, my friend." Lorenzo said, as he reached for Trent's money and then placed it in the cash register.

"By the way, how's your band coming along?" Lorenzo asked.

"Great man, we're actually playing tonight."

"Really? Where at?" Lorenzo asked surprisingly.

"It's just a few blocks from here, a place called The Cave. It's a club right here in the village and my father has known the owner for years, so I was able to get my band in for tonight. We're only going to play a few songs, but it's a start."

"Hey I know exactly where that place is, I've been there a few times myself in my younger days." said Tony.

"Good for you my friend, that sounds great, I wish you all the luck," said Lorenzo.

"Thanks guys, I really appreciate that, I'm a little nervous, but it should be a lot of fun". Trent said with a smile.

"What's the name of your band again?" Tony asked.

"City Rats," replied Trent proudly.

"Nice." Tony said while nodding his head.

Trent smiled once again then turned to find a seat. He looked around the vacant pizzeria, but decided to slide into a booth by the front window so he could view the street. As he sat and waited patiently for his meal, he looked back at the homeless man and his uncertain feelings returned. His mind concentrated back on the man's eyes and the long, relentless stare he held upon him.

"Your pizza's ready and here's your Coke too," said Lorenzo, interrupting his thoughts as he placed his food on the counter. Trent slid off the seat and approached the front counter.

"Man, I can't get over the homeless man across the street." Trent said to Lorenzo.

"Who, NED?"

"Yeah, today he gave me this unusual stare when I stopped and gave him some money. Do you think maybe the cold weather is having some strange effect on him? I mean it's just so cold, why doesn't he go somewhere warm?"

"I don't know, he appeared on the avenue several months ago and he's been just sitting on that same corner ever since." said Lorenzo.

"I know, I see him all the time, but isn't there a homeless shelter somewhere around here?"

"Yeah, I think it's about five or six blocks away."

"Well why wouldn't he just go there? I mean he should do something to get out of the cold." Trent continued the conversation.

"I don't know, I'm sure the place must be packed on a day like today, but I think after living on the streets for so long, he's probably become immune to the cold weather. I mean you can tell he's been homeless for a while."

"Besides that, he's not well upstairs." Tony said pointing to his head. "You can tell that by just looking at him."

"Yeah, I've noticed that too, but he just freaked me out a moment ago." Trent said to Tony.

"Why, what happened?"

"I don't know, I gave him a dollar and a second later, he looked like he wanted to kill me," explained Trent.

"Nah, he doesn't bother anybody," said Lorenzo.

"Yeah, but something's not right with him, especially today," said Trent.

"I've always wondered how he became homeless," said Tony.

"I see him almost every day, and I've never seen him say a word to anybody." Lorenzo told Trent, trying to ease his worries.

"I'm surprised he's still alive," said Tony.

"Do you think he might be dangerous?" Trent asked.

"Nah, he's harmless. Like I said before, he doesn't bother anybody," said Lorenzo.

"Hey, have you've ever noticed how tall that son of a bitch is?" Tony said to Trent.

"Yeah, like I said, I occasionally stop to give him money, and I've stood by him many times before, he towers over me."

"You really can't tell how big he is when he's sitting down like that, but from here, sometimes he looks like a giant standing on the corner." Lorenzo said, as he looked out his front window towards the homeless man.

"Yeah, he's gotta be way over six feet tall," said Tony.

"Yes, but honestly, I just can't imagine being homeless, it must

14

be horrible," said Trent.

"Well, something must have happened for him to have wound up on the streets," said Lorenzo.

"Again, are you sure he's not dangerous? I mean, he gave me such an intimidating look earlier."

"Nah, I'll say it again, he's harmless." Lorenzo said with confidence.

"Yeah, but just the other night I heard on the news, that recently a bunch of crazy shit has been happening around here. People are being mugged, beaten up and even killed. Have you heard anything like that?" Trent asked both men.

"Man, this is the lower east side of the New York City, shit is always happening around here, and besides, these are desperate times and there's a lot of desperate people out there," said Tony.

"Yeah, but do you think maybe NED is responsible for it? He seems desperate."

"No, he's so harmless that we even give him free food," said Lorenzo.

"Really?" asked Trent.

"Yeah, sometimes towards the evening, he'll walk up to the window and we'll motion for him to go out back to the alley and we'll give him some pizza or a sandwich, whatever we have leftover. I don't mind," said Lorenzo.

"There have been many times we arrive in the morning and found him sleeping in the alley, and believe me, he's scared the fucking shit out of us a few times." said Tony.

"I bet he has." Trent said under a small laugh.

"I said it once and I'll say it again, you guys are the best." Trent said to both of them, as he grabbed his food and returned back to his seat.

He sat back down and took another bite of the warm slice. He then turned his head once again, looked back out the window towards the man across the street and re-read the sign one more time, **HOMELESS – NED**.

As Trent took another bite his cell phone rang. While chewing, he reached into the inner pocket of his jacket and pulled it out. As the phone rang again, he looked at the identifier and saw that it was Vince, the drummer in his band. He pushed the button on his phone, then held it up to his ear.

"Hey Vince, what's up?"

"Hey dude, are you home?"

"No, I'm at Lorenzo's pizzeria."

"Lorenzo's, where is that?"

"Just around the block from my house, why, where are you?" Trent asked.

"I'm just walking out of the subway."

"You're early."

"Yeah, I told my boss I was sick and he let me leave."

Trent began to laugh and then said, "Well meet me here."

"Where is it again?"

"Walk to the corner, make a left and it's just down the block. I'm sitting by the window, so you'll see me."

"Cool, see you in few."

"Sure man, see you soon," said Trent.

He clicked off his phone, placed it on the table and grabbed what was left of his first slice of pizza and shoved it in his mouth. As he began to chew the last bites, his head turned back towards the man across the street and again he began to stare. Seconds flowed into minutes when his trance was broken, as Vince suddenly appeared at the front window of the restaurant. As he opened the front door, he saw Trent sitting in a booth and walked over and slid into the opposite side. .

"Hey man, how's it going?" Vince asked his friend.

"Fine, I'm just getting something to eat, are you hungry?"

"No man, I ate something right before I came here."

"I'll just be another minute," said Trent, as he picked up his second slice of pizza and took a big bite out of it.

"Take your time, if feels good just to get out of the fucking cold," said Vince.

"Enjoy it while you can, because the basement feels just as cold as it is out there," said Trent pointing to the outside.

"Dude, once I start playing, I warm up quickly." Vince said with a laugh.

"I see you wore your black leather jacket today, cool." Trent said.

"Yeah, I thought I'd pull it out for the show tonight. We gotta look cool when we walk in the place, you know, appearance is half of it, right?

"You know it man," said Trent.

Vince unzipped his jacket and then reached up and pulled off his New York Yankees baseball hat, exposing his spiky blonde hair.

Trent looked at Vince and said "Dude, did you get another haircut?"

"Yeah man, not everybody that plays in a band has long hair; the

16

80's are long gone, brother." Vince said with a grin.

Trent returned the smile and turned around and yelled over to Lorenzo and Tony "Hey guys this is Vince, he's the drummer in my band."

"Nice to meet you," said Lorenzo.

"What's up?" Tony said, as he lifted his head and nodded.

"Hi guys." Vince said, before he then turned his attention back to Trent.

"Dude, I'm really excited about tonight."

"Yeah, me too," said Trent.

"Hey is your dad going be there?"

"No, he left yesterday with his band for a mini Eastern tour. He won't be back until next week."

"You know, he might not be a full fledge rock star, but he still makes a living being a musician, and that's fucking cool in my book," said Vince.

"Yeah, he taught me everything I know." Trent said, while making a silly air guitar gesture towards his friend.

"So what's the deal tonight? I know we're the first band up, is there going to be a drum set already there?"

"Yeah, all you're gonna need is your sticks. Shane and I will have to bring our instruments, but we'll just plug them into their amps and we're ready to go. It's going to be real simple, I hope," said Trent, as he took another bite.

"That's fucking cool man, by the way, how was your first day back to college? Was it a drag?" Vince asked.

"No, it actually turned out better than I expected," said Trent, grinning from ear to ear.

"Oh really? O.K give me some details." Vince asked curiously.

"Well, I'm only taking a few classes this semester, so that will give me the afternoons off, and I can already tell that some of the classes are going to be somewhat easy, plus I met this really cute girl today." Trent said, as an even bigger grin graced his face.

"A cute girl, really, what's her name?"

"Allison."

"How did that all go down?" Vince asked, wanting more details.

"Well, I walked into my first class and I saw her sitting towards the back of the room and we immediately made some eye contact. I then noticed that the seat next to her was empty, so I walked over and asked her if the seat was taken, she said no, so I sat down."

"Good for you man, what does she look like?"

"She's got long blonde hair and really pretty blue eyes. I'd say she's medium height, with a real sexy body." Trent said, as he made a slight sexual gesture with his hands, describing the young girl's figure.

"How old is she ya think?"

"She said she just started college, so I would assume she's eighteen."

"That's cool, she's eighteen, and you're twenty one. That's a good age difference, then what happened?" Vince asked, maintaining his curiosity.

"Well, we started chatting before the class began, and once our conversation started, it just continued to flow. First she said she really liked my leather jacket and thought I rode a motorcycle, but then I mentioned that I had a car and that seemed to really spark her interest. I didn't hide anything from her, I told her it was an old piece of shit, but she still thought it was cool. She was a little intimidating at first, but I tried to maintain my cool. Throughout the class, I'd occasionally look over at her and smile, and then after class I followed her out into the hall and invited her to come watch us play tonight."

"Really, well what did she say, did she say she'd come?" Vince continued with his questions.

"Yes, she said yes, and then she gave me her phone number. She told me to call her later so she can give me directions to her house; I think she lives somewhere uptown." Trent said as he took another bite.

"That's so fucking cool."

"I told her that Shane's girlfriend will be there too, so she wouldn't feel so awkward."

Their conversation was suddenly interrupted as Trent's phone began to ring. He picked it up off the table and quickly looked at the identifier.

"Speak of the devil." Trent said to Vince, as he pushed the button and brought the phone to his ear.

"What's going on Shane?" Trent said to his other band mate.

"Trent, I'm sorry but I'm stuck at work and I can't leave."

"Stuck? Dude, your dad owns the company, what do you mean you can't leave?" Trent asked with concern in his voice.

"Man, it's so busy here today that my dad will flip the fuck out if I ask him if I can leave early."

"I wanted to get one more practice in before tonight." Trent fired back.

"I know, I'm so sorry, but I can't do anything about it," said Shane.

Trent paused for a moment and took a deep breath. There was an uncomfortable silence between the two, but then Shane said "Don't fucking worry, I know the songs, we'll be fine, I promise."

Trent took another deep breath and then said "Alright, if there's nothing you can do about it, it is what it is."

"Again, I'm really sorry." Shane said.

"Alright." Trent said with a disappointed voice. He then asked, "By the way, is Beth still coming tonight?"

"Yeah man, why?"

"Because I might have a date tonight and it would be cool if she wasn't the only girl there."

"You're bringing a date? Great! Yeah, she's coming. Her parents went to Vegas for a few days so she'll be there, and don't worry about tonight, we'll be fine, I promise." Shane said with confidence.

"Alright, and if this all goes down the way I'm hoping, I'll swing by and pick you two up tonight," said Trent.

"That's cool, look, I have to get back to work, my dad is standing here just staring at me, call me later dude."

"One more thing, wear your black motorcycle jacket tonight," said Trent.

"Really ….. Why?" Shane asked.

"Because Vince and I are wearing ours, and I want to make a good first impression."

"No problem, I gotta go, talk to you later."

"OK." said Trent, as they both hung up their phones.

Trent tossed his phone back on the table and looked at Vince with a frustrated face.

"Don't tell me anything. I heard the whole thing," said Vince.

"Damn it, I wanted this gig to be flawless, especially if this girl comes tonight." Trent said angrily.

"We'll be fine man, we know the songs," said Vince, trying to comfort his friend.

"Dude, I don't want to tarnish my dad's reputation with the club owner. I worked hard to convince him that we were ready for this gig, and we can't blow it."

"We'll be fine. We're gonna rock the fucking roof off that place." Vince said as he looked at Trent, trying to make him smile.

Trent looked back at Vince, then turned his head and looked out the window, trying to hide his true feelings. His inner temper was still flaring until his eyes fell back upon the homeless man across the street, who was still sitting there, wrapped under his blanket, fighting the harsh

19

winter elements.

"Here I am complaining about something that hasn't even happened and a true sense of reality was sitting across the street. If there's anyone that should be complaining, it should be that poor man." Trent said to himself, as he shook his head out of shame.

"I'm really sorry; I know everything will be fine tonight. I have total confidence in you two." He said in a low calming voice to Vince.

"It really will, don't worry," said Vince.

Trent picked up his last piece of pizza and took one last bite. It tasted cold and not as appealing as it was about twenty minutes ago.

"Alright, let's go make some noise." Trent said to Vince, as he slid out of the booth and stood up. Vince nodded and followed Trent's cue. He grabbed his Yankees hat and put it back on his head, as he too slid out of the booth and stood up. Trent grabbed his trash and threw it in the garbage pail, before turning to Lorenzo and Tony and motioning to them that he was leaving.

"Take care guys, and thanks again Lorenzo." Trent said, as he grabbed the zipper on his jacket and pulled it back up.

"Nice meeting you two, next time I'll bring an appetite." Vince said, trying to have a sense of humor, as he too started to zip up his jacket.

"Hey, you two look like you're part of the Hell's Angels gang, wearing those motorcycle jackets," said Lorenzo laughing.

"It's all about appearance boss," Trent said with sarcastic arrogance.

"Again, good luck tonight," said Lorenzo."

"Hey, one more thing …watch out for Homeless NED, he's gonna get ya," Tony said, lifting his hands up in a Frankenstein monster type manner and then laughing in a sinister tone.

"Dude, don't be such an asshole." Trent said, shaking his head back and forth.

"Hey, I was just joking with you," said Tony.

"If that was a joke, then I guess I missed the punch line." Trent said with a very serious look on his face.

"Hey man, I'm sorry if I offended you, I was just teasing, that's all," said Tony, immediately wiping the smile off his face.

"I know, I just got a lot on my mind, it's cool," said Trent, looking at Tony then cracking a small smile, showing an acceptance to his apology.

"Homeless NED, who the fuck is that?" Vince asked his friend.

"I'll tell you later, let's go."

"I'll see you guys sometime during the week." Trent said as he pushed open the front door and they walked out.

Both Trent and Vince stood outside for a moment as the cold, frigid air began to sting their warm faces. Trent's eyes returned to the man across the street and saw that once again, he too was staring back at him. As their eyes connected, he shook his head and repeated, "Man, what the fuck is wrong with you today?"

***

The homeless man focused on the two figures that emerged from the restaurant and was shocked to now see two black leather jackets standing together. His heart began to race, causing his fingers to immediately grab the top of the hidden object, preparing him for any trouble that might lie ahead.

***

"Hey man, I gotta run across the street to the grocery store and grab a pack of smokes, do you mind?" said Vince.

"No, let's go," said Trent, as he and Vince walked to the corner.

They waited for a moment until the light turned green and then crossed. As they walked across the icy avenue, Trent kept his eyes on the homeless man and once again, the man kept his eyes on him, but he also noticed that he was now watching Vince too.

***

The homeless man watched as the two young men crossed the avenue, coming back to his side. He noticed that the taller one with long hair kept staring back at him, as he kept a watchful eye on them, not knowing what their intentions were. Again, he didn't know if the two young men were affiliated with the gang from earlier, but he wasn't going to take any chances as he gripped the hidden object tighter.

***

Both men stepped up onto the curb as Trent continued to look at the homeless man with concern. His eyes stared in his direction until he was out of sight upon entering the corner store.

"So who's Homeless NED?" Vince asked Trent once again, as

they waited in line.

"He's the guy sitting around the corner on the sidewalk."

"The guy wrapped under the blanket? I noticed him, so what about him?"

"He's just a homeless person that has been seen around the neighborhood for several months now."

"So why did Tony say all that crazy shit to you?"

"He's just fucking with me," said Trent as he shook his head.

"Yeah, but I can tell it definitely had an effect on you, what gives?" Vince continued.

"I don't know, I told him and Lorenzo that I gave the man a dollar today and then afterwards he reacted really weird towards me, I'm not sure why?"

"Maybe he thinks you're just cheap with your one dollar donation," said Vince as he began to laugh.

"Don't be an asshole like Tony. It's bad enough I'm freaked out about it." Trent said, with a serious look on his face.

"Freaked out over what? The homeless guy is probably fucking crazy, so why even bother with him?"

"Because he's homeless and I feel sorry for him, that's why."

The small line in the store moved quickly and soon Vince and Trent were standing in front of the counter and the cashier.

"Can I help you?" said the grocery store clerk.

"A pack of your cheapest cigarettes," said Vince.

The store clerk turned, grabbed a generic pack of cigarettes and placed it on the counter.

"Can I get you anything else, maybe a lotto ticket? The jackpot is up to forty two million. Tonight could be your lucky night."

"I wish I could get lucky tonight, but no thanks," said Vince with a smirk.

"Six dollars and forty five cents please."

Vince reached into his jeans pocket and pulled out a ten dollar bill. He handed it to the cashier and then grabbed his pack of cigarettes off the counter.

The clerk rang up the purchase and then handed Vince his change.

Both Trent and Vince walked out of the corner store and stood outside for a moment, as Vince tucked his pack of cigarettes into his jacket. They both cringed, as the ice cold wind once again brushed up against their faces.

"So why are you so concerned about this one particular homeless

22

guy?" Vince asked.

"I don't know, I guess throughout the months of seeing him around, I've grown to have a soft spot for him," said Trent in a sympathetic voice.

"Dude, you can't help someone who won't help themselves."

"Yeah, but every dollar helps unfortunate people like him."

"Look, if it will make you feel any better, I'll give him a dollar too and that will give him enough money to buy a beer," said Vince.

"You're missing the point," Trent said.

"No, dude, this is your hang-up, I couldn't care less about him," said Vince, giving Trent his honest opinion.

"Exactly, and that's what's wrong with everybody," said Trent, now getting agitated.

"Listen dude, I rode here today to play some music, not argue with you. I told you I'll give him a buck too, so let's go because I'm fucking freezing," Vince said, putting an end to the conversation.

"Fine, let's go." Trent said as he and Vince began to walk around the corner.

***

The man's eyes were immediately fixated on both Trent and Vince the moment they came back into his view. He was waiting with anticipation, to see which way the two black leather jackets were going to go after they left the grocery store, but it looked like they were now coming towards him. He fingers grew even tighter around the object, as he waited for the inner voice to return for guidance, but within seconds, the two young men were now standing before him. He began to get nervous, as his eyes began to alternate back and forth between Trent and Vince.

***

Trent once again felt an immediate feeling of fear as he looked into the homeless man's eyes and saw the same eerie look like he had before.

"Hi, how you are doing?" Vince said.

The man was silent as he turned his attention and focused on Vince.

"Here's a dollar for you NED," Vince said cheerfully, as he bent down and dropped his money into the man's open shoe box. He then

23

turned, looked up at Trent and gave him a wink.

The man suddenly looked at Vince and then proceeded to stare directly into his eyes. Vince saw the man's sudden response and quickly stood up and turned his head, looking back at Trent. He too felt an immediate jolt of anxiety from the homeless man's strange reaction.

"Come on man, let's go." Trent responded quickly, upon seeing another angered gesture from the man.

Vince just stood there, frozen with fear. The man, confused and still not knowing what the intentions of the two young men were, began getting up from his once placid position. Still holding onto the object within his coat, he pushed himself up, and off the garbage bag that lay upon the snow-covered sidewalk. His large framed body struggled at first, as he used the wall of the grocery store for leverage, but he soon began to quickly move upwards. The old cardboard sign he had on his lap fell to the ground, as the woolen blanket fell off his shoulders and soon followed. Vince remained paralyzed, with his eyes wide open and now in a state of shock. His head began tilting backwards as it followed the tall rising man.

"Come on, let's go!" Trent said once again.

The man was now standing completely upright, as he looked down at Vince and stared directly into his eyes. Vince's body began to shake out of fear as he tried to move, but his feet still wouldn't respond. Trent suddenly became frightened too, as he noticed the man's hand was digging for something within his coat.

"I said let's fucking go!" Trent shouted as he suddenly grabbed Vince by his arm and pulled him away from the tall and now infuriated homeless man.

They made an attempt to run, but their feet immediately began to slip out from underneath them. They began to stumble and even grabbed onto each other, trying to prevent themselves from falling, but they quickly lost their balance and fell to the ground.

Upon their hard descending impact, Vince's Yankee hat flew off his head and tumbled towards the wall of the grocery store. People on the street immediately stopped to see what all the commotion was and saw the two boys on the ground and the tall homeless man hovering over them. As usual, nobody wanted to get involved, so they began to scramble off the sidewalk and into the street, trying to avoid any possible danger. Within moments, the sidewalk was clear of all pedestrians as they all scattered in different directions, trying to escape the current hostile situation.

Still lying down on the icy sidewalk, Trent and Vince quickly turned their heads and looked over their shoulders. They saw that the tall man was just a few feet away and was staring down at them with hatred in his eyes. They began to panic, as they both realized that they were still in grave danger.

"Oh my god, he's going to kill us!" Vince shouted at Trent.

Trent looked into Vince's eyes and saw genuine fear. "We gotta get the fuck outta here man!" Trent screamed back at his friend.

Desperately, they began digging their hands and pushing their feet against the icy concrete, as they hopelessly crawled forward, trying to get away from the man. Trent was the first to get up and onto his feet and he immediately reached down, grabbed Vince by the back of his jacket and began dragging him across the snow.

"Get up man, get the fuck up!" Trent shouted again.

He pulled his friend several feet before Vince was able to get to his knees and then eventually to his feet. After taking a few more awkward steps, both Trent and Vince were able to finally get themselves away from the tall, angry man and the dangerous situation that was mistakenly created. Then, like bullets from a gun, the two young men began running as fast as they could down the avenue's sidewalk, towards their safety. They got about thirty yards down the block, when they stopped and turned. Their eyes squinted against the cold wind, as they looked back to see if the man was possibly coming after them

"Do you see him?" Vince shouted at Trent.

"No, but are you alright?"

"Yeah, I think so, how about you?"

"Yeah, I'm fine."

They continued staring down the street, as they began to brush the snow and ice off their faces and clothing. They looked at each other and tried to exchange smiles, but it seemed difficult. They stood there for a moment in total silence, as they tried to catch their breaths and ease their distress. Then their eyes shifted back towards the other end of the block, once again looking for the big man.

"I think we're safe." Trent said.

"Damn it!" Vince shouted.

"What?"

"I lost my fucking Yankee's hat!" He shouted again.

"Do you want to go back and get it?" Trent said sarcastically.

They looked back at each other and finally cracked two genuine smiles that came deep from within. Their smiles were a natural reaction, from the feeling one would get if one had just cheated death.

"Lorenzo kept telling me he's harmless, but I'm not really sure anymore," said Trent.

"Harmless my ass, that fucking guy wanted to kill me. You saw the look in his eyes." Vince responded.

"I don't know what just happened, but it all happened so quickly. You called him NED, why did you do that?"

"I don't know? I thought that was his fucking name."

"I told you that wasn't his real name. It was just some nickname that the neighborhood gave him." Trent said, as he began getting irritated.

"I don't know? I was just trying to be friendly." Vince said in his defense.

There was another long silence between the two friends, as they both continued to take deep breaths of the cold winter air. When their pounding hearts finally eased up, they both looked back down the block one last time to assure their troubled minds.

"I think we're safe." Trent said.

"Did you see him reaching inside his coat? I'm sure he wasn't going to pull out a bible and hand it to me." Vince said with a scared and shaky voice.

"Yeah, I saw that too, that's why I grabbed your arm and pulled you away from him."

"What do you think he was reaching for?"

"I don't know? It could have been anything, a knife, a gun, who knows, I just know he definitely had bad intentions," said Trent.

"Fuck you, you, crazy motherfucker!" Vince held up his finger and yelled down the block.

"Come on let's go." Trent said laughing.

Both young men turned and began to walk. They reached the corner and made a left towards Trent's house. Halfway down the block, Trent looked back over at his snow covered car but he didn't stop, he just shook his head and again thought to himself that he would deal with it later. They finally reached Trent's house, turned into the alley and walked down the icy path, until they reached the stairs that led down to the basement.

"Wait a second," said Vince, as he unzipped his jacket, reached into his pocket and pulled out a joint and a lighter. He quickly lit the tip, inhaled it deeply and then passed the joint over to Trent.

"Here man, want a hit?" Vince asked.

"No thanks, you know I don't smoke weed," said Trent.

"Fuck, after that incident, I need something to calm me down."

"I agree, when we get inside, I'll run upstairs and grab one of my father's bottles, I'll bring it down and we'll both have a couple of drinks.

I'm sure he wouldn't mind due to the circumstance."

Vince took one more hit off the joint and then said, "Did you see the look in that man's eyes? He's fucking crazy!"

"Well, he's been sitting on that corner for several months now and he hasn't bothered anyone."

"Yeah, well doesn't just sitting on a corner sound fucking crazy to you? Vince said sarcastically.

"Like Lorenzo said, he's harmless; you just somehow pissed him off."

"Alright, so the scary homeless man is harmless until you piss him off, then he fucking kills you," said Vince.

"That's not true, he hasn't killed anybody," said Trent in the man's defense.

"How do you know that?"

"I guess I don't know," was Trent's feeble response.

"So as far as you know, he hasn't killed anybody... or, he just hasn't killed anybody yet," said Vince, trying to confirm his point.

Trent nodded his head as if he was almost agreeing with Vince, before he turned and said, "Come on, let's go inside."

"Hold on one more second," said Vince, as he put out the joint, reached into his other pocket and pulled out his pack of cigarettes.

"I just need a couple of drags," he said, as he unwrapped the cellophane off the new pack; pulled out a cigarette and placed it in his mouth.

Again, his hands were still shaking, as he flicked his lighter and brought it up towards his face to light the end of the cigarette. He took a few quick drags off the tobacco then tossed it into the snow.

"Feel better now? Trent said with a smirk on his face.

"Yeah man, I'm okay, thanks again," said Vince, as he returned a small smile back to his friend.

"Good, now let's go inside and make some music," said Trent and Vince agreed, nodding his head.

Holding onto the cold handrail, both young men made their way down the icy stairs to the steel basement door. Trent reached into his jacket, pulled out his keys and inserted the correct one into the keyhole. As he turned the knob and pushed the door open, he instantly felt the slight warmth of the basement against his face as he stepped forward. Vince followed him inside and let out a low moan as a sign of relief upon entering the dark room. Trent flipped on the lights and then quickly shut and locked the door.

27

***

    The homeless man walked over, bent down and picked up Vince's hat off the small bank of snow. He held it in his hands as he looked at the New York Yankee's emblem and carefully touched the white embroidered letters on the front of it. The feeling of the material caused a small smile to appear under his long, grey beard, as he walked back over towards the wall of the grocery store. He looked at the hat one more time, then tossed it into his rusty shopping cart, which ironically landed next to his newly found baseball. He then reached down, grabbed the blanket off the sidewalk and wrapped it back around his shoulders, before proceeding to sit back down. Next, he picked up his cardboard sign, brushed off the excess snow and placed it back onto his lap.

    Just then, the sun peeked out from behind the dark gray clouds once again. Its bright rays brought some temporary comfort as it penetrated into the old man's face. He closed his eyes, took a deep breath and sat there in silence, as a slew of memories began racing back to haunt him. He automatically reached into his overcoat and began to touch the top of the hidden object, bringing forth the imaginary voice to somewhat settle his nerves.

    The sun continued to shine, allowing him to fall momentarily into a tranquil trance, but just a few seconds later, the sun disappeared, bringing back the cold winter's gloom. He suddenly became aware of the sounds of the passing bystanders walking along the icy sidewalk, causing him to quickly open his eyes, and frantically turn his head from side to side. His paranoid mind then instantly focused on every individual who was in sight, trying to observe if anyone else might be wearing a black leather motorcycle jacket.

Chapter 3

Allison was on her way home after completing her first day of college. She stood patiently waiting on the subway platform, when she decided to lean over and take a peek down the darkened tunnel. She saw the light of the oncoming train and prepared herself for the arrival, by grabbing her book bag and holding onto her pocketbook. As the train rumbled into the station, it caused a gust of wind that wildly blew her long, blonde hair and the scarf that was wrapped around her neck.

The train then came to a typical screeching halt, as Allison moved towards one of the doors and waited for it to open. As it slid open, she stepped aside, allowing the other passengers to exit, then she quickly entered the subway car. She was lucky to locate a vacant seat between a construction worker and an elderly woman. She sat down and placed her book bag on the floor between her feet, then reached up to loosen her scarf.

A minute later, the doors slid shut and the train began to move. It started off slowly bucking back and forth, but the ride gradually became smoother as the train began to gain speed. Allison's eyes glanced over at the other passengers riding along in the same car, when the older woman seated next to her turned her head and gave her a warm, friendly smile.

"Hi, how are you?" Allison said politely to the woman.

"Fine dear, how are you?" The woman responded back.

"Fine, thanks."

"Are you a college student?" The woman asked, after noticing her book bag.

"Yes … yes I am, and today was actually my first day."

"So, how was it?"

"It wasn't bad, it actually turned out better than I expected."

"Well good for you, I remember when I went to college, which was many years ago, and I loved it."

"Well, I wouldn't go as far as that, but it wasn't bad." Allison said, as she began to laugh at the woman's humorous comment.

"Well, stick with it, a good education is the basis of your future," the woman said in a diplomatic tone of voice.

"Now you sound like my father," Allison said sarcastically.

"Well your father sounds like a real smart man."

"Yeah, he's actually too smart." Allison said, shaking her head back and forth.

"You can never be too smart," said the woman.

"If you only knew," said Allison, as she rolled her eyes.

"College is important, especially for a young woman of today. By the time you graduate, it will bring you to a new level of maturity." The woman continued advising Allison.

"Really ... and what did you become ...when you grew up?" Allison asked the woman with a slight sense of humor.

"I became a school teacher."

"Gosh, I guess you really did love school." Allison said, followed by a small laugh.

"I was a high school teacher for over forty years, I taught English," the woman said proudly.

"Really? Were you strict, because I hated most of my high school teachers?"

"I know times have changed and so have teachers, but back in my days, I was strict enough to keep my students interested and motivated. Over the years, I've watched several of my best students go on to become some of the greatest people in today's society."

"Good for you, you should feel proud. I wish I would have had you as one of my teachers. Maybe I wouldn't have such a bad attitude towards them." Allison said, continuing to prove her point.

"Well, then change your attitude. Start college with a clear conscience, set some goals and take your studies seriously, you'll be amazed how far it will take you." The woman said in a stern tone of voice.

"That sounds like good, strong advice," said Allison, agreeing with the elderly woman.

Their conversation was interrupted as the conductor came on the loudspeaker and announced the next stop. The train pulled into the station and began to slow down.

"Well, this is my stop dear, it was a pleasure talking to you," said the woman, as she gathered herself together.

"Thanks, it was nice talking you too," Allison said politely back to her.

"By the way, my name is Mildred."

"Nice meeting you Mildred, I'm Allison."

"Well Allison, I hope we meet again sometime soon."

"Thanks Mildred, same here."

"Stay in school and study hard." She said, smiling at her new-found friend.

"I'll give it my best," said Allison, smiling back.

The train came to a stop and the woman got up and headed towards the open door. Before she got off the train, she turned and looked back at Allison one last time and smiled at her. Allison looked at Mildred, lifted her hand and waved goodbye. The elderly woman, along with a small crowd of people, quickly exited the subway car. They were soon replaced by another group of people who entered. Mildred's vacant seat was soon occupied by a young man, who Allison turned and ignored like she had the construction worker.

She reached around and pulled her pocketbook off her shoulder. She set it on her lap, opened it up and began shuffling through its contents. She pushed aside her makeup case, moved her hair brush out of the way and grabbed her IPod. She pulled it out, turned it on and carefully unraveled the wires of the ear buds. She placed the small speakers into her ears one at a time, then began shuffling between her favorite songs. She finally settled on something nice and easy, as she sat back into the seat and slowly closed her eyes.

Her mind began to race around all of the day's activities. It teetered back and forth between the morning argument with her father over breakfast, and meeting the cute guy in her first class. After the conversation with Mildred, her mind naturally veered off to the argument she had with her father.

"I hope you take this seriously today, you're not in high school anymore," said Walter Thompson.

"Oh no, were not going to have this conversation again, are we?" Allison said to her father with an attitude.

"I want today to be the beginning of something positive, a step in the right direction."

"I know dad; I've heard this speech before." Allison said, as she began rolling her eyes with disrespect.

"And you can start by eliminating that attitude." Walter said in a stern voice.

"I told you I'd go to college if you would stop treating me like a child."

"Well after all the crap you pulled last year, I'm just making sure you're going to stay on the right track." Walter began preaching his point.

"Please, not this speech again …Mom!" Allison shouted at her father and then called out for her mother, who was in the kitchen.

"Yes dear?" Grace Thompson said to her daughter.

"Dad is starting to preach at me again, please come in here." Allison hollered back to her mother.

"I'll be right there dear," Grace responded.

"Hey, don't get your mother involved, this time she's on my side," Walter said to his daughter.

"You know, I was actually excited about today, but you're already ruining it …Mom!"

"Coming dear," said Grace as she entered the dining room, holding plates of breakfast items.

"Please tell him to stop, I can't take it anymore, even if I try to do something good it's just not good enough, nothing will ever be good enough!" Allison began screaming at both her parents.

"Come on honey, let her go to school today with a nice positive attitude. Don't upset her, please." Grace said, pleading with her husband as she placed the plates upon the table.

"I just don't want my daughter starting college and making all the same mistakes like she made in high school, that's all." Walter said to his wife.

"I agree Walter, but just give her a chance," Grace said peacefully to her husband as she sat down at the table.

"How many chances are we going to give her?"

"I don't know dear, she's our only child, please, please." Grace said, desperately trying to calm her husband down.

"Listen, I don't want you getting involved with all the wrong people, skipping school, doing drugs and ruining your life again." Walter said sternly to his daughter.

"You told me if I went to college you would treat me like an adult, for god sakes I'm eighteen, I'm an adult according to the rest of the world's standards."

"Yes, but you still act like a child," Walter said, not letting up on his daughter.

"I'll try to do my best. I'm sorry if I'm not an honor student like you were and I probably won't become a lawyer, but I'll do something with my life." Allison said, trying to convince him of her maturity.

"You should be grateful that I'm a lawyer, after everything you've done, you would be in jail right now if it wasn't for me." Walter said, as he pointed his finger at his daughter, showing her again how serious he was.

32

"Walter, please, you're not helping the situation," said Grace again, pleading with her husband.

"What are you really going to do with your life; do you even have a goal?"

"At this point I don't know. If my future really concerns you, maybe I just marry a fucking Rock Star, does that sound like a fucking goal? I've had enough of this, I'm leaving!" Allison screamed at her father as she got up from the table.

"Allison, please sit down and eat your breakfast," Grace said, trying to calm her daughter.

"I lost my appetite; maybe I'll just stop at the city jail and grab something to eat there." Allison continued to scream at her father as she grabbed her coat, pocketbook and book bag.

"Listen young lady, don't you ever talk to me like that again, do you hear me?" Walter yelled back at his daughter.

"Yes, I heard you, I heard every single word you said to me this morning …dad." She said angrily, as she walked out the door, slamming it behind her.

Allison's thoughts were interrupted as the train pulled into the next stop. She opened her eyes and glanced around the subway car. Her mind began to calm down, as she tried to tuned back to the song that was playing softly in her ears. She began to tap her foot to the rhythm, as an attempt to change her previous unsettled thoughts.

The train came to an actual stop and she watched as several more people came and went. She noticed two middle-aged women getting on and sitting directly across from her. She stared at the two ladies as they sat down and began talking to each other. She couldn't hear their conversation due to the music playing in her ears, but she could tell by their actions that they were good friends, maybe even best friends. Just then, a vision of her best friend Meaghan popped into her mind, causing her to have a warm, secure feeling.

Allison continued to watch the two women converse as the doors closed and the train began its journey back down the track. The music continued to play as she once again closed her eyes and forced herself to think about something pleasant. Her mind then wandered to the young man she met earlier today, which caused her to smile as she remembered his name, Trent.

He instantly caught her attention when he walked into her first class. He looked like a rebel with long black hair, accompanied by a black leather motorcycle jacket. The moment she laid eyes on him, she was instantly attracted. He was tall, handsome and looked like a Rock

Star. She recalled him standing at the front of the classroom, checking out where he might want to sit as they made eye contact. They stared at each other for a couple of seconds, but then shyly looked away. As their eyes returned back to each other, he cracked a small smile then proceeded to walk down the aisle to where she was sitting. There was an empty seat next to her and he politely asked if the seat was taken. She said no, so he dropped his book bag on the floor and sat down. After a few exchanged glances and a couple of awkward smiles, he introduced himself.

"Hi, I'm Trent," he said, as he extended his hand towards her.

"I'm Allison" she said, as she reached out and shook his hand.

"Hi Allison, how are you?"

"Not bad for my first day here."

"Your first day, good for you, what are you taking up?" Trent asked lightheartedly.

"Space," Allison said with a smirk on her face.

"Space ... I didn't know this college had a space program," Trent said with a confused look on his face.

"It was a joke... taking up space ...get it?" Allison said sarcastically.

"I got it," said Trent as he began to laugh, enjoying Allison's sense of humor.

"Do you ride a motorcycle?" Allison asked, pointing to Trent's leather jacket.

"No, I drive an old, beat up piece of shit," he said with disappointment.

"You have a car?" She asked surprisingly.

"Yeah, it's just an old Mustang. It was free; my mom and step dad gave it to me so I really can't complain. Do you have a car?" He asked in return.

"No, I take the freaking subway everywhere."

"I usually do too; it's just easier, and besides, it's such a drag trying to find a place to park in the city."

"By the way, I love your jacket," Allison said with a big smile.

"Really, thanks, I got it in the village; it was a Christmas present from my dad." Trent said, as he took it off and placed it on the back of the chair.

"Well your dad has good taste." Allison said politely.

"Yeah, he's real cool."

"Well, then consider yourself lucky."

"Oh really, and why's that?" Trent asked.

"Because my dad is a real asshole," Allison said, as her smile abruptly left her pretty face.

Allison's thoughts were interrupted again as the train came to a sudden stop. She opened her eyes and naturally looked around at the other passengers on board. She then noticed that the two women across from her had the look of concern on their faces. She reached up, removed her ear pods and tried to listen in on their conversation. She tuned into their voices and overheard them talking about an incident that just recently happened.

"Last week this train was stuck for almost an hour," one woman said to the other.

"Why, what happened?"

"They found a homeless family living down here in the subway tunnels. It seemed that one of the trains almost ran one of them over." She began telling the story.

"Oh my god, what did they do?" Her friend asked with interest.

"They had to call the authorities to remove them; I saw the story later on the news that night. They showed pictures of the whole family, it was a man, his wife and their two little kids. They all looked like they were starving and hadn't bathed in months, it was horrible," the woman said, describing the incident with a sad expression on her face.

"I also saw a story on the news, and the commentator said due to the recession and the state of the economy, the homeless population in New York City has doubled, even tripled, in the last few years. They said it has become a city wide epidemic," said the other woman, also showing signs of anguish.

Allison listened to the two women conversing back and forth. Her thoughts pondered on what she had just heard. A homeless family living in the subway tunnels, the homeless population tripling over the course of a few years. For a moment, she thought about the privileged life she had lived, and then thoughts of guilt entered her mind about how most people would kill to have her life.

Several minutes passed, but eventually the train began to buck back and forth as it started to move again. She noticed the relief on the women's faces, as the train began to gain its momentum back down the track. Nobody knew what caused the train's delay, but thank god it wasn't the removal of another homeless family from the dark subway tunnels. Feeling somewhat relieved, Allison put the little speakers back into her ears and once again closed her eyes.

The train continued to make several stops along the way as passengers came and went, but Allison remained lost within her thoughts. Her mind raced back to Trent, but this time her focus was towards the ending of the class and their departure.

"Hey, make sure you save me this seat on Wednesday, okay?

"Sure," said Allison, as she began putting her books back into her bag.

"It was really nice meeting you today," said Trent, as he stood up and put his leather jacket back on.

"Thanks, same here." Allison said, smiling and looking into his eyes again.

"Let me walk you out." He said in a gentleman type manner.

"Okay, let's go," said Allison, as she too got up from her seat.

The two walked up the aisle and out the classroom door. In the hallway, Allison smiled at Trent once again and said," Well I'll see you on Wednesday."

"Yeah…hey, wait." Trent said spontaneously.

"What?" Allison said with hesitation.

"What are you doing later on tonight?" He asked her.

"I'll probably just do some homework. Why, what's up?"

"Well, my band is playing tonight down in the village and well, how would you like to come see us play?"

"I don't know, I just met you, and besides its Monday; nobody goes out on a Monday." Allison said again with hesitation.

"I was fortunate enough to get an open spot at the club. We go on around nine. We're only going to play a few songs and then I'll take you back home."

"Well, who else is going? Am I going to be the only girl there?" Allison asked.

"No, my bass player is bringing his girlfriend, so you can hang out with her," Trent said, hoping to convince her.

"I don't know, I can't stay out too late," said Allison, still being somewhat leery.

"I won't keep you out late and my friends are really cool, and it will just be for a couple of hours. We'll have a blast, I promise." Trent said one last time, trying to get Allison's approval.

"Well, okay take my phone number and call me later."

Trent quickly pulled his phone out of his jacket and began typing in her number as she spoke.

"Cool, I'll call you." Trent said with a big smile on his face.

"Great, I have to get to my next class; I'll talk to you later."

"Okay, by the way, what part of the city do you live in?" Trent asked, as Allison began walking away.

"Uptown, call me and I'll give you directions."

As she quickly walked down the hall, she turned and looked back. She saw that he was still standing there, holding his phone and smiling. Their eyes met one more time, causing her to smile back at him. She then turned and continued walking down the hall, but the smile remained on her face.

The train began to slow down as it approached the next station. The loud screeching sound of the brakes returned, as Allison opened her eyes and realized it was her stop. She shut off her IPod, pulled out her ear buds, and then tossed them back into her pocketbook. Out of curiosity, she glanced up but saw two different people sitting where the two women where once seated. The vision of the two talking ladies remained in her head as a reminder to call her friend Meaghan and tell her about her first day of college and all about Trent.

When the train finally came to a halt, Allison pulled her scarf tightly back around her neck, then bent down and grabbed her book bag. She lifted herself up and out of the seat, as the doors slid open, and along with several other people, she stepped onto the familiar platform of her station. She quickly trotted up the steep steel stairway, pushed herself through the exiting turnstile and made her way back out to the part of the city known as her neighborhood.

Stepping onto the snow-covered concrete and immediately feeling the ice cold wind whisk against her face, Allison adjusted her scarf as she glanced upwards and noticed how dismal the sky looked. She then reached into her coat pocket, pulled out her gloves and slipped them on, before reaching into her pocketbook and pulling out her phone to call Meaghan.

With her phone pressed firmly against her ear, she began walking briskly along the icy sidewalk towards her home. She heard it ring once, then twice, before she heard the voice of her best friend.

"So how did it go?" Meaghan asked.

"I can honestly say … It was quite interesting," replied Allison.

"Interesting, what does that mean?"

"Well, I met a really cute guy in one of my classes," Allison said, with excitement in her voice.

"A cute guy … on the first day …I can honestly say … It already sounds like trouble," said Meaghan, knowing all about Allison's past.

"No, he's really nice."

"You said he's cute, well what does he look like?"

"Well, he's tall and he has long black hair," said Allison, trying to describe Trent.

"He has long black hair?" Meaghan said in shock.

"Yeah, he's in a band," Allison said, trying to defend Trent's appearance.

"Your father will freak out if you bring a guy with long hair home."

"Don't worry; my father will never meet him."

"It still sounds like trouble to me."

"Come on Meaghan, you know me," said Allison.

"Exactly, I do know you. My advice, don't get involved." Meaghan said, trying to convince her friend to use good judgment.

"Too late, we're going out tonight," said Allison as she began to laugh.

"What?" Meaghan said surprised.

"He sat next to me." said Allison, trying to explain her situation.

"Long hair, in a band, that has trouble written all over it," said Meaghan, interrupting her excitement.

"Yeah, but look on the bright side, I met him in college, that's something positive."

"Yeah, well, good luck with that …call me later." Meaghan said in a disappointed voice.

"Okay, I will," said Allison and then they both hung up.

She was a bit stunned by her friends' reaction as she put her phone back into her pocketbook, but knowing Meaghan, she was just being overprotective like she always had been. Allison was about to turn down her block, when she came upon an unusual sight. She was startled when she saw an old woman sitting on her corner, holding a cup and begging people for money. She stared at the woman and saw she looked dirty, pitiful and probably homeless. Allison instantly felt sympathy as she then noticed her torn coat and the filthy red hat the woman wore upon her head.

Allison remained staring at the woman, until the woman looked up and noticed her standing there. The woman immediately made a waving gesture in an attempt to call her over. She was franticly waving her cup and wanted Allison to give her a small donation. Allison cautiously walked over to the woman and thoughtfully pulled out whatever change she had in her pocketbook and placed it in her cup.

"Thank you sweetie," said the woman, as she looked up and smiled.

Upon getting closer to the woman, Allison was now able to get a good look at her and it was quite obvious she was homeless, based on her image. Her harsh, wrinkled face showed evident signs of what years of living on the city streets had done. Her hair was long, gray and brittle.

Her halfhearted smile revealed a mouthful of rotted teeth, and to make matters worse, the poor woman wore a black eye patch over one of her eyes, making her appearance seem downright frightful.

"Thank you again sweetie," the old woman said to Allison, after she looked into her cup and saw how generous she was.

"Do you live around here?" Allison asked unknowingly.

"Around here?" The woman laughed.

"Yes." Allison nodded innocently.

"No sweetie, I'm just kind of working here tonight, trying to get enough money to eat something other than what they feed us folks at the shelter. I thought this would be a good corner to sit down on for a couple of hours and just see what happens, I don't need much," the woman said sadly, as she looked back up at Allison.

"Aren't you cold sitting out here?"

"Just a little bit, but it's not that bad."

"Are you going to stay out here all night?" Allison asked.

"No, I'll be in one of the shelters by the time it gets dark, besides, I never stay on the streets late at night, it's too dangerous."

"Dangerous? In what way?" Allison asked curiously.

"There are gangs in the city, and some of them like to prey on us homeless people. They'd kill you for the clothes on your back, for the food you eat, or just for the fun of it." The woman said despairingly.

"Really? I haven't heard anything like that," said Allison.

"They did this to me." She said, pointing to her eye patch.

"They did what to you?" Allison asked.

The woman lifted up her eye patch ever so slightly, to give Allison a small glimpse of her wounded eye. Her eye was red, swollen, and oozing an abundance of excessive white fluid, down her cheek. The sight of the old woman's eye was so grotesque, Allison quickly turned away, trying to avoid seeing it. She then shook her head, trying to erase away the horrible image she just witnessed. The woman nonchalantly wiped her face with her coat sleeve, trying to eliminate the slimy substance off her face.

"Are you okay?" Allison asked.

"Sure, I just can't see too well out of this one." The woman said, pointing to her swollen eye.

"And a street gang did this to you?"

"Yeah, they sure did, and they've done a lot of bad things to all of us."

"All of us?" Allison asked a bit puzzled.

"All of us homeless people. There's a gang of young guys going around the city, beating us up and taking everything we have. The leader is a guy that carries a knife and he'll cut you up, if you make him mad." The woman said nervously, remembering back on her instance.

"Did this man use his knife on your eye?" Allison asked with concern.

"No, he and his gang just beat me up. There were several of them and one guy had a large stick, and he kept poking me in my face."

"Oh my God!" Allison said, still in a state of shock.

"They told me they'd kill me the next time they see me," the old woman added, with fear in her voice.

"What are you going to do?" Allison asked.

"I won't go down there anymore," said the woman.

"Down where?"

"Downtown. It's not safe, especially at night." She said, as if she was warning Allison.

"Maybe you should see a doctor about your eye."

"I did, at the shelter, that's where I got this patch." The woman said, trying to smile again.

"And what did they say to you?"

"They told me it'll get better, and then they sent me on my way."

Allison, for once in her life, was at a loss for words. She just stood there and stared at the poor old woman. A wave of emotional sorrow passed through her, as she suddenly felt a deep compassion. Allison had come face to face with a person who had lost everything and was now an old broken-down human being who was just trying to survive another night on the streets.

"I'll be alright, always have, and always will." said the old woman under a hopeless grin.

"Did this happen to you recently?" Allison asked, pointing to the woman's eye.

"About a week ago, but it'll be okay. The doctors at the shelter said so." She said, with some hope in her voice.

Again, Allison was absolutely speechless. For a moment, she thought about helping the woman, but what could she really do for her.

"You will definitely be off the streets tonight, right?"

"Like I said, I'll be in one of the shelters sometime before dark," the woman responded.

"That's good." Allison said.

"As good as it gets," the woman said, trying to laugh.

"By the way, what's your name?"

"Violet." said the old woman.

"Violet, that's a real pretty name."

"Thank you sweetie, and what's your name?"

"Allison."

"That's a real pretty name too."

Allison smiled and then reached into her pocketbook and pulled out her purse. She opened it up and handed Violet a ten-dollar bill.

"Here you are Violet, please get yourself a nice warm meal somewhere tonight." She said with sympathy in her voice.

"Thank you so much, I will." Violet said, reaching out and grabbing the money.

"Have a good night and stay safe."

"You too."

Allison, feeling like she still didn't do enough for the old woman, reached around and pulled off her scarf from her neck and said, "Here please take this for these colder nights."

Again, the woman thanked Allison, but this time she reached out to touch her. Allison reacted by jumping back for a second, as the woman's hand came towards her.   The sight of her hands matched the rest of the poor old woman's attire. They were wrapped in a pair of torn gloves, with her fingers protruding out of the holes. Allison thought twice about the touch from the woman, but then accepted the woman's gratitude.

"Here please take my gloves too." Allison insisted, as she removed them also and gave them to Violet.

She gave the old woman another smile and said. "I have to go now, but please enjoy your meal tonight."

"I will sweetie, thank you for everything and may God bless you". Violet said, giving Allison her biggest smile yet and once again showing her rotted, blackened teeth.

As Allison began to walk down her block, a strange man suddenly approached her.

"Excuse me," he said.

"Yes?" said Allison.

"Why did you stop and give that old homeless woman money?"

"Because she was hungry, what's it to you?" Allison immediately snapped back.

"Because homeless people are like stray animals, you feed them once and you'll never get rid of them. I don't want her wandering around my neighborhood." The man said angrily to her.

"I'm sorry, but I didn't realize that this was your neighborhood."

"I live here and I don't want to see scum like her hanging

41

around."

"She has as much right to be on this street as you do." Allison said.

"If you or anybody else continues to give her money, next thing you know, she'll bring all of her friends here too. Mark my words; you'll see her again tomorrow and then the next day because of people like you, who feel sorry for them. Most homeless people are either drunks, drug addicts or insane, and now they want us to help them by giving them money." The stranger continued reprimanding Allison.

"Excuse me sir, but I think you're insane, now get away from me," Allison said sharply.

"Listen; don't ever give her another thing, you hear me!" The man shouted.

Allison stepped back, reached into her pocketbook and grabbed her small can of mace. She pulled it out, showed the stranger her defense mechanism and made him realize that she will defend herself if needed. The man, seeing the dangerous situation he was now in, raised his hands and tried to cover his face.

"Get away from me or I swear I'll spray you." Allison said, as she pointed the can directly at the stranger eyes.

The man backed away from Allison and said to her once again "Mark my words, she'll be back here tomorrow, you'll see."

"Have a little compassion for the less fortunate, asshole." Allison said, getting in the final word, before she turned and quickly walked away from the man.

Knowing the stranger was now gone, Allison turned around and focused her eyes back towards the end of the block. Just then, the sun broke through the gray midday clouds and brought a few seconds of warmth against her face. It almost seemed like an appropriate sign from above, confirming that her intentions and motives were warm hearted and correct. She squinted against the bright light to get one last glimpse of Violet. She could still see her silhouette seated on the corner. For a moment, Allison pictured Violet sitting down in a restaurant, eating the warm meal she graciously provided, but then she pictured her walking into a liquor store to make a purchase like the stranger had mentioned. Allison began to wonder if maybe the stranger was right. What if she did return tomorrow and she brought along her friends? Allison knew, she too didn't want homeless people wandering around the neighborhood.

Her memory flashbacked to the conversation she overheard of the two ladies on the train earlier. The homeless population had now tripled in New York City, and seeing Violet in her neighborhood today

42

was living proof. But just like everyone else walking along the avenue, she too was also shocked to see the old homeless woman sitting on the corner. Allison's mind began to repeat all the harsh words the stranger said to her, as haunting visions of Violet's face intertwined within her mind. With her hand still shaking from the brief confrontation, she slowly placed the can of mace back into her pocketbook, as the warm sun rays vanished and the cold bite of winter returned.

Allison turned and began to briskly walk up the block towards her building. As she arrived at the front door, she was greeted by James, the familiar friendly doorman.

"Hello Allison, how are you today?" He asked, as he opened the door for her to enter.

"I'm alright now James, but I'm just a little shaken up."

"Why, what happened?" James asked with concern.

"Did you happen to see the homeless woman sitting on the corner?"

"No, there's a homeless woman?" He asked, with a confused look on his face.

"Yes, she's sitting on the sidewalk, begging people for money," explained Allison.

"Hmmm, I've been employed in this neighborhood for over fifteen years and I've never seen a homeless person in this particular part of the city."

"Neither have I, but I know there are homeless people living in New York, it was just very strange seeing this old woman begging on Park Ave."

"Well what happened, and are you okay?"

"Well I stopped, and gave her some money because I felt really sorry for her, and afterwards, this stranger confronted me and then started yelling at me."

"What did you do?"

"I pulled out my can of mace and pointed it at his face. It was so scary because I've never been in a threatening situation like that before."

"Well, what did he do?" James asked, as he released the door and then took a few steps out onto the sidewalk, to see if maybe the stranger had followed Allison home.

"Well, once I threatened him, he quickly walked away from me."

"Well, thank God nothing happened to you," said James, as he turned and focused his attention back to her.

"Like I said, it was all really scary. This poor homeless woman was badly beaten by a gang that threatened to kill her. She said she didn't

43

feel safe where she was anymore and that's why she decided to come up to this area. But just seeing her sitting there suffering, really touched me and I felt like I should do something, then afterwards a strange man started yelling at me for helping her. He said if people like me start giving money to the homeless they'd never leave."

"Please don't hold this against me Allison, this is just my opinion, but the man did have a good point. I mean do you really want to see a homeless woman sitting on the corner of this block from now on? I'm not condoning what that man said to you, but he was just reacting to the obscure situation also."

"I know, but I couldn't help but feel sympathy for her, especially after she showed me her injured eye."

"Her eye was injured?"

"God, it was so gross." Allison continued with her story.

"I understand, Allison and believe me, you did a good thing for that poor woman, but you have to realize that you put yourself in a real dangerous situation. You don't know what that woman could have done to you and then afterwards, resulting in a confrontation with the angry stranger. I'm just concerned for your safety. The last thing I would want is for anything to happen to you, I mean I've known you since you were a little girl. Again, please excuse my opinion, but I'm just concerned for your safety, that's all."

"Thanks James, I really appreciate that," said Allison, as she reached out and gave him a small hug.

"You're welcome," said James.

"I have to get upstairs; you have a good night, okay?"

"Thanks Allison, same to you." He said, then grabbed the handle of the door and held it open, while tipping his hat.

Allison walked into the lobby of the building and headed towards the elevator. She stopped in front of the metal door, pushed the top button on the wall and waited. As she stood there, she once again thought about what James had just said and knowing deep down, she hoped that she'd never see Violet again.

Allison's thoughts were interrupted by the sound of the elevator's bell. The door slid open and Allison entered the small compartment. She pushed the button for her floor and within seconds, the door closed and the elevator began to rise up to the apartments. Allison shook her head one more time, trying to clear the image of Violet and soon it was replaced by sweet thoughts of Trent's handsome face.

As the elevator continued its ascending climb, Allison began to wonder what was in store for her date with Trent. The thought of going

44

out with a musician sounded interesting and just downright fun. She pictured him on stage, playing his guitar and it gave her butterflies. Despite what Meaghan had said to her earlier, she just adored his long hair and his whole Rock Star persona. Besides having a bad boy look, she saw a nice pleasant side to him and she knew he was different from anybody she has ever met.

"He'd better call me," she said.

The elevator's bell once again interrupted her thoughts, as it reached its destination and stopped at her floor. The door slid open and she exited into the hallway and walked towards her apartment. She stopped in front of her door, reached into her pocketbook and grabbed her house key. She inserted it into the doorknob, then pushed the door open.

"Mom, I'm home!" Allison shouted as she entered.

Chapter 4

The season brought the evening darkness early upon the snow covered city. The day's frigid temperature seemed to have decreased even more, holding the neighborhood in a cold, captive state. The ice and snow that lay upon the streets was nowhere close to extinction, as the bleak winter's climate continued its brutal assault. The blackened skies also brought the avenue to a mere halt, with the neighborhood beginning to wind down from the day's regular activities.

The homeless man's mind remained cautious and unsettled throughout the passing hours, ever since the two incidents that had occurred earlier. He diligently kept a close watch on every single person within his vicinity, just waiting for the next and unexpected confrontation. His thoughts repeatedly relived the altercations he had, from the young men wearing black leather jackets. He knew that after today, he was in grave danger if he remained in this part of the city. He had profound feelings of sadness, knowing his once peaceful domain was now threatened and his comfortable corner was going to be just another memory.

Knowing the lower east side's streets were far too dangerous to walk at night, he decided to spend one more evening in his current surroundings, hoping and praying that nothing else would happen. He knew for his own personal safety he couldn't remain out on the open avenue and he'd be better off hiding out in the alleyway behind the restaurant. It has always been an ideal place to shelter him from any threatening night prowlers and especially for tonight from the recent gang members. He thought that tomorrow would bring a new day, where he could get an early start on a much needed journey in search for another safe place to call home.

He looked across the avenue and his eyes focused on the pizzeria. Another twinge of sadness fell upon him, as his mind wandered to the gentleman inside and how they had provided him with many generous offerings. Even when he'd offered to pay with the money he had collected from the neighborhood citizens, they just smiled at him and then graciously refused. The restaurant was yet another reason why, over the past several months, he would return to this specific inconspicuous corner. He had witnessed immeasurable hospitality from the owner and it always made him feel like there were still some good people left in the city.

Keeping his large blanket tightly around his shoulders, the homeless man placed his cardboard sign against his side and leaned forward to grab his shoebox. He looked down into the open box and began to shake it back and forth, trying to mentally calculate what the day had brought. He noticed that the cold winter days weren't as plentiful as some of the passing warmer ones, but a few individuals still found compassion to offer him a small donation. He focused on the two one dollar bills that lay flat on the bottom as he recalled their origin.

Another sudden flashback of the two young men wearing leather jackets appeared within his mind. He once again recalled the two incidents when they both approached him and then placed the dollar bills into his open shoebox. He remembered the familiar face of the long hair fellow showing up alone at first. It seemed like he must live locally, right here in the neighborhood, because he had seen him many times before. He also recalled that the two young men weren't aggressive like the three punks he had encountered earlier by the park, but he was still uncertain and cautious of their motives. They both seemed unpretentious, but he knew he couldn't take any foolish chances. He was already threatened once and the affiliation between all five young men is they all wore the same style jacket he now associated with danger.

The homeless man turned his head and peered through the rusty steel of his shopping cart, trying to focus only on the Yankee baseball hat on top of the rest of his belongings. His memory summoned up the face of the young man who once wore it, and then he suddenly remembered he'd called him an odd name. He sat there dumbfounded as he tried to remember what the young man had called him. It was a name he'd never heard anyone call him before. His face began to slowly twitch, as he desperately tried to conjure up what was said.

"He called me a short singular name," he said to himself.

"Was it Ed ... or Fred? No ...it was NED. Yes, that's it, NED... but why would he call me that?" He then questioned the young man's motive behind the unusual name.

He thought intensely about why some stranger would just call him NED... NED ...NED." He repeated it over and over as he closed his eyes with confusion, trying to understand the meaning behind it.

"Excuse me." A low distinct voice suddenly rang out that broke the man's concentration.

"Ah, excuse me, sir?" The voice repeated.

The homeless man opened his eyes and slowly lifted his head to see a tall prominent male figure standing before him. Startled, he automatically reached into his coat and placed his fingers on the top of the object within the inner pocket, as he prepared himself for yet another unexpected confrontation. With his free hand, he rubbed his eyes to get a clearer vision of who was within his presence. He quickly inspected the man and instantly saw a shiny brass badge proudly displayed upon the chest of a uniform, identifying him as a police officer. He then tilted his head and looked past the officer, to see his patrol car parked at the corner curb. He wasn't sure why the police officer had stopped to talked to him, but he was about to find out. With his fingers still touching the hidden object, he said in question, "Yes?"

"The temperature is supposed to drop severely again tonight, with high chances of another snow storm. Why don't you go down to the neighborhood shelter for the evening?"

"The shelter is full, it's always full," said the man in a low growly voice.

"Well I can't have you sitting out here on this corner, freezing to death. The last thing I want to do is come back tomorrow morning and have to pick up your dead, frozen body and take it down to the morgue." The police officer said in a stern, but humorous voice.

"They won't let me in. I've already tried, it's full," the man repeated his spoken lie.

"I've seen you sitting on this corner, minding your own business over the past several months and that's why I've haven't said anything to you, but I can't have you dying on my street tonight. Christ man, it's already way below the freezing mark and it's going to get worse."

"I'll be just fine sir, believe me, I've been through worse." The seated man said, looking up and into the officer's eyes.

Staring down at the cold and pathetic man, the police officer reached into his coat pocket and pulled out a small card and a pen. He turned it over and began to scribble something on the back. He then reached out and kindly handed it to the homeless man.

"Here, this is my card with my signature on the back. Give this to whoever is in charge and they will let you in. I can't guarantee you a bed, or even a pillow, but this will at least get you inside and off the street for tonight."

Finally, with a feeling of assurance, the man slowly removed his grasp from the hidden object as his hand peered out from under the blanket. He then reached up, grabbed the officer's courteous offering and read it.

Thomas Phillips – N.Y.P.D – Police Officer

He then flipped it over and verified the man's signature. Unseen and unaware to the officer, a small smirk appeared hidden under the man's long gray beard, as he tucked it into the side pocket of his overcoat.

"Please take advantage of my generosity and get out of this bitter cold, its brutal out here."

"Thank you sir, I will," said the lying man in a low calming voice.

He stared up at the officer once again, paying particularly close attention to his badge. The street lights above praised the shiny piece, catching the embossed details and making it flicker in the night. The man closed his eyes and imagined that maybe it was a sign of glimmering hope. That maybe this gentleman appeared as an angel from above, to save him from this horror he now calls life. For a second, he surrendered to the idea but he knew it was all a mental façade, and his bleak reality returned as he reopened his eyes.

Just then the officer's handheld radio went off. He grabbed the receiver and began to speak to the dispatcher on the other end.

"Yes this is Officer Phillips, what can I do for you?" He asked.

There was a few moments of silence then the officer responded, "Really? Well we're just a few blocks away and we can get there within a few minutes …yes I will … over."

Just then, the passenger window on the police car rolled down and a voice from inside yelled out, "Did you get that call from the dispatcher?"

"Yes, I sure did and I told them that we would respond to it, I'll be right there."

The officer tucked his radio back onto his belt, looked back down at the man and kindly said, "By the way, what's your name?"

The man sat there momentarily in silence because he was completely stumped by the question. Nobody had asked him his name in many years and he honestly could not come up with an answer, except for the one that was just recently mentioned to him. "NED." He said.

"Well, it was nice meeting you NED but I have to go, I hope for your own safety, you get out of the cold tonight. Damn, I wish I could, I can't wait to get home to my nice warm ……." The police officer stopped in mid-sentence, as he realized what he was about to say to a homeless person.

"Ahhh," he uncomfortably paused and then said "Take care NED."

With a simple nod and a small sympathetic smile, the police officer turned and walked back to his car.

The man watched as the officer got into his vehicle and moments later he heard the loud screech of the siren and then saw the flashing red and blue lights suddenly illuminate. For a few seconds, the whole corner instantly lit up like a firework display on the Fourth of July, as the lights ricocheted off the buildings and the store front windows. Seconds later, the car quickly sped away in its pursuit, causing the man's hidden smile to remain on his face, as he secretly hoped the officers were called to a situation that involved the leather jacket gang.

With the corner now back to its gloomy haze, the man sat there confused about what he had just said. He once again tried to remember his name but couldn't. He closed his eyes and tried to recall something that had his name on it; his previous address, a letter, even the sign that once graced his prestigious office door, but he continued to draw a blank. He racked his brain but all he could come up with was the name NED.

He reopened his eyes and pushed his thoughts aside as he looked down into his collection box. He once again began to thumb through his money while he tried to mentally add up the day's accumulation and by the looks of it, he knew he had more than enough to get something warm to eat from the pizzeria. He grabbed the dollar bills and all the loose change and tucked it into the side pocket of his coat.

The man then grabbed his shoe box, his tattered cardboard sign and slowly stood up. He stretched his tight arms and his numbing legs and then pulled the blanket off his shoulders. He slowly bent back down and grabbed the torn garbage bag off the sidewalk and placed it into the cart with all the rest of his items. He then reached back in and pulled the Yankee hat and the soiled baseball and placed them on top of the blanket. He stood there and studied both items so intensely, that it brought a slight rush of warmth throughout his body. He smiled for a moment, then instantly frowned as he patted the object hidden inside his coat pocket.

The homeless man shook his head a few times, trying to clear his unwanted memories as he placed both of his hands upon the cart's horizontal bar. He slowly pulled it away from the grocery store, sliding the stubborn wheels across the cold slushy ice. He then began to push the rusty box of steel towards the street corner.

The cold relentless wind assaulted his face, but his eyes stayed focused. Not for a second did he let his guard down, as he waited for the light to change. His vision shifted from all angles of the street, watching carefully for anyone wearing a black leather jacket.

The light changed and he quickly dropped the two front wheels onto the icy tar. Then with a heavy shove, he quickly pushed his cart across the avenue. When he reached the other side, he spun the cart around and lifted the back wheels up onto the sidewalk and then pulled back strongly. He then pushed the cart up to the restaurant's window and looked inside. He paused for a moment and pretended to feel the warmth that was confined within the walls. Next, he put his hand in his coat pocket, withdrew the dollar bills and waved it, trying to get Lorenzo or Tony's attention.

The tall, monstrous figure leering into the window startled Tony at first, but once he recognized who it was he laughed. "Look Lorenzo, we have a customer, and a paying one at that." Tony joked.

Lorenzo turned, smiled and waved at the man. He made a gesture with his hands as to ask him what he wanted, but he knew he was cold and hungry.

"What do we have for our fine and always scary friend?" Lorenzo laughed along with Tony.

"There's a few slices left over. I can give him those."

"Sure that's fine, toss 'em in the oven for my old buddy."

Lorenzo walked over to the window and signaled to the man to choose what he wanted to drink. He pointed to the soda machine and then to the coffee pot. The man nodded his head and pointed to the coffee pot. Lorenzo smiled and waved for him to meet him outback as usual. Through the glass, the man once again waved his money, but Lorenzo smiled then shook his head, refusing.

The man's eyes shifted as he saw a young couple sitting in a booth. He stared at them for a moment, admiring their happiness until they looked up and noticed him. The look of disgust on both of their faces immediately defined their feelings. He quickly turned away and lowered his head with embarrassment.

The homeless man had never been inside the pizzeria. He knew his limits and never wanted to over step his boundaries. The owner had been giving him free food since he first arrived in the neighborhood. He met him in the alley one morning and had just taken for granted, that's where he would always extend his graciousness. He was not ignorant, and was well aware of the ghastly picture he had become, and the last thing he wanted was to cause any trouble for the kind-hearted owner.

The man pushed his cart towards the edge of the building and around the corner. The side street was dark and quiet, with low radiant street lamps that lit his way. With each forward step he made, he surveyed every aspect of the street as he continued to look over his shoulder, assuring his path was unthreatened. About a quarter down the block, he entered the darkened alleyway. He stopped and stood there for a moment, while his eyes adjusted to the serene blackness. He first looked at the dumpster closest to him and then focused down the alleyway, reassuring his safety. He took a deep breath of the ice cold air and then slowly exhaled, showing a small sign of comfort and relief.

The man pushed his cart up to the back of the restaurant, when suddenly the light came on, followed by the opening of the thick steel door. It was Lorenzo; he was smiling and holding a plate of food and a large cup.

"Here you go big guy; here are a few slices of warm pizza and a large cup of hot coffee, that'll warm up your insides."

"Thank you." The man said gratefully.

Always astounded by the size of the homeless man, Lorenzo looked up as he began a small conversation with him. "I saw that cop talking to you before, is everything okay?"

"Yeah, everything's fine."

"Was he harassing you?"

"No, he just wanted me to go to the shelter to get out of the cold, that's all."

"Well that was nice of him to be concerned about you, why don't you do that?"

"I don't know, I really don't like the shelters, there's too many people," said the man, before he took a big bite of one of the slices of pizza.

"Well, you know you're always welcome to stay back here. Has anybody ever bothered you back here before?"

"No, it's always been safe and very quiet too."

"That's good," said Lorenzo.

Just then, Tony walked out the back door, holding two bags of garbage and heading toward the dumpster. He lifted the lid and tossed them in as he said to Lorenzo, "Hey boss, that last couple left and the front doors are locked. Are we ready to go?"

"Yeah, let's get out of here; it's been a long day."

"It sure has," said Tony, as he disappeared back into the restaurant.

"We're getting ready to leave now; do you want me to leave the light on for you?"

"No, I prefer the dark," the man said, knowing he needed to be as inconspicuous as possible. "But thanks anyway." He said, followed by a

53

small nod.

"Well, have a good night, and if it starts to snow, you might want to take that cop's advice, at least for tonight. You don't wanna catch pneumonia," Lorenzo said kindly.

"I'll think about it, thanks again," said the man, as he took another bite.

Lorenzo turned and pulled the door shut and within a few seconds, the back light was turned off. The man was back in total darkness again so it took a moment for his eyes to re-adjust. He turned and looked out of the alleyway and onto the street to see if anyone had witnessed his brief conversation with the owner, but the street remained desolate.

Happy, his eyes shifted up at the street lamp that always provided a small ray of light upon his secret hideaway. He stared at the iridescent glow as he popped the lid off the coffee cup and took a sip. Between the warm amber shining from the lamp and the hot comforting beverage, he felt a secure feeling deep inside. He placed the cup and his plate on the snow-covered ground and began to dig through his cart. He grabbed his garbage bag and placed it on the ground next to the wall, then he grabbed his blanket and wrapped it around his shoulders. He positioned himself against the wall, then slowly slid down until he was seated. He leaned forward, picked up his food and took another bite, followed by a sip of coffee.

Inside the restaurant, Lorenzo and Tony were finishing up the last of the closing procedures when Tony said, "You're so fucking nice to the big guy, I wouldn't be surprised if one day you'd take him home and ask your wife make him dinner."

Lorenzo laughed and said, "Hell, aren't you the one looking for a roommate?"

"No, I was looking to get a watch dog."

"Well think about it, He would scare the shit out of anybody that broke into your apartment. He'd be better than any watch dog that you can possibly get for protection."

"Yeahhhhhhh ... but, no!" Tony said laughing. "It's funny, but every time I see him back there, it always reminds me of that old saying; I wouldn't want to run into him in a dark alley."

"I've said it once and I'll say it again, he doesn't bother anybody and honestly, I don't think he'd hurt a fly. Come on let's go," said Lorenzo, as they both walked out.

Lorenzo turned and locked the door, then Tony pulled the steel gate down to the ground and secured it.

"See you tomorrow, stay warm." Lorenzo said.

"Yeah, it's so cold, I'm actually gonna run to the subway tonight, see ya," said Tony, as they quickly parted ways.

As the man sat there enjoying another complementary meal, he began to think about what he was really going to do about his situation. His thoughts began to intertwine amongst the different options he possibly had.

"Should I really leave tomorrow after all I've been through? Maybe I should take the advice of the police officer and stay at the shelter, or I could possibly go live under the streets in the sewer again, but I know there are more people down there than ever, Scavengers, families and now even rumors of cannibals, indicating that there's no safe place anymore. Maybe my option is to just stand up to these punks," The big man thought to himself.

"Damn it, what should I do?" He now said aloud.

He paused for a second and took a deep breath of the cold air, trying to come back to his senses. He slowly exhaled, trying to calm his sudden burst of rage. He closed his eyes and sat perfectly still for a moment, as a calming and final thought came to him, "I think I'll be alright for tonight, there's no danger here, I'll just decide what to do tomorrow."

He picked up the cup of coffee and sat there holding it with both hands, trying to soak up whatever warmth was left as the evening's temperature continued to drop. Looking up, he saw the winter's moon peeking through the dark, overcast sky and got lost in the beauty behind the big white star, as he sat there in silence.

With his head pressed against the wall, his mind began its daily ritual of reminiscing about his tragic past. As his thoughts began to wonder, he reached into his coat and began to touch the object hidden inside. He delicately caressed the top of the item, before he slowly withdrew it from its home.

He gripped it from the small marble base and held in front of his face like he had a thousand times before. He stared at the tarnished, gold-plated piece of metal with deep sadness. He reached out and with his filthy calloused fingers, softly touched the tiny, exquisite features that graced the face of the item. A small teardrop began to fall down his cheek, as he heard the familiar haunting child's voice begin to speak within his head.

"A baseball, a bat and a glove, Wow! Santa did hear my prayers, Daddy. Look Mom …look what Santa brought me!"

55

"Good things always come to good little boys, Scotty." Marcia said to her son.

"I love everything else he brought me, but these are what I really wanted! This is the best Christmas ever! Can we go play baseball in the park, can we? Can we go today, Daddy?"

"Maybe later...maybe after our Christmas dinner that your mother prepared for us." The man said, as he patted his blonde son.

"After dinner...but we didn't even eat breakfast yet." Scotty said, disappointed as he began to stomp his feet.

***

The man laughed to himself, as he squeezed his eyes shut tightly. He reached up and wiped another tear, as he continued to touch the face of the small object as another painful segment from his memory arose. This time, it was a warm spring day and he and his son were down at the park.

"Alright Scotty, concentrate this time and pitch it right down the pike," the man said, as he bent down and crouched into a catchers position.

"This one's gonna be perfect pop, watch this." Scotty said, as he wound up his arm and then threw the ball to his father.

"Good boy Scotty, you've definitely gotten a lot better over the past few years."

"Thanks to you dad, you're the one who taught me how to pitch like this and like you always say, practice makes perfect."

"Yes it does. Alright, let's see you throw another strike."

"Okay, are you ready?" Scotty asked, as he wound up his arm once again.

"Ready when you are."

"Do you think I'll be good enough for Little League next year?" He asked as he paused for a moment.

"Absolutely!"

As another perfect pitch was thrown from the boy's hand, they both exchanged huge grins.

"Abso-freakin-lutely," said the proud man to himself.

The man pulled the tarnished gold object towards his chest and hugged it tightly. He held it there for several minutes, as his mind raced into his next flashback.

***

"What do you mean I have to come into work? My kid's big game is this Saturday, it's the city championship and he's pitching, I can't miss it." The man said to his boss.

"We cannot afford to lose this account. Saturday is the only day available for this meeting before these clients leave, and I'm depending on you to be there." The boss said in a stern and demanding tone.

"But, I ..." he said, until he was rudely interrupted.

"But nothing, get your priorities straight. There will be other baseball games, other championships, but there won't always be opportunities like these. This is a big deal, millions of dollars, you will be here no matter what, and that's final, end of conversation." The boss said, as he turned and stormed out of the man's office.

"Fucking asshole." He said quietly to himself.

The man's intense thoughts were broken, as he found himself gripping the object with such aggressive hatred. He'd squeezed it till his hands were numb and his knuckles had turned white. He began to grind his teeth, as another unsettling segment of his previous life rushed forward.

"What do you mean you have to work this Saturday? You'll miss Scotty's big game," asked Marcia.

"I can't do anything about it, I tried, but Rodney was just being a dick about it. The only thing that greedy scumbag ever thinks about is money. You know him, there's nothing on this planet that's more important."

"Well, why don't you just call in sick or something?" asked Marcia innocently.

"I can't do that, I have to go to this meeting. But I'll try to somehow cut it short, and get down to the ball field to at least see the last couple of innings."

"Scotty's going to be so upset." She said.

"Scotty? What about me? I've been waiting for this moment since the day he was born."

The man's psychotic trance was momentarily broken as he found himself trembling. He tried to physically get a hold of himself, but between the bitter cold and his harsh unrelenting memories, his body shook uncontrollably. He took another deep breath and closed his eyes, as he mentally prepared himself for the next, and worst, flashback.

***

"Just sign right here gentlemen and on Monday, I will personally see that both of our accounts will show the deal was finalized. I'm glad we came to a mutual agreement today and we look forward to representing your company. Thank you again and I will contact you early next week with all the final details. Have a safe trip back and enjoy the rest of the weekend." The man said in a courteous but hasty way.

Back in his office, Rodney entered and said, "You were great; honestly I couldn't have done it without you, thanks again for coming in today, I will make it up to you."

"Sure...listen I've got about thirty minutes to make it across town to catch the last inning of my son's game. I will see you on Monday."

"I will make it up to you, I promise." Rodney said, still grinning from ear to ear.

"Sure ... enjoy the rest of your weekend."

"I will, and hey ...good luck today ...I hope your boy wins."

"Me too." The man said, as he darted out of the office towards his car.

He grabbed his cell phone and speed dialed his wife as he ran through the parking lot.

"Hello," answered Marcia.

"What's going on? Who's winning and what inning are they in?" he asked franticly.

"It's the bottom of the sixth and their losing by one, but Scotty is pitching an incredible game, you'd be so proud if you were here watching him."

"I'm in the car and on my way, I'll be there as soon as I can," he said as he pulled out of the parking lot.

"Drive safely, dear," begged his wife.

"I will baby, I love you."

"I love you too, see you soon."

About thirty minutes later, he arrived at the ball field. He saw a crowd of people walking to their cars through the parking lot; it was quite obvious the game was over. He drove up and down a few aisles, until he finally found an empty spot and pulled in. He quickly got out of the car and began to rush towards the entrance of the field, where he saw a few of Scotty's teammates exiting the front gate, along with their parents. They were cheering and smiling and high fiving each other; he also saw some of the kids from the opponents team with tears in their eyes. He quickly scanned the area looking for his wife and his son. As if the sun was just shining down upon him, he noticed Scotty's bright blond hair from afar, and holding his hand with a big bright smile on her face, was Marcia.

"Scotty!" He yelled from the parking lot as he got closer to them.

Little Scotty turned his head and quickly noticed his tall, towering father coming towards him. He released his mother's hand and began running, while waving a bright golden object high above his head. By the gigantic smile on his face, it was quite obvious it was the award for winning today's game.

"Dad, dad, we won. We won!" He yelled with excitement, while he proudly waved the shiny golden trophy in the air.

Subconsciously, the man heard a loud roar from an engine but he didn't see a car. He quickly turned and then suddenly witnessed a red sports car speeding through the parking lot. It was like he saw the whole scene in slow motion, watched his son running towards him, unaware of the fast moving vehicle.

"Scotty stop, stop right there!" he yelled out, but the loud roar of the engine and his child's adrenaline seem to silence his command. The last thing he witnessed was the sun's reflection off the smile on his child's face and the gold trophy before the fatal accident.

He heard the loud screeching of brakes and then a loud, sudden bang. At that very moment, he felt his heart stop. He desperately ran through the parking lot, as he suddenly came upon the scene of the accident. As he arrived, he saw the driver of the vehicle, a young teenage boy, and his friends had gotten out of the car to see what had happened and what they might have hit. He then saw his son lying on the ground, unconscious. He quickly pushed the driver out of the way and grabbed his son, but he was unresponsive.

"Scotty! Scotty!" He screamed.

He then heard a gut-wrenching scream come from his wife, as she too ran up to the scene of the accident. She immediately bent down and together they held their son, as their uncontrollable tears began to flow.

"Oh my God! What have you done? What have you done?" Marcia screamed at the teenage driver.

"I didn't see him, I swear, he's so little, I didn't see him. I didn't see him!"

They held their son's lifeless body as they both screamed, "Please open your eyes Scotty! Please open your eyes!"

The child remained still, but his fist was still tightly clenched around his winning trophy. They laid Scotty back down on the pavement and then the man reached over and pried the golden object out of his dead child's hand.

***

The homeless man relived these horrifying moments daily, and over the years they had taken a drastic toll on his mind, body and soul. He sat there, holding the tarnished gold item in front of his face as his tears continued to flow. He brought his son's championship trophy to his lips and lightly kissed its slightly corroded face.

"I still love you Scotty, I love you so much. Not a second goes by that I don't think about you."

The man then held the trophy up and into the beam of light coming from the streetlamp outside the alley. The ray of light caught the trophy's tiny little face as he slowly twirled it around, giving it a new and revived radiance.

***

The three punks from earlier were walking the neighborhood, doing some early night patrol, when one of them happened to see the tiny sparkle reflect off the man's trophy, down the dark alleyway.

"What the fuck was that?" The short, bald one asked.

"What?" The blonde leader asked.

"There was a flash of light or something in that alley."

"Huh?"

"Look, there it is again."

"Yeah I saw it too." The dark-haired one said as he tightly gripped his stick.

"Let's check it out; it's probably another homeless person stinking up the neighborhood," said the leader.

As they walked into the alley, the man noticed three shadowy figures walking towards him. He could not see their faces due to the streetlight being behind them, but he immediately recognized the large stick in the one's hand. He brought the trophy to his face one more time and gently kissed it again, before quickly tucking it back into the inner pocket of his coat. As his heart began to race, he immediately stood up because he knew that trouble was upon him once again.

As the three men advanced closer, he could see the shine off their black leather jackets and realized it was the same punks that threatened him earlier. Trying to avoid another conflict, he quickly

60

grabbed the handle on his shopping cart, but in just a matter of seconds it was too late. The three of them were now standing before him.

The leader stepped forward and began his malicious rant. "Well look who it is. Hey, I thought I told you to leave and never come back. You see, earlier today, out of the kindness of my heart, I gave you a chance. But I guess you didn't listen, I guess you didn't understand, but then again why would you? If you were smart, you wouldn't be homeless. You wouldn't be out here, living and begging on the streets and ruining our neighborhood. You see, earlier today, you had a chance to fucking leave; but now you don't have that opportunity anymore. Now you're going to pay, pay the consequences for not listening to me, and I mean pay with your fucking life." Just then, the leader's hand slowly reached into his back pocket and withdrew the weapon he was about to use on the man.

Chapter 5

Trent and Vince approached the rear of the snow-covered vehicle. With his arm, Trent brushed a thick layer of snow and ice off his car's trunk, then inserted the key into the lock. He grunted as he slowly pried the back lid open, due to the cold weather freezing the hinges. It made a loud squeaking sound as he continued to struggle, trying to lift it completely up.

"God damn it," he said as he strained to complete such a simple task.

"It's like everything in the whole fucking city is frozen solid," he continued complaining, as he bent down and picked up his guitar case and carefully placed it inside the trunk. He then reached inside and grabbed the shovel he kept for emergencies such as these.

"You have a shovel, for what?" Vince asked laughing.

"To dig my car out of any unexpected snowstorms, and to dispose of the bodies of people who ask stupid questions." Trent answered sarcastically.

Vince laughed again and then said, "Hey, give me the keys so I can sit in the car and get the hell out of the cold, I'm fucking freezing."

"Sure, God forbid if you maybe help me."

"How many times am I going to tell you, I'm just a drummer."

"I'll dig the car out and you can do a drum solo on the ice that's frozen to the windshield; use the scraper, it's in the back seat." Trent said as he tossed Vince the keys.

"And start the car so it'll warm up and we'll be able to go in a few minutes."

"Hey man, I don't know how to drive, that's why I take the subway."

Trent gave Vince a dirty look and said, "Give me back my fucking keys."

Trent dropped the shovel and walked around to the driver's side of the car. He opened the door, reached in the backseat and grabbed the windshield scraper.

"Here, do something will ya." He said to Vince, tossing the tool over to him.

He then sat down in the driver's seat and stuck the key in the ignition. He pumped the gas pedal and then turned the key. The cold engine turned a few times but didn't start. He paused for a moment, pumped the gas pedal a few more times and gave it another try, but once again the engine didn't start.

"Fuck!" Trent yelled, as he hit the steering wheel with both hands.

Vince came around to Trent's open door and asked, "Is it going to start?"

"I hope so."

"I don't know much about cars, but what I do know is that doesn't sound too good." Vince said sarcastically.

"Just scrape the windshield, it'll start." Trent responded.

He turned the key again and the car began to shake as the engine continued to turn. He pumped the gas pedal several more times while holding the key in the on position.

"Come on!" He screamed.

Then suddenly, the car's engine roared. He immediately pressed down on the gas pedal, causing the car to backfire as the car sputtered with minimal power.

"Yes! Thank you Lord!" Trent yelled.

"Hell yeah!" Vince yelled out too, as he patted the hood of the vehicle.

"Try to scrape a little more ice off on my side of the window so I can see clearer. It'll take me a few minutes to dig the snow away from the tires, then we're out of here." Trent said, before he got back out of the car and grabbed his shovel again.

He quickly circled the car as he dug away some of the snow, then he threw the large tool back into the trunk and slammed down the lid. He sat back in his car, reached over and opened the passenger door lock.

"Let's go." He said.

"Rock and Roll!" yelled Vince.

He handed the scraper back to Trent, then went around to the other side of the car. He reached into his leather jacket and pulled out his drumsticks, then opened the door. He threw the pair down onto the seat and got in.

"Damn dude, it's fucking colder in here then it is out there, does your heater work?" Vince asked pulling up the zipper on his jacket.

"Yeah, maybe, things work on this car whenever they want to,

64

but we might get lucky, wait till the car warms up a bit then I'll give it a try, but until then there's a few blankets in the backseat, grab one or two."

"What about the stereo?" Vince asked, while reaching into the backset.

"It's like the only thing that does work."

"Well, crank the bitch up!" Vince insisted.

Trent pushed a button and instantly, the car was filled with the loud sounds of heavy metal music. He revved the engine one more time then fastened his seat belt. He turned on the headlights and then put the car in drive.

"Fuck yeah!" Vince blurted out.

Within a few maneuvers, Trent got his car out of the tight parking space. The cold engine continued to sputter as the car began to move. As they slowly approached the corner stop sign, both Trent and Vince turned their heads with curiosity. Both sets of eyes leered down the block, looking for the homeless man.

"Do you see him?" Trent asked.

"No I sure don't, and I hope I never see him again for as long as I live."

"I'm telling you, I've seen that guy a hundred times before and he's never acted like he did today, never." Trent said, trying to defend the homeless man once again.

"That guy scared the shit out of me." Vince said, as he kept staring down the block.

"I can honestly say I was pretty scared too. Maybe, you pissed him off and he decided to leave the neighborhood." Trent said.

"Maybe, your buddy NED decided to kill himself. That would make me a lot happier," Vince said, as his eyes remained focused on the far corner.

Trent laughed as he pushed back down on the gas pedal.

"Where are we going first?" Vince asked, as he turned his head and attention back to Trent.

"We'll go get Shane and his girl, and then we'll make our way uptown and pick up Allison."

"Where does she live again?"

"She texted me her address after we spoke earlier, she lives somewhere off Park Avenue."

"You found yourself a little rich girl, huh? What does her father do?"

"I don't know, I guess he's probably some big shot, but I'll never meet him."

"And why's that? You're a respectable guy, with long hair, that wears a leather jacket and plays guitar in a rock band. What super-rich guy wouldn't want you dating his daughter?" Vince said sarcastically with a smirk on his face.

"My thoughts exactly, honestly, I can't believe this girl even agreed to go out with me tonight."

"And why's that?"

"Well, first of all she's gorgeous and second, she's rich."

"So? Nobody's perfect."

"Yeah, but she's fucking close, so there's gotta be something wrong with her. I bet she has severe daddy issues." Trent said, smiling back at his friend.

"Yeah, and I bet you'll be the final nail in the old man's coffin." Vince said, laughing at his own remark.

***

Allison was in her room, looking through her closet, trying to decide what to wear. At dinner, she failed to mention to her parents about her date, knowing they would only disapprove and the conversation would end up into another argument. After the early morning fiasco with her father, she thought she would get dressed and just tell them she was going over to Meaghan's. She remembered Trent telling her they would be the first band to play and that he would get her home early, so she figured they would never find out.

"He said wear something black," she said to herself, recalling their earlier phone conversation as her fingers continued to rummage through her closet of clothes. She pulled out a few black items and tossed them on her bed. She started mixing and matching jeans with blouses and dresses with stockings, but also thinking what does it matter, because she's just going to wear her winter coat over everything anyway.

Her thoughts were interrupted when her phone rang. She picked it up and saw that it was Meaghan. "Hello." She said.

"So are you still going out tonight with the rock star guy?"

"Yeah, and I need you to cover for me because when I leave, I'm going to tell my parents I coming to your house."

"Great, here we go again," said Meaghan in a frustrated voice.

"I thought you were my best friend?"

"I am, you know that."

"Well, that is what best friends do for each other, they help each other out, and besides, why don't you come with us? I'm sure it will be alright."

"Ah, no thanks, you know I hate rock music."

"Yeah, I know, but it might be fun."

"Again, no thanks."

"Alright, I have to get ready; the rock star guy said he'll call me when he pulls up to the building and I'll meet him downstairs. So once again, our story is that I'm coming to your house for a few hours, alright."

"Yeah, I guess. What's his name again?"

"Trent."

"If Trent only knew what he was getting himself into." Meaghan said with a hint of sarcasm.

Allison laughed and then said "Listen I really have to go, I'm already running late but I'll call you later."

"Okay."

"Thanks again." Allison said.

"Yeah, yeah, yeah …Bye." Meaghan ended their conversation with a slight attitude.

***

Trent's car continued to sputter its way through the cold dark city of Manhattan. From the lower east side up to mid-town, the traffic proved to be just as stressful as Trent's nerves, as the two band mates continued their conversation.

"You don't understand. I'm really nervous about tonight. I've got everything riding on this one gig. My reputation, the band's reputation, my dad's reputation, I mean the owner of the club has known him for years and, and, I just don't wanna fuck it up. Maybe I jumped the gun by booking this show; I mean we've only been playing for a few months and, and, also this girl, maybe I should have waited a week or so, but I played like I was some rock star today and, and…"

"And what, she bought it, didn't she? Dude you are a rock star."

"Yeah, a wannabe rock star."

"We're all wannabe rock stars, it's called being a musician."

"Yeah, I guess."

"Hey, do you think your heat will work yet, it's still freezing in here?"

"I don't know, let's check it out." Trent said, as he flipped a switch on the car's console.   Just then, ice cold air immediately blasted

67

from the vents, giving Vince an instant chill.

"Brrrrrrr, well at least we know the air condition works." He said jokingly.

Vince then reached into his jacket and pulled out his pack of cigarettes. "Do you mind if I smoke." He asked.

"Yes."

"Dude, a cigarette will warm me up."

"I'm not breathing in your second hand smoke, nor am I opening a window."

"Can I smoke a joint? I rolled up another one back at your place."

"No, I don't want my car reeking of weed either."

"You know I like to catch a buzz before I play."

Trent just shook his head as he continued to drive through the city. Within ten minutes, he pulled up to Shane's apartment building, where he saw him and his girl standing outside waiting. He beeped his horn to draw their attention, then rolled down the window.

"It's about freaking time; I was just about to call you." Shane yelled out to him.

"Sorry, traffic was a bitch due to all the ice still on the streets. Believe me, I hate driving in the winter," said Trent as he got out of the car.

"Sorry man, I'm just anxious about our gig tonight that's all," said Shane.

"Me too man, I've been stressed all day."

"Hey, you remember Beth."

"Absolutely, Hi Beth, glad you can come tonight," Trent said politely.

"I wouldn't miss you guy's first gig if my life depended on it," Beth responded with a smile.

"Cool, thanks so much," he said.

He then turned and said to Shane, "Hey man, let's put your bass in the trunk. Hold on, let me grab my keys."

Trent reached into his car, pulled the keys out of the ignition and walked to the back of the car. Shane grabbed his guitar case and followed him. The loud squeaking sound of the trunk's hinges cried out once again, as the back lid was reopened.

"Just toss it on top of my case," He said to Shane.

"Sure." He said, as he placed his guitar case into the trunk and then reached up and slammed the lid back down.

"You and Beth can sit in the back; Vince will let you in on the

68

passenger's side." Trent said, as he walked back to the front of his car and got in."

Vince got out and pulled the bucket seat forward, allowing Shane and Beth access to the back seat of the vehicle.

"You remember Vince." Shane said to Beth.

"Yes I sure do, nice to see you again."

"Same here," said Vince, holding the seat forward for them as they entered.

Once they were both in and seated, Vince pushed the bucket seat back into place. He then got back in the car and pulled the door shut. Trent rolled up his window, turned around and said "Sorry, it's so cold in here, but my heat doesn't seem to be working. Wrap yourselves in one of those blankets back there; maybe that will keep you warm."

"No problem, Beth will just give me a little body heat," said Shane, grinning at his girlfriend.

Trent put the keys back into the ignition, then turned and looked at Vince. A slight look of concern was drawn on both their faces for that moment when Trent turned the key. The engine sputtered once but then started right up, also bringing the music alive once again to the silent car. Both guys immediately smiled at one another as a sign of relief, knowing they were on their way again and nothing was going to stop them from performing tonight.

"Rock and Roll!" Trent yelled out to pump up his band mates.

"Hell yeah!" Vince yelled too, feeling the excitement.

"Let's tear this mother up!" Shane hollered from the back, bringing an instant smile to Beth's face.

"Look out New York, the City Rats are coming to devour Manhattan tonight." Trent said, as he put his car in drive and pushed down on the pedal.

***

Allison, wrapped in a towel, stepped out of her bathroom and glanced at her alarm clock on her night stand. She realized that she was still running behind and began hurrying through the motions of getting prepared for her date. She quickly finished drying her body off, then slipped on a matching pair of undergarments before she dodged back into the bathroom. She looked at the distorted image of herself as she quickly rubbed the mirror with her dampened towel, trying to remove the mist that had formed from her hot shower. She pulled open the top drawer of her vanity then began pulling out all of the necessities needed. She scattered all the items on the counter and then grabbed her hairbrush and her blow dryer. She plugged in her dryer, turned it on and then aimed it towards the mirror. The hot air instantly cleared the condensation from the reflective glass, giving her sight more clarity. She gently ran the brush though her long, wet, blond hair then proceeded to apply the basic make-up she uses to make herself beautiful.

"A little bit of this and a little bit of that," she said to herself, as her hands kept switching back and forth between her beauty products.

"I guess I already made a good first impression, but the second one has to simply dazzle him."

As Trent's car was idling at a stop light, Beth asked him a question. "So, I hear you're bringing a date tonight, where did you meet her?"

"I met her in one of my classes today. To make a long story short, I walked in, saw her and then noticed an empty seat next to her and the next thing you know, I've got a date."

"Well good for you. It's all about having confidence, that'll get a girl every time."

"Yeah, I'm still a little overwhelmed to be honest with you, I was telling Vince that I played the rock star card today, but I hope I can live up to my own hype."

"Dude, don't worry, everything will be fine, just you wait and see." Shane said, patting Trent on his shoulder, reassuring him.

"Thanks man," said Trent, as the light changed and he drove forward.

"Hey by the way, thanks again for wearing your black leather jacket tonight, I think we all look really cool, don't you agree?" Trent said to Shane.

"Hell yeah, we'll look like we rode to the gig on fucking Harley's," said Shane.

"I think we look like a gang of bad asses." Vince added.

"I think you guys look sexy." Beth said, complementing the whole band.

"Thanks," said all the guys simultaneously.

"What part of the city does your date live in?" Shane asked.

"She told me she lives off Park."

"Rock on brother," Shane said, patting Trent on his shoulder once again.

"Yeah, I'm a bit nervous about that too, I'm not used to dating upper class girls. I tend to date girls that live by me, you know, villagers."

"Well, maybe things are starting to look up for you Trent, this could be a whole new change in direction for you," said Beth.

"Maybe," said Trent, as he looked into his rear view mirror, nodding his head while making eye contact with her.

"We're almost there right? This traffic is starting to dig into our time," said Shane.

"Yeah, I'm gonna cut through the park; we'll be there in about ten minutes."

As the car made its way through the winding road of Central Park, it finally came out on the other side. Driving just a couple of streets over, they were now on Park Avenue as the car continued along.

"That's it, that's her block." Trent said, as he turned his car down her street and began to check the addresses. About half way down, the car slowly pulled up in front of the posh building. Trent looked out of his window and saw the door man standing just inside the big glass door. He reached into his jacket pocket, pulled out his phone and said, "She told me to call her when we arrive and she'll meet us down here." He hit the previously called button then held the phone to his ear. As the phone began to ring, it rang once, twice then three times before Trent said, "Come on Allison, answer your phone." The phone unfortunately went to her voicemail when she failed to answer.

"Damn it, what the fuck!"

"Well, call her again," said Shane.

Trent hit redial and held the phone back to his ear. Once again, the phone rang until it automatically went back to Allison's voicemail. This time he left a message.

"Hi Allison, this is Trent, aahhh, we're downstairs waiting for you, give me a call back. OK."

"What's up?" Vince asked.

"I don't know, I talked to her earlier and she said she was coming, let's give her a minute or two."

"Sorry man, but maybe she changed her mind," said Shane.

Trent felt discouraged and a bit like a fool as he sat there waiting. "What should I do?" Trent asked his friends.

"Call her back one more time, maybe she's just getting ready and didn't hear her phone," said Beth.

Trent hit the redial button one more time but after a minute, he got the same results. "Damn it, what should I do?"

"Well, you have two options; you can say fuck it and drive away, or get out and go get her," said Shane.

71

"I can't just walk up there. What will the doorman say?"

"Well, he's probably gonna ask you who you are and what you're doing here," Shane answered.

"Just tell him you're here to pick up your date and see what he says," added Beth.

"Damn it!" Trent said, as he paused for a moment to collect his thoughts and then said, "Fuck it, I'll be right back," as he got out of his car and walked towards the big glass door. The door was suddenly opened and held, as he was immediately greeted by James the doorman. "Can I help you?" he asked Trent.

"Yes sir, I'm here to pick up a girl. Maybe you can help me."

James looked at Trent and was not familiar with his face or his type coming to this particular building.

"Do you know her name?" He asked.

"Her name is Allison, she's a real pretty girl with long blonde hair, and she gave me this address. Do you know her?"

"Do you know her last name?" James asked with skepticism.

"Aahhh, no I don't, I met her today in school and I invited her to come see my band play tonight."

"You're in a band?" James asked.

"Yes sir,"

"And you met her where?"

"Today in class, I go to college and she was in one of my classes."

"Hmmmm, one moment, I'll be right back." James said nodding his head, knowing exactly who Trent was looking for. He walked over to the lobby phone and dialed up to the Thompson's apartment.

The internal phone rang a few times before it was answered by Allison's father.

"Hello, this is Walter Thompson."

"Good Evening, Mr. Thompson, this is James down in the lobby."

"Yes James, what can I do for you?"

"Well, sorry to bother you sir, but I have a gentleman down here looking for your daughter Allison."

"A gentleman? Looking for Allison? I am unaware of this, are you sure?"

"Yes sir, he described her perfectly."

"Well what does he look like?" Walter asked.

"Well, he said he's in a band. To describe him, he has long hair and he's wearing a black leather jacket and torn faded jeans. He said he

72

invited your daughter to go see him and his band play tonight somewhere."

"Really? Again, I am unaware of this but honestly, I'd like to meet this so-called gentleman."

"Are you going to come down to the lobby sir?"

"No James, give him my apartment number and send him up."

"Yes sir, I will do just that, thank you sir, have a good night."

"Thank you James," said Walter before he hung up. He then called out to his wife, who was in the kitchen putting away the leftovers from the evening's dinner.

"Yes dear," Grace answered as she walked into the room.

"Were you aware that Allison has a date tonight?"

"Allison has a date tonight? No dear." She said with a confused look on her face.

"Well, she does, and he's on his way up."

"Well who is he?"

"I'm not sure, but I think we're in for a big surprise."

***

Back down in the lobby, James wrote down all of the Thompson's information on a slip of paper and handed it to Trent.

"Here you go sir; this is the floor and apartment number, the elevator is down the hall."

"Well, what did they say?" Trent asked.

"They informed me to tell you to just go upstairs." James answered.

"Cool, thanks for your help," said Trent, as he turned and looked back at his car and signaled to his friends that he would be right back.

He walked down the lobby hall of the posh building, admiring all the exquisite furnishings and art work that graced the internal surroundings. He thought to himself "I'd better stay in school if I ever want to live like this someday, man, this is the life."

He approached the elevator, pushed the top button on the wall and waited. Within thirty seconds the car landed, a single bell rang and the door opened. He walked inside and turned to the all the buttons upon the elevator wall. He looked back at the slip of paper, pushed the floor indicated from the doorman and watched as the door closed.

He felt the tremble of the elevator rising, but it didn't compare to the now tense feeling he had in his stomach. He wasn't sure what to expect and wished that Allison would have just answered her phone, hoping to avoid this particular situation. As the elevator continued to climb upwards, Trent reached back into his jacket and grabbed his phone. He once again checked to see if Allison had called, but he knew that she hadn't. The elevator car began to slow down as it approached Allison's floor. Trent stood perfectly still and waited for the door to open. He heard the bell ring once again and watched as the door slid to the side. He stood there, paralyzed for a moment as he contemplated about the whole scenario.

Here was his only chance to back out of it, if he'd just push the lobby button. His feet were frozen in place as all these thoughts ran through his mind, but then he thought he'd feel like a fool in front of his friends if he showed up downstairs without Allison. That motivation alone pushed him to step off the elevator. As the elevator door closed behind him, he stood in the hallway and took a deep breath of the warm comforting air, while tucking his phone back into his jacket's pocket.

"Well, this is it, time to grow a pair," he said to himself, as his nerves escalated even higher. He took one more deep breath of the warm air and then proceeded to walk down the hall towards Allison's parent's apartment. He checked the information on the slip of paper one more time, verifying that the apartment number was correct as he stood in front of their door.

"Well, here goes nothing." He mumbled to himself, before he moderately knocked. He stood there patiently waiting, as he overheard footsteps approaching the door from the other side, then the turn of the lock. A few seconds later, the door opened and Trent was standing face to face with a middle-aged man. He could instantly tell by the look on his face that he wasn't that pleased to see him.

"Hello, my name is Trent and I'm here to pick up Allison, is she here?"

"Yes she is, please come in."

Trent walked through the doorway and into the Thompson's living room and saw what must be Allison's mother standing there looking at him.

"My name is Walter and this is my wife Grace," said Mr. Thompson, as he reached out and extended his hand to Trent.

"Hi, how are you?" Trent said to both of them, as he grabbed Walters hand and firmly shook it.

"Nice place you have here." Trent said politely, as he looked around the posh apartment.

"Thank you, lord knows I worked really hard for it."

"May I ask what you do for a living?"

"I'm an attorney."

"An attorney, well that's good to know; you never know when you might need a good lawyer right?" Trent said, trying to bring some humor into the conversation, before realizing he was the only one laughing.

"So I heard you're in a band?"

"Yes Sir and we're playing tonight at a club downtown."

"I see, and you're taking Allison with you?"

"Yes, I invited her to come see us when I met her earlier today."

"And where did you happen to meet my daughter."

"I met her in one of my classes; we go to the same college." Trent said, smiling.

"I see," said Walter, nodding his head.

***

Allison was busy blow-drying her hair and failed to hear her phone ring. As she continued trying to hurry through the process, she looked over at her night stand and noticed the time again. She thought to herself, "Hmmmm, I wondered why Trent hasn't called yet."

She walked over to her bed and grabbed her phone. She looked at it and realized that Trent had called three times.

"Holy Shit! God I hope he didn't leave!" She said, as she pushed redial to call her date.

***

Trent suddenly heard his phone ringing from within his jacket and he reached inside to grab it. He excused himself for a moment, as he looked at the identifier and saw that it was Allison. He shook his head and then answered it.

"Hello." He said in a confused voice.

"Oh my god, I'm so sorry. I was getting ready and I didn't hear my phone ring, are you still waiting downstairs?"

"No, actually I'm standing here in your living room, talking to your parents."

"What?" Allison said in shock.

"Yeah, where are you?"

"I'm in my bedroom, ahhh…I'll be right out." Allison said nervously.

She hung up her phone, threw it down on the bed and said to

75

herself, "Oh my God, I'm screwed."

She immediately sat down on her bed, trying to think of something quick, but she knew she couldn't leave poor Trent out there too long with her father. She quickly got up and began putting on the rest of her clothes, as she continued to mentally torture herself for being so ignorant. She then grabbed her winter coat and prepared herself for the worst.

***

"That's funny," said Trent.

"What is?" Walter asked.

"That was Allison; she just called me from her bedroom, hmmmm, that's strange."

"Yes it sure is," said Walter, as he patiently waited for his daughter.

"I just figured she already knew I was here waiting for her."

"Yes, I bet she's going to be really surprised, just like we were."

Trent didn't know what to say after that remark, so he said nothing.

***

Allison opened her bedroom door and was instantly greeted by her mother, who was waiting for her in the hall.

"Allison, what is going on tonight?" Grace asked with an irritated tone in her voice. "What do you mean?" Allison answered, trying to playing dumb.

"Who is this long haired derelict standing in our living room?"

"His name is Trent and he's not a derelict, he's my date."

"Date? Tonight? It's a school night, why didn't you mention this at dinner?"

"What, and start another argument like we had this morning? No thanks."

"I know, but what were you thinking, and who is this guy?"

"I met him today at school, he sat next to me, he asked me to go see him and his band play, and I thought he was cute so I said yes. What's the big deal?"

"The deal is that you're already back to your old habits, what's next Alley?"

"I know dad treats me like a child, but now you?"

76

"You always do such stupid things; I mean honestly, what were you thinking?"

"I was thinking about going out and having a nice time and escaping from this hell hole. Now if you'll excuse me, I have to go meet my date before daddy eats him alive, if he hasn't already." Allison said, as she walked past her mother.

"Hi Trent, I am so sorry," Allison said as she walked into the living room.

"That's okay, but we're running late and we really have to go."

"She's not going anywhere." Walter said to Trent.

"Daddy please, I'll be home early."

"Yes, I promise to have her home right after we finish playing, it won't be late." Trent said in a comforting voice.

"I'm not talking to you; I'm talking to my daughter." Walter said, turning his attention towards Allison.

"Daddy please, I said I'll be home early."

"And I said you're not going anywhere." Walter said in a stern voice.

"Sir, please, I said I will get her back early."

"Trent, no offense to you but I think it's time for you to go." Walter said, as he walked over to the front door and opened it.

"Sir, please ..." Trent said, trying to remain cool.

Allison turned and looked at her mother, who was now standing there in silence. She could tell by the look on her face that she was just as equally upset and knew that she wasn't going to get any help or sympathy from her on this one.

"Sorry," said Trent, as he looked Walter in the eye, then made his exit out of their apartment,

"Trent, wait." Allison called out.

She then turned to her parents and said, "You have to stop treating me like a child. I said I will be home early and I will. When will you trust me?"

"When you grow up," said Walter.

"Thanks for embarrassing me; I can always count on you to do that." Allison said, as she walked out the open door.

"Allison, come back here now," Walter yelled to his daughter.

Allison ignored her father's command and ran down the hall to Trent, who was waiting by the elevator.

"I can't even begin to apologize to you." Allison said.

"That's alright, are you sure it's cool for you to come tonight, because I don't want to get you into any more trouble?"

"Please, my father has been like that since the day I was born."

"Allison!" Walter yelled out, as he walked into the hallway and saw both her and Trent standing there.

Just then, they heard the sound of the elevator bell as the car arrived to the floor and then they watched as the door slid open.

"Quick, let's go," said Allison, as she grabbed Trent's arm and pulled him into the elevator. She quickly pushed the lobby button, as she overhead her father calling out to her one more time before the door closed. They stood in complete silence as the car descended, until Trent said, "By the way, you look gorgeous."

"Thanks." Allison said, as she looked up into his eyes and smiled.

He smiled back at her then they rode the rest of the ride down in silence, hearing nothing but the subtle humming coming from the car's moving cable. Their slight tension was broken, when they landed and they heard the single ring before the door opened.

"Are you ready to Rock and Roll?" Trent said to Allison, trying to get her to smile again.

"I sure am," said Allison with a girlish giggle.

"Cool let's go," said Trent, as they got off of the elevator and began walking towards the front door.

James saw the two youths walking in his direction and he immediately went into his professional mode and held the door open for them.

"Have a good evening, Ms. Allison." He said to her with a big smile.

"Thanks James, you too."

"You too Sir," he said to Trent as he tipped his hat.

"Thanks man, same to you."

As they walked outside, James pulled the door closed behind them and stood back at his post. They instantly felt the bitter cold sting their faces and then the soft touch of icy snow flurries falling from the dark winter sky.

"Damn, just like they predicted, another snowfall tonight," said Trent.

"Honestly, once Christmas is over, I hate the remaining winter months." Allison said, complaining about the miserable weather.

Trent looked out towards his double parked car and he could see his band mates were definitely impatient at this point. He could see Shane was telling them to hurry up through the closed back window.

"I am so sorry once again; I hope I didn't ruin your evening."

78

Allison said.

"No, but we're definitely running late, but we should be fine, come on let's go." Trent said, as he held Allison's arm as they quickly walked across the icy sidewalk. He escorted her over to the passenger side of his car and opened the door.

"Everybody, this is Allison, Allison, this is everybody. I'll introduce you to them once we get in the car and get going." He said to her.

He looked at Vince and said, "Jump in the back and let her sit up front."

"Absolutely," said Vince, as he reached back in and grabbed his drumsticks, before he pushed the seat forward and got in the backseat. Trent pushed the seat into place and waited for Allison to sit down before he closed the door. He quickly dashed around the front of the vehicle and then got back into the car.

He fastened his seat belt and then made sure she had hers on too. With an apologetic face, he looked over at Allison and said, "Sorry it's so cold in here; my heat doesn't seem to be working, but hang on and I'll give it another try."

He flipped the switch on the console and once again, ice cold air blew out the vents, causing Allison to cringe but then miraculously, the air began to get warm. Trent held his hand up in front of the vents, smiled and said, "See, good things are starting to happen, I can just tell this is going to be a great night."

"Yeah, well you better get this car in gear or we'll never make it to the club on time," said Shane.

"I got this." Trent said as he nodded his head, put his car in drive and once again pushed his foot down on the gas pedal.

Chapter 6

The blonde-haired leader raised the object above his head, allowing the homeless man to get a good look at it. The long, black and chrome handle enabled the man to quickly identify it as an unopened switchblade. The leader looked into the eyes of the man, smiled, and then pressed the release button. The man heard the click and then watched, as the thin steel blade swept through the air, locking securely into place. The leader began to wave it gracefully through the air, making the blade dance within the darkness as he laughed out loud. His sinister laugh demonstrated the unstable mind he possessed, giving the man a sense of fear. He had a threatening grin upon his face as he looked up at the man, pointed the knife at him and said, "I know we weren't formally introduced earlier today, but I like to let you know my name is Jack. On the streets, I'm known as Jack the Knife, for reasons, well, it's quite obvious. You see, I like to let my victims know my name, because I want it to be the last thing they remember. Oh and by the way, these are my colleagues; the one holding the stick is Slugger, I call him that because he likes to hit homeruns with people's skulls, and the name of the bald headed guy is Spaz, basically, because that's what he is."

The leader's deranged sense of humor caused a trickle of laughter amongst his two companions. They both looked at each other smirking, showing the man they also had irrational minds.

"And by the way, what's your name?" Jack asked.

The man stood there in silence. He looked at them one at a time and once again began sizing them up like he had earlier in the day. His attention was particularly drawn to Slugger. The way he was holding his stick over his shoulder made the man think of the golden trophy within his coat pocket. He slowly raised his hand and subtly patted the hidden object from outside his coat, just for security measures.

"I'm going to ask you one more time, what's your fucking name?"

The man's eyes instantly returned back to Jack. He stared down at his face, not knowing what to say. Again his mind raced, trying to remember his actual name, but just like before, he didn't know. He paused for another second then said "...NED."

"Well NED, unfortunately, after tonight you'll be known as Dead NED." Jack said as he began to laugh again, but this time at the expense of the man and at his own immature rhyme. The comment made the other two punks laugh out loud as well, as they began to tease the big man by calling him, "Dead NED, Dead NED, you're going to be dead ...NED!"

"Shut up!" Jack yelled abruptly at both of them, showing them this wasn't some game and this was no time to be fooling around.

"You see, NED, I'm going to cut you up into little pieces and throw you in that dumpster so when they come and empty that thing, they will have taken you where you belong, at the city dump with all the rest of the garbage."

The man made one more attempt to leave by giving his shopping cart a quick shove but just like earlier, Spaz instantly reached out, grabbed the cold steel cage and stopped it dead in its tracks. As if he started playing a game of tug of war with the man, Spaz began to shake it back and forth like a maniac. The man tried desperately to hold onto the cart's handle, but he eventually lost his grip, making the cart topple over. Suddenly, all of the man's belongings tumbled out and scattered onto the snow-covered ground. Again showing how despicable they were, the leader's henchmen began kicking all the items around. Next, they began to rummage violently through the objects, trying to get a good look at what he had.

"Look at all this fucking shit!" Spaz shouted.

"Hey Jack, do you need a new, old pair of shoes?" Slugger said to the leader, as he began picking up some of the man possessions. He then grabbed the tattered cardboard sign and read it "**HOMELESS** – **N**eed **E**very **D**ollar".

"Hey look Jack; I just got myself a new job." He said sarcastically, holding the sign in front of himself, before throwing it back to the ground.

The big man remained silent and still as he watched his situation worsen. He turned his head and stared directly into Jack's eyes, showing a deepened sense of anger. Jack returned the stare as to accept the man's challenge and said, "Oh yeah, and what the fuck are you going to do about it, NED?"

Both Slugger and Spaz continued to comb through the man's belongings, trying to find anything of value, but kept coming up short. Spaz bent down and suddenly burst into laughter when he saw something's that caught his eye. The long stare between Jack and the big man was abruptly interrupted when they both heard Spaz's voice yell out, "Hey look, a Yankee's hat and a baseball!"

Excitedly, Spaz put the hat upon his bald head and smiled with a big devilish grin. He then gripped the baseball and proceeded to yell over to his fellow gang member, "Hey Slugger, let me pitch one to you, let me see you hit a homerun over the building."

Also getting into the thrill, Slugger immediately got into a typical batters stance and waited for Spaz to pitch the ball to him. The two began laughing out loud like children on a playground as their horseplay continued. Jack momentarily took his eyes off the big man and turned to see what all of the commotion was between his two henchmen.

Once again annoyed, Jack yelled at them for the second time, "Hey, I said this isn't a fucking game!"

The big man realized that if he had any opportunity it was now and he quickly reached into his coat and grabbed the prized trophy. He gripped the figure tightly and extracted it from his coat then quickly raised it high over his head. He stretched his arm and held his hand as high as he could to gain the greatest downward momentum possible for the deed that he was about to accomplish.

Out of the corner of his eye, Jack saw the sudden flash of movement occurring in front of him and he quickly turned back around. His eyes looked at the face of the man then traveled upwards to see his arm extended high. A split second wasn't enough time to save Jack from receiving the hard initial blow, as the solid marble base of the trophy came plunging down. The combination of the big man's strength, and the trophies hardened edge, caught Jack and instantly ripped open his forehead. The intense, sudden impact also made him drop his knife as he fell to the icy ground. He then lay upon the snow, holding his head and screaming out loud in severe, agonizing pain.

His two henchmen quickly turned around and were simultaneously shocked to see what they were witnessing. Somehow, the tables had been turned and their fearless leader was lying on the ground, helpless and screaming. They both took a few quick steps forward as if they were going to try to help, but then stopped and had second thoughts after seeing what happened to their leader. They both looked at each other, knowing their whole sinister plan of stealing, and then killing this particular homeless man, had backfired.

The big man was looking down at Jack, when he slowly lifted his head and focused his attention on the other two. He stood there for a moment and stared at Slugger and Spaz as his anger began to fuel. They recognized hatred within the man's eyes but thought they still had him outnumbered, until they noticed the gold shiny object in his hand.

"Holy shit," said Slugger under his breath.

"What the fuck are we going to do?" Spaz asked his friend.

They didn't have much time to decide because within seconds, like a vicious bull, the big man came charging towards them. Slugger prepared himself for the worst as he tightly gripped his stick but without having a weapon to defend, Spaz panicked and tried to run. With his adrenaline racing and no traction under his feet, he began to slide upon the icy snow and soon plummeted to the ground. The big man was upon him first, as he swung his trophy-loaded fist at his head. The initial blow instantly knocked the Yankee's hat off of Spaz's head and then the second hit pierced his skin and drew blood.

With his arms flaring up in the air, Spaz tried desperately to protect himself from the man's aggravated rage, but like an uncontrollable sledgehammer, the big man brought the trophy swiftly down upon Spaz again and again. Spaz cried out "Help me! Help me!" until he was semi-unconscious.

Knowing this might be his only chance to save his fellow gang members, Slugger gripped his stick with both hands and swung it with all his might. He connected across the back of the big man, but between the man's enormous size and his thick layered clothing, the shot did nothing except draw his attention to Slugger. He turned his head, and with bloodshot eyes, he stared at Slugger for about a second before he lunged at him.

Still gripping the trophy, the man grabbed Slugger's leather jacket with his free hand and flung him across the alley. Slugger slid across the ice and snow and slammed into the dumpster. His body hit the sturdy iron box so hard that he literally bounced off of it. With his body feeling immobile, he now lay upon the ground scrambling for his life.

"Please stop! I'm sorry! I'm sorry!" Slugger screamed as he pleaded with the man, but by now his rage was unstoppable. He grabbed Slugger by his leather jacket once again and with one hand he lifted him up off the ground. Slugger watched through his tearful eyes, as the golden trophy was raised high above the man's head and then came barreling down, hitting its mark. Slugger screamed out in pain as he felt the shiny prize strike his skull, tearing deeply into his flesh too.

"Help us!" Spaz suddenly let out a loud scream like his life depended on it. "Somebody, please help us!"

The man stepped back and took a good look at both Spaz and Slugger and felt some satisfaction for his accomplishment. He took several breaths of the cold air in order to revitalize himself, before he was about to finish what they had started. Both men looked across from each other, bloodied and lying helplessly and finally realized they'd messed with the wrong guy.

"Jack! Help us! Help us!" Both Slugger and Spaz began to yell to their still grounded leader.

They saw him moving but he wasn't getting up. Jack was still in severe pain, bleeding profusely from his wide-open gash. He continued to roll around, trying desperately to regain his senses, but as he wiped the blood and tears from his eyes, he saw a shiny vision. It was his switchblade and it was directly in front of him.

"Fuck yeah," he said out loud.

He reached out and grabbed his knife and then slowly staggered back to his feet. He made another attempt to wipe the blood and tears off his face, but the pain was immeasurable. He cringed as he took a few steps forward, towards the big man and his wounded men.

"God damn mother fucker, I'm going kill this bastard," he said to himself, as he retightened his grip on his knife.

The big man's attention was still focused on Spaz and Slugger, unaware of Jack coming up behind him. Still staggering and still in a slight state of confusion, Jack quickly plunged forward and stabbed the big man in his side. The sharp knife instantly cut through the big man's coat and into his flesh.

"Arrrghh!" the big man yelled from the unexpected attack.

Jack pushed the knife deeper, twisted it and then pulled it out. The man quickly turned around and saw Jack holding the bloody blade and pointing it back up at him.

"Come on mother fucker!" Jack yelled at the big man, as he began to wave his knife once again, while desperately trying to remain on his feet and somehow regain control.

The big man looked at Jack's bloodied face and gave him a sneer. The injury to his head from the trophy's marble edge was severe and his blonde hair line was crusted with thick blood. Jack looked down and witnessed the amount of blood he was losing and knew he was badly hurt, but he also knew he couldn't back down at this point.

"I'm going to carve my name into your fucking face you stupid motherfucker!" Jack yelled his threat, as he continued to stagger and point his knife up at the man. The man just stared back at Jack, as he held his side with one hand and his golden trophy in the other. He was not sure how deep the cut was, but he knew he was hurt too as the pain sharpened. He looked deep into Jack's eyes and like a crazed wild animal, growled as his anger increased.

85

Jack stood confident but inside he was really scared. Throughout his life, he had never backed down from a fight and had maintained a solid reputation as being one of the toughest people on the street, but tonight, he knew he'd finally met his match and was definitely in a do or die situation.

He continued his threat by waving the knife, but was still unsure of his next move. He knew he wanted to kill this man, but currently he didn't see a way how to. He heard Slugger and Spaz still moaning in pain. He looked past the man and saw them both trying desperately to get back to their feet. He thought maybe he could bide some time and soon they would be able to get back into the battle, but he also knew as the leader of the gang he really couldn't rely on them. Besides, he should be the one protecting them.

As Spaz continued his attempt to get back up, he noticed the old baseball lying in the snow and plunged forward and grabbed it. He held it firmly in his hand and basically prayed for a miracle, as he threw it with whatever strength he had left towards the big man. The ball sailed through the darkness and fortunately hit the man directly on the back of his head, causing him to instantly drop to one knee. Jack, also suddenly shocked, tried to take advantage of the opportunity, by quickly thrusting his knife towards the face of the kneeling man.

Luckily, the homeless man saw it coming and swung his trophy-loaded fist around, blocking Jack's fatal attempt. The two pieces of metal collided, but the hard impact made the knife fly back out of Jack's hand. Once again, in a state of panic, he dove back to the ground, trying desperately to regain possession of his weapon. His fingers feverishly filtered through ice and snow, as they hurriedly tried to reach for the blade.

Both Spaz and Slugger finally staggered back to their feet, but they knew they wanted no part of continuing this fight. They saw the big man still on one knee and they too took advantage of the opportunity, and began to quickly run towards the exit of the alleyway.

"Run for your fucking lives!" Spaz screamed, as he grabbed Slugger by the sleeve of his leather jacket.

"Don't be fucking stupid Jack, run!" Slugger screamed back at the leader, as he and Spaz stumbled to the street.

Jack immediately grabbed his knife, got back up and stood there for second, contemplating what he should do next. Should he try to charge the big man and continue this battle, or should he run to safety like the other two did? He looked past the big man, saw that both Slugger and Spaz were now gone and felt a sense of resentment, as he knew he was now truly alone, negating the meaning of the word 'gang'.

The man kept one eye on Jack, knowing that his knife was back in his possession, but he turned his head slightly and acknowledged the other two had fled the scene. He smiled and then tightly gripped the trophy, as he mentally and physically prepared himself, knowing this fight wasn't over yet. He slowly stood back up, held his wounded side, then leered back down at Jack and said, "Well, it looks like it's just you and me."

"You don't scare me motherfucker, I'm going to cut you apart, you fucking son of a bitch!" Jack said, trying not to show his true fear.

"There's only one way out of here, and that's through me," said the big man.

Jack paused for a moment and took a deep breath. As he exhaled, he stared deep into the man's eyes and for a second, saw a vision of his own death. He felt a cold chill run down his spine, as he knew he had to somehow escape this predicament if he wanted to get out alive. Then, with a sign of desperation, he began viciously swinging the knife back and forth. The sharp whirling blade made an intense swooshing sound, as it cut blindly through the night, forcing the man to take a couple of steps back.

Once again, in another attempt to defend himself, the man quickly raised the trophy, trying to block Jack's violent incoming attack. Like an old time fencing dual, the sharp blade and the golden piece of metal connected, once and then twice; but on the third clash, the two pieces were locked together and so were their eyes. Jack's blade was tightly lodged under the arm of the bat boy and it was now down to a test of strength, as both men drove their weapons close to each other's faces. The big man's size soon overpowered Jack and forced him downwards into a submissive position. Struggling for dear life, Jack was lucky and able to lift his leg, to get a swift kick into the area of the man's open knife wound.

Wincing in pain, the big man fell backwards and eventually lost his balance. He fell hard to the icy ground, as he tightly held his golden possession in one hand and his side with the other. Jack looked down at the now grounded man and realized this was his only chance to escape. Then, like a raving lunatic, he quickly shuffled his feet and staggered towards the exit of the alleyway.

"Come back! Come back! You fucking coward!" The big man screamed, as he turned his head and watched Jack running away. Jack paused for a moment, as he heard the man's insulting and threatening plea. He turned, looked back into the alleys bitter darkness and for a moment, wanted to go back to defend his honor. He then lifted his hand and felt his forehead, which brought forth an acute sting, which immediately contradicted his second thought.

"Fuck you!" He screamed back into the alley, before he turned and finally disappeared.

The man rested his head back down into the soft snow and then screamed as loud as he could into the cold darkness. "I will get you! I will get all of you!"

He laid there for a minute or two, then slowly and painfully pulled himself up to a sitting position. He brought the tarnished trophy up to his face and stared at it like he had a thousand times before. He then held the shiny object back into the streetlamp's ray of light, and watched it as it began to sparkle like it was new once again. The man returned to admiring all the tiny features upon the face of the object, like he was doing before all the trouble started.

"Thank you Scotty. Thank you for saving my life tonight," he said, as he reached out with his bloody fingers and touched the small nose on the face of the golden object.

"You are and always will be my hero, Daddy." The imaginary voice rang out within the man's mind.

He smiled under his long gray beard and then brought it up to his lips and softly kissed the trophy's face.

"I will get you Jack and all the rest of your punks," he whispered and then stopped and corrected himself by saying "No ....NED will get all of you."

Chapter 7

The sudden spark of the evening's snow continued to fall, as Trent drove southbound towards Greenwich Village. He turned on his windshield wipers, hoping to clear the front glass, but just like everything else on the car, the blades were old and just smeared the icy windshield, obstructing his view.

"What a drag, now because of the snow, the traffic will probably slow down even more. Man, could we have any more bad luck," said Shane.

"God I hope not," said Trent.

"Just be careful," said Allison in a low, concerned voice.

"Yeah, the last thing we need is to get into an accident." Trent said, trying to stay focused on his driving.

He then took a moment and personally introduced Allison to his band members, and then to Beth. Everybody still gave her a warm welcome, considering she was responsible for the tension they were all feeling. She once again apologized to everybody, trying to ease all of their stress levels, but she knew deep down she had messed up. She also felt embarrassed over her father's reaction toward Trent, making her less talkative as she sat there quietly. Trent looked over at her and smiled, reassuring her that everything was fine, as he continued to drive towards their destination.

"Come on guys, let's not lose our positive energy. Tonight will be a night you'll remember for the rest of your lives." Trent said trying to pump his band back up.

"I'll feel better when we get there," remarked Shane.

"We'll be there in about twenty minutes or so." Trent said, still trying to ease the tension.

"Can't you drive any faster?" Shane asked.

"Dude, I'm doing the best I can, just sit back and relax, because you're beginning to stress me out and I've already been through enough already."

"I'm really sorry." Allison said once again.

"Sorry, I didn't mean to say that." Trent said to her.

"Why, what happened?" Shane asked.

"Nothing, everything's okay." Trent said, as he turned towards Allison, looked her in the eyes and smiled once again.

***

The homeless man laid the golden trophy upon the icy ground as he tried several times to get to his feet, but the pain from the knife wound persevered. He turned his head and noticed that the tipped-over shopping cart was just a few feet away, so he turned himself over and slowly crawled towards the steel apparatus. His fingers finally grabbed hold of the cold steel and he was able to push himself to his knees. He paused for a moment, took a deep breath and then with profound strength, forced himself to progress upwards into the alley's darkness.

As the man stood tall, he felt a mist of snow flurries that began falling from the sky, upon his face. The cold, icy flakes felt somewhat revitalizing, as he unbuttoned his coat to get a look at his injury, but then he felt both angry and saddened upon the gruesome sight of his shirt, saturated with the color red.

"God damn it." He said to himself.

He reached inside his coat and softly touched the knife wound from the outside of his shirt. He cringed as he felt the severe pain that instantly made his eyes fill with tears. He didn't know exactly how deep the wound was, but he knew he couldn't just stay in the alley, or he'd mostly likely bleed to death. He knew the local hospital wasn't close to his vicinity, meaning his only option was the neighborhood shelter located several blocks away. He couldn't remember if the shelter had a doctor, or even a nurse on staff, but he thought if he could just make it there, they wouldn't let him die.

Trying to endure the intense pain, he mustered up every ounce of strength he had left, knowing all of his possessions were scattered all over the alleyway and he wasn't about to leave them behind. He struggled as he first crouched down and slowly pulled the shopping cart back onto its wheels. Then, with every agonizing step and every painful strain, he slowly gathered up all of his snow-covered items. He wrapped the thick woolen blanket over his shoulders, in an attempt to shield himself from the cold, and from the now constant snow fall. He then limped over to where he once laid upon the icy ground, retightened his bloody fingers back around his deceased child's golden prize and then the old soiled baseball.

90

He slowly stumbled back over to his shopping cart and tossed the baseball in on top of his gathered items. He then pushed open the child seat and placed the golden trophy upon the flat piece of worn plastic. In the past, he had always kept the precious prize inside his coat, but he wanted to keep it in plain sight, as a sign of hope and determination. He placed his hands upon the cold horizontal bar, as he began his slow and painful walk to the shelter, but he suddenly stopped and looked back at the preceding battleground. His eyes focused specifically on the four patches of blood that stained the icy white covering. He grinned for a second, then trembled, knowing that one of them was his.

***

As Trent's vehicle continued towards the downtown area, Allison kept to herself and just looked out of the passenger side window. She was a bit stunned to see how many people walking the streets, resembled the homeless woman she had seen earlier today. She began to realize there were more homeless people living on the streets of Manhattan than she had ever imagined. Between hearing the story told by the ladies on the subway, of the family living in the sewer, then meeting poor Violet on the corner of her block and now seeing dozens of poverty-stricken people just wandering aimlessly in the cold, she couldn't help but feel heartbroken over their situations. She turned to Trent and said, "I can't believe how many homeless people there are, wandering around the city."

"Funny you bring that up. Vince and I had a run in with a homeless man earlier today."

"Really, so did I, it was with a homeless woman, but that's beside the point; what happened to you?" Allison asked.

"Make a long story short, several months ago, this homeless guy started hanging out around the corner from where I live. He would just sit there, minding his own business and begging for money …you know, like most homeless people do. But today, when I gave him a dollar, he just seemed different."

"Different in what way?"

"I don't know, like abnormal or pissed off, like something must have happened to him. Then Vince showed up, and on our way back to my house, he too gave him some money and then for some ungodly reason, called him NED."

"NED? Is that his name?" Allison asked.

"You told me that was his name," said Vince from the backseat,

91

listening in on their conversation.

"I told you that was his nickname."

"NED? Why would NED be a nickname for someone?" Allison asked.

"It's derived from a cardboard sign he holds; everybody in the neighborhood calls him Homeless NED, but anyway, at one point this guy got up and started chasing us."

"Oh my God, what did you do?"

"We ran like hell."

"That scary son of a bitch scared the shit of me," said Vince, leaning forward.

"Now tell us your story." Trent said to Allison.

"Well my story involves a homeless woman. I was walking home from the subway and there she was, standing on my corner. She too was begging for money, so I stopped just like you did and I gave her some, and then afterwards, this guy came up and started yelling at me."

"Well what did you do?" Trent asked.

"I pulled out my can of mace to protect myself."

"That's crazy!" Vince shouted again from the backseat.

"What's sad is the homeless woman was beaten up. She actually had a patch over one of her eyes; she even showed it to me, it was so gross."

"Did she tell you who beat her up?" Trent asked.

"She said there's some gang that's going around, threatening homeless people. She said that's why she was up in my area; she didn't feel safe being downtown anymore."

"Hmmm, that makes me wonder if maybe the homeless guy had a run in with that particular gang. That might explain why he was acting so weird," said Trent.

"That would just be a coincidence, but you'd never know. But honestly, I couldn't imagine living on the streets, begging for money. It just seems so horrible; I think I'd rather be dead."

Without saying a word, everyone in the car nodded their heads, agreeing with Allison's statement.

***

The screeching sounds of the shopping carts wheels once again pierced the cities silence, as the man made his way out of the alley and back onto the dimly lit street. With the snow falling down upon him, he looked up at the street light and said a small prayer, hoping the worst was behind him. He then pushed his cart forward, keeping an eye out for the return of the leather jacket gang and his other eye on the golden trophy, as it bounced back and forth within the confines of the cart's child's seat.

"We're going to make it Scotty; we're going to make it." He whispered to himself.

With every grueling step he took, he could feel the tormenting pain from the deep laceration. He began to channel his agony, using the faces of the three punks as a reminder of who was responsible for it. The image of Jack's evil grin appeared within his mind, as he kept recalling the moment when he felt the knife pierce his skin, and when the edge of the trophy tore into his enemies head. He then looked down at the bouncing award and actually saw the marble corner coated with Jack's blood. He grinned, knowing that nobody walked away tonight unscathed and that the punks in this particular situation were not victorious. The warm feeling of self-accomplishment gave the man another reason and the die-hard motivation to take another aching step forward, as he approached the corner of the avenue.

***

"We're almost there, we're actually back in my neighborhood," said Trent, as he drove into The Village.

"Good, because we're still running behind," said Shane.

"I know, we'll be there in about five minutes, then hopefully we can find a parking spot, you know that's always a challenge."

"So this is where you live, in the artsy fartsy part of the city. My personality fits in better down here than where I live." Allison said.

"Really? And why's that?"

"Everyone is so uptight and I'll use my father as a perfect example."

"Ahhhhhh …just forget about it," Trent said, hearing a bit of annoyance in her voice.

"As a little girl, I've always dreamed of living a bohemian lifestyle, you know being an artist, writer or even a musician like yourself. Not having all the pressures of being my father's only child. It would absolutely kill him if I didn't live up to his expectations."

"Well, what does he expect you to be?" Trent asked.

"Successful."

"Well, we all want to be successful."

"Yes, but I've lived in that world my whole life and honestly all I want to be is …" Allison paused for a moment and then said, "Happy."

The car went silent after everyone heard Allison's sad remark. The feeling everyone had when they first pulled up to her beautiful apartment building seemed to vanish, as they looked at her now with a different set of eyes. They actually felt sorry for her, knowing she was living the life of a poor little rich girl.

"Well, for tonight you can just forget about it. You came out with me to hear my band play and I guarantee you're going to have a great time."

"Hey look, there's Lorenzo's." Vince said.

"Do you see our homeless friend anywhere?" Trent asked, laughing.

"No, I bet you we'd scared him off."

"Yeah, with your scary face." Trent continued joking as he drove a little faster, trying to make up time, but it all came to a screeching halt when the traffic light turned red.

***

As the homeless man began to reach each and every corner, he would go through the routine of getting his shopping cart up and down onto the curbs. Every time he pulled the cart up, the strain would tear at his wound, causing him to let out a small agonizing moan. His feet would also occasionally slip, due to the fresh snow making every curb a tedious and hazardous task.

He knew he had just a few blocks to go before arriving at the shelter, and eventually had to cross the main avenue. He noticed that the early evening's traffic was scarce, but there were still a few cars sporadically on the main street. As the cars would pass, he noticed that some of the drivers would turn their heads and stare, but then just continue driving, as they were all oblivious to his injured condition. To them, he was just another homeless person wandering around the downtown district.

He came to a corner when he noticed the light had changed and he thought this was his chance to get across. He took a deep breath of the cold air and then dropped the cart's front wheels onto the black icy pavement. The hard, sudden impact with the street made the golden trophy bounce about an inch high within the small circumference of the child's seat. He quickly placed one hand on the precious item, securing its position back down against the plastic protector and then with a sharp painful shove, he began to push his cart across the avenue. With the wind

94

and the snow sweeping hard against his face, his pace was slower than usual. Time passed quickly, as he noticed that the crossing sign was beginning to flash. He tried to hurry but every step he took showed another sign of his growing weakness. The crossing sign eventually stopped flashing and the light turned green for the one car that was idling at the red. He realized that he was only half way across the avenue when he saw the car make a sudden advancement.

***

With his head turned and his attention focused on Allison, Trent did not see the man crossing the intersection until he heard Shane say, "Damn it, with all this talk about homeless people, we now have one right in front us, blocking the street."

Trent turned his head, immediately looked out of the vehicle's blurry windshield and was instantly shocked to see who was standing before him. His foot slipped off the brake pedal for a second, as his body quivered in fear, making the car jump about an inch before he immediately pressed back down on it.

Everybody in the car suddenly looked forward, witnessing the horrifying sight of the big man. They all stared at his long, gray hair and his elongated beard blowing furiously in the wind, giving him the appearance of an old, hideous giant.

"Holy shit! That's him, that's fucking NED!" Vince screamed out from the backseat.

***

Although all the windows on the car were tightly closed, the homeless man could not overcome hearing the name that had haunted him since the early afternoon. With his feet frozen to the icy street, he turned and stared deep through the windshield. Despite the constant movement of the wipers, he leered at all the passengers and immediately recognized the driver as one of the leather jacket gang members from earlier. His eyes quickly pivoted back and forth as he tried to get a good look at all the rest of the passengers. He quickly noticed Allison's long, blonde hair, along with a horrified look on her face within the vehicle's darkness. Next, he saw a couple of young men from the backseat lean forward and began to scream obscenities at him. Once again, the sound was muffled, but he could definitely hear the name NED being repeated, as the green light swaying over his head turned back to red.

"Hey NED, get the fuck out of the way!" Shane yelled.

"Yeah, fucking move NED!" Vince also shouted.

"Calm the fuck down, what the hell is wrong with you?" Trent hollered at his band mates.

"We're already running late and this homeless asshole is just standing there," Shane hollered back at Trent.

"Well, what do you want me to do, run him over?"

"If I was driving I would. Look, he already made us miss the light once and now he's just standing there like a fucking idiot." Shane began arguing with Trent.

As the light once again turned green, the man just stood there in the middle of the avenue. "God damn it, get the fuck out of the way!" Shane screamed out again.

He then reacted by reaching over Trent's shoulder and pressing down on the car's horn. The strong beeping sound rang out, piercing the avenue's silence, as he held his hand firmly down in the middle of the steering wheel, until Trent grabbed it and pulled it off.

***

The loud sound of the horn startled the man, breaking the trance he fell in from staring at the people inside the idling car. He once again felt his inner rage beginning to erupt, after recognizing and associating the driver and the passengers with the leather jacket gang. In his mind, he contemplated many decisions, as he laid one of his hands back upon the golden prize for protection. He squeezed it firmly, trying to regain some strength, but he also knew he was in no condition to properly defend himself from so many enemies. He decided to try to avoid another conflict as he took a tiny step forward. With one hand on the horizontal bar and the other on the trophy, he slowly pushed himself and the shopping cart across the avenue. His eyes remained focused on Trent and vice versa, as he made his way to the corner curb and then turned around to perform his normal routine.

***

The stop light once again turned green, but Trent's eyes were still fixated on NED. He watched his every move as he slowly backed up onto the curb.

"Are you okay?" Allison asked, but Trent ignored her, keeping his eyes focused on the homeless man.

"Hey man, for god sakes let's go," said Shane, redirecting Trent's attention back to reality.

Trent looked up at the green light, then pushed down on the gas pedal. The icy street caused the tires to spin in place, as they tried to gain traction. The car suddenly slid to the side, as it began to hydroplane across the avenue. Trent spun the steering wheel, trying to regain control of his vehicle, but the back end moved quickly towards the corner curb and the homeless man. He immediately pushed down on the brakes, but the momentum of the vehicle could not be stopped, as the rear of the car continued to slide and inevitably collided with the front of the homeless man's shopping cart. The man tried desperately to maintain his grip upon the horizontal bar, but the hard impact made his feet slip on the icy sidewalk, thus causing him and the cart to topple over.

His large body hit the slushy concrete, causing him to release his grip upon the bar. As he landed upon his back, he looked over and saw all the contents of the steel cart fly out, including his precious golden trophy. He lunged towards the airborne item, trying desperately to retrieve it, but it was beyond his reach. He dug the back of his heels deep into the snow, making one last attempt to push himself forward, towards the uncontrollable plight of his deceased son's only tangible memory. The street light above made the tarnished golden item intermittently sparkle, as it began its descent towards the corner of the avenue. With his useless arms fully extended, he watched with desperate eyes, as the trophy soon disappeared below the surface of the curb. He quickly turned over onto his stomach, dug his fingers deep into the slush and pulled himself blindly towards the edge of the sidewalk. When he peered over the perimeter of the concrete, he was stunned to see that the trophy was nowhere to be found. The only vision he had was that of the corner's black sewer grate and the darkness below it. He swiftly stuck his arm into the narrow opening and franticly waved his hand, grasping for anything, but his fingers felt nothing. He quickly raised his head and with furious eyes, watched Trent's car accelerate down the avenue. His rotted teeth automatically began to grind and his throat discharged a low guttural growl, as his mind immediately triggered an uncontrollable sense of vengeance towards the driver and the passengers in the departing vehicle.

Chapter 8

All the passengers in the moving vehicle heard the loud thump that came from the back end of the car. They quickly turned and looked out the back window, to witness the homeless man and his shopping cart plunging towards the ground.

"Oh my god, you knocked his ass over," said Vince.

Trent looked up into his rear view mirror and saw the man hitting the ground as he sped away. He reached up and grabbed the mirror, adjusting its angle to keep the fallen man within his sight, as the car continued gaining distance away from the accident.

"You're not going to stop and help him?" Allison asked Trent.

"Ahhhhh …I don't think it's such a good idea to go back, and besides, I didn't run him over. I think I just knocked him over. I'm sure he's fine." Trent said, as he continued driving forward.

"How do you know he's not dead?" She asked.

Trent kept his eye in the rear view mirror and said, "Because I see him moving on the ground."

***

As the man stumbled to get back to his feet, he quickly looked up at the street signs to mentally mark his territory. He held his side, trying desperately to numb the pain, as his eyes focused on the back of Trent's car. Then, without giving it a second thought, he set his agony aside and left all of his belongings behind, as he began to run as fast as he could towards the moving vehicle. His unstable mind quickly expedited feelings of hatred and revenge as his pace quickened.

***

Trent drove a few more blocks and then turned down the street the club was located on. His foot trembled upon the gas pedal, as he continued to speed towards his destination. His heart was rapidly beating, as his anxiety over the incident played over and over in his head. He knew he had done an erroneous thing by driving away, but he also knew he felt a genuine fear of the man and he wasn't about to stop and help him. His feelings continued to teeter between right and wrong as he pulled up in front of the club.

"I'm really sorry." He said to Allison.

"I can't believe you didn't stop to help that man, I mean it's bad enough that he's homeless and then you knocked over everything he had left in his life."

"I said I was sorry."

"Yeah to me, but not to him,"

"You did the right thing," said Shane.

"No he didn't; if you think about it, he was involved in a hit and run accident," said Allison.

"Yeah, but nobody was around to see it, so fuck it," said Shane.

"Believe me, I feel terrible about what just happened, but I didn't intentionally try to hit him, it was an accident. The car slid and I had no control over it, it was a fucking accident."

"Yeah, well then I guess you got lucky that no one saw you," said Allison in a disappointed voice.

Trent lowered his head, as he now felt ashamed at what he had done. He sat there for a second in silence and thought about the unexpected turn of events. What he imagined would be such an incredible evening was turning out to be a nightmare.

"I can't believe how many people are here, considering it's a Monday," said Beth, changing the subject.

"Yeah, this club is always packed, no matter who's playing. Hopefully sometime soon, we'll be the headliners." said Shane.

"I don't see any place to park. Let me drive around the corner and hopefully there will be a spot. Since it's still snowing, do you guys want to get out now and I'll go find a parking place?"

"After what just happened I don't want you walking the streets alone; how about letting the girls out and they can wait for us inside the club," said Shane.

"That sounds like a great idea," said Beth.

Trent looked over at Allison and she also agreed. He got out of his car and ran around to the other side to open up the passenger door. He reached out and grabbed Allison's hand as he helped her out, then pushed the seat forward, allowing Beth access to climb out of the backseat. She turned and kissed Shane on his lips and said, "Please hurry up." He smiled at her and said, "We'll just be a minute, just wait for us." She

100

smiled back at him and gave him another kiss.

"Wait, let me get out first," said Vince.

He stood outside the car and waited until Beth made her exit, then he pushed the seat back into place and sat up front. Trent looked at Allison and said "We'll be right back; once again, I'm really sorry."

Allison looked Trent in the eyes and said "It's alright; let's just have a good time tonight." He turned and closed the passenger door, ran back around and got back into his car.

"Thanks guys." Trent said to his band mates.

"No problem," said Vince.

"You better hurry up, I say we have roughly fifteen minutes before were on," said Shane.

Trent nodded his head, dropped his car in gear and proceeded forward.

***

The big man continued running down the avenue until he came to the corner where he saw the car turn. He stopped momentarily to catch his breath, as his unstable mind fueled his vengeful pursuit. His hateful eyes peered down the dark street, hoping to see the car, but it was nowhere to be found. What he did notice in the snowy haze, was a well-lit establishment not far from where he was standing.

Once again, he fought through the pain and pushed himself forward, allowing curiosity to overcome his obstacles. Step by step, he steadily advanced until he was just a block away from the luminous site. Camouflaged within the shadows, he stood silently pressed against the adjacent corner building. His eyes began to search for his prey, as he heard the opening of a car door.

***

As Trent turned the corner, he noticed a parking spot just a couple of yards away.

"Wow, how lucky can I get?" He said, as he began to parallel park his car.

"See man, everything is going to be just fine," said Shane.

"God I hope so."

"Why? What now?"

"I'm still upset about what just happened." Trent said, as he

101

pulled the keys from the ignition.

"In my eyes, nothing happened. Some stupid homeless man, who was obviously drunk out of his mind, got in our way. For what I saw, you were actually the good guy"

"I guess," said Trent to his band mate while opening his door. He then got out and walked back towards the trunk.

Vince opened the door and pushed the seat forward, allowing Shane to get out. With snow falling on his head, he stood outside of the car and reached into his leather jacket, pulling out his pack of cigarettes and his lighter. He searched through his pack until he came upon the joint he'd previously stashed inside. He pulled it out, placed it in his mouth and then brought the lighter's flame to the tip. He deeply inhaled the sweet-smelling substance and then repeated his action again.

As Trent stuck his key into the lock of the trunk, he looked around to see if the homeless man had possibly followed them. His eyes quickly scanned all four corners of the avenue for any sudden movement, but his mind was immediately relieved to see nobody. Then the loud sound of the frozen truck broke the silence, as Trent struggled to raise the lid once again.

"Wait, let me help you," said Shane walking back.

"Just hold the trunk open," said Trent, as he reached in and pulled both of the guitar cases out.

"Are we ready?" Shane asked, as he slammed the trunk shut.

"Hell yeah." Trent said, as he handed Shane his guitar case and then called out to Vince. "Hey man, are you ready?"

"No not yet, I'm still smoking my joint." Vince said, coughing as he responded.

"Dude, smoke that shit as we walk to the club," said Shane.

"Yeah, come on stoner, we have to go," said Trent.

"Go on, I'll be right behind you, I'm not putting this motherfucker out, this shit is way too good."

"We have like ten, maybe fifteen minutes" said Trent.

"By the time you plug your guitar into an amplifier, I will be sitting behind the drum set, waiting on you."

"Aren't you scared of staying out here all alone? What about the homeless man?" Shane asked.

"After that bullshit today, he better hope he doesn't run into me." Vince said, acting tough.

"Well hurry the fuck up, I'm stressed enough as it is," said Trent.

"Yeah me too, that's why I have to smoke this." Vince said, holding up his joint.

102

"Just hurry the fuck up." Shane said
"And don't forget to lock my car." Trent said as his final words.

***

The man watched as the driver of a parked car exited and walked towards its rear end. He then saw the passenger door open and witnessed two more men getting out. He focused on their dark silhouettes roaming about the vehicle, as he tried to identify if that was the car he was searching for. His squinting eyes then opened widely when he recognized that it was and that all three men were also wearing black leather jackets. He stared with anticipation, as his heart began to race and his unstable mind pondered the steps needed to achieve his retribution.

Out of habit, his hand automatically reached into his coat's inner pocket, but this time his fingers came up empty. With a closed fist, he pounded the wall behind him as his anger expelled. He took a small step forward from the hidden shadows of the night, but stopped as he saw two of the men walking off leaving one behind. His patience grew shorter, knowing that the odds were now in his favor, as he began his vengeful pursuit towards the soon to be victim.

***

Vince continued to puff down on his euphoric herb, as he began to mentally prepare himself for the gig. He started to sing Trent's songs out loud while tapping his foot against the icy street. As the joint got shorter and his mind became buzzed, he slowly tapped it out. He reached back into his leather jacket and grabbed his cigarette pack once again. He slid the half smoked joint back into the box and pulled out a cigarette. He lit the end of the smoke as he began to walk away from the car, when he suddenly stopped.

"Fuck, I almost forgot my sticks, and to lock the fucking door too. Damn, Trent would have killed me." He said to himself.

He turned, opened the door and leaned inside, as he reached into the backseat to retrieve his wooden possessions. As he crawled out back first, he bumped into something that prevented him from exiting the vehicle.

"What the fuck?" He said.

With a big shove, he forced himself out and turned around, thinking it was either Trent or Shane, but was completely stunned to see the homeless man looking down upon him. His tall, monstrous figure

103

made Vince's hand instantly release his drumsticks, causing them to fall to the ground.

NED was the only word he was able to say, before the homeless man reached out and grabbed him by the throat. With a firm grip, he slowly raised him up and off the ground. Vince grabbed hold of the man's arm with both hands, desperately trying to break free from his restraint. His dangling feet began to kick uncontrollably, but there was no means of escape. His body continued to rise into the snowy night, as the man lifted him high above his head. He stared deep into Vince's tearing eyes, showing him the level of anger he had towards him. Vince's body finally fell limp within the man's grip, but that still wasn't enough to fulfill his hateful satisfaction. He turned and took Vince's seemingly lifeless body, and then threw him hard against the wall of the building behind him. The back of Vince's head hit the solid brick with such an impact, that it instantly split wide open. His body bounced forward from the hardened blow and his blood splattered across the untouched snow.

The man reached down, picked up Vince's drumsticks and slowly walked over towards his body. With a vengeful grin, he stared down at him and watched his bloody face still gasping for air, while buried half way in the snow. His smile remained constant, knowing he was still alive and was still able to feel the wrath of the cruelty in store for him. The man bent down and grabbed Vince by his neck one more time. He pressed him against the building while he observed the damage he had caused. He stared at Vince's mouth as it pleaded for sympathy and tried to take another breath. The man then leaned forward and whispered in his ear, "You will all die for taking away my little golden boy." He proceeded to raise both of Vince's drumsticks up towards his face and then with careful aim and one hard thrust, he drove them both deep into one of his eyes.

***

Trent and Shane entered the club and immediately saw Allison and Beth waiting. They walked over to them before approaching the cashier.

"Hi, we're on the list for tonight." Trent said.

"And your name is?"

"City Rats."

"Yep, you're actually first, are you guys ready?"

"Ahhh, almost." Trent said, as he looked back at the front door, hoping to see Vince.

104

"Well, you've got a few minutes, I suggest you get it together."

"Okay, we will."

Just then, Mike, the owner of the club walked up to the front. Trent immediately introduced himself and thanked him for adding his band to the bill.

"No problem Trent, I'm more than happy to help. I've known your father for years." He said.

"Cool, I'm just waiting on my drummer; he'll be here in just a minute."

"By the way, how's your father doing?"

"He's fine; he and the band are on a mini tour. He'll be back sometime next week."

"Great, make sure you tell him I said hi."

"I will, and thanks again for letting us play tonight."

"I'm sure you're a chip off the old block."

Trent nodded at Mike and then looked towards the front door, hoping to see Vince walk through it, but he didn't. He walked over to Shane and the girls and said, "Where is Vince?"

"Fucking stoner probably got so blasted he forgot where the club was," said Shane.

"God damn it!" Trent yelled, as his stress level began to rise.

"He'll show up any minute, let's just get ready." Shane said, before he leaned over, kissed Beth, then picked up his guitar case and began heading towards the stage.

Trent smiled at Allison, trying to hide his obvious nervousness, as he too picked up his case and followed Shane.

"Let's just plug ourselves in and like he promised, he'll be sitting behind the set before you strum your first chord." Shane said, trying to comfort Trent, as they made their way through the crowd then walked up onto the lit stage. They opened up their guitar cases and wrapped their instruments around their shoulders. Then they both walked over to each of the amplifiers and plugged themselves in. Trent looked over at Shane as they both stood there, waiting for Vince. Trent lowered his head, then walked up to the microphone and said. "Hello everybody, we're City Rats and … we're waiting on our drummer."

As Trent stared out at the crowd, they all stared back at him with a blank look. Trent's eyes began to bounce between Shane, the crowd and the front door. The minutes seemed like hours, as he continued to wait for Vince's arrival, until Mike walked over to the stage and motioned for them to him to get off.

"Fuck!" Trent said, as he looked at Shane with a face of

disappointment.

As they gathered their equipment and quietly exited off the stage, Trent walked over to Mike.

"I'm so sorry, I don't know what happened."

"That's okay, I've been in the business for years. I'm use to unexpected mishaps. Maybe your drummer just got stage fright, I've seen that before," said Mike, trying to be understanding.

"Again, I'm sorry."

"Look, go find your drummer and I'll get the next band to play and then I'll send you up after them. That will give you about forty five minutes."

"Really?" Thanks so much Mike," said Trent.

He walked back over to Shane and the girls and shook his head. Allison responded by reaching out and touching his arm, in an attempt to comfort his disappointment.

"What the fuck do you think happened to Vince?" Trent asked, as his eyes looked back towards the front door.

Everyone looked at him but said nothing. They too were baffled by Vince's delay.

"Well I'm going to take a walk back to the car, just wait here." Trent said to everybody.

"No, you stay here Trent, Beth and I will go see what happened to Vince. I bet he smoked so much weed, he's just passed out on your front seat, and believe me if that's the case, I'm going to kick his ass."

"Are you sure?" Trent asked in a concerned voice.

"Yeah man, watch my bass and we'll be right back ... along with Vince."

***

The deranged homeless man held the drum sticks that were imbedded inside Vince's head. The wooden weapons caused a trail of blood to slither down his snow-covered face and onto the icy ground. The man's mind unleashed a sense of gratitude, knowing he had eliminated at least one of the gang members posing a threat to him earlier. As he held Vince high, he studied his bloody face and soon recognized him as the young man that had called him NED. Again, he was not sure why, but he had now come to accept the new name as his vengeful alter ego.

106

Chapter 9

Jack's feet pounded the icy pavement. His blood boiled with deep anger and bitter frustration. He didn't know what hurt more; his head from the near fatal brawl, or his mind over the abandonment from his fellow gang members.

"Those fucking scumbags left me to die!" He said, over and over to himself.

The snow continued to fall, as he briskly walked through the cold, dark city. He held a hand over his injury, because he knew he was badly hurt but he didn't know to what extent. His curiosity made him suddenly stop in front of an abandoned store, where under a dim street lights' glow, he peered at his reflection within the dirty window. He took a deep breath, then removed his hand slowly from his face. He was initially shocked at the sight of the deep, bloody gash, but then his sudden anger flared his next response.

"Bastard!" Jack screamed, after bringing up a mental picture of the hideous homeless man in his head. He saw the old man's beady eyes, surrounded by his long, gray hair and straggly beard. The image made Jack cringe at first, but then it triggered a reaction of hatred, forcing him to clench his fist to a white knuckle degree.

"NED!" He shouted, as he reached back and grabbed the switchblade from out of his back pocket.

While still staring at his vision within the store's hazy glass, Jack slowly raised the closed knife and then pressed the trusty release button, causing the blade to quickly whiz through the cold air and lock into place. He then held the knife up and said, "I will find you old man, and then, I'm gonna cut you into pieces …little fucking pieces."

He began to wave the sharp knife back and forth, as his mind raced with violent thoughts, but they all came to a screeching halt, when he suddenly remembered the word the man had called him before he fled away from the fight.

"Coward!" The scratchy voice of the homeless man cried out loudly within Jack's head.

"He called me a coward." Jack repeated the old man's insult.

He was completely speechless for a moment as he tried to collect his thoughts, but that one word was mentally killing him.

"A coward! ... A fucking coward!" Jack then shouted loudly into the dismal night.

The insult resonated deep into Jack's psyche and he began to mentally question his own dignity behind his manhood. It was a real challenge and strain against his egotistical mind, but he finally confessed to himself that he did indeed run from the fight, thus validating the truth behind the homeless man's harsh, one word statement.

His twisted mind repeated that one word so many times, that it actually triggered a happy and treasured childhood memory. He pictured himself sitting on the living room couch, alongside his older brother Jeffrey, who was three years his elder. He recalled both of them giggling, while watching The Wizard of Oz on their television set. He remembered the movie was near the end, where all the characters were receiving their personal gifts from the great and powerful wizard, when suddenly their dad walked into the room. He recalled the happy look on his father's face when he said to us, "This is one of my favorite scenes. The part where the scarecrow gets his brains, the tin man gets his heart and the cowardly lion get his courage.

"Courage? ... What's courage, dad?" Young Jack asked.

"It means that the lion won't be a coward anymore."

"Coward? ... What's a coward?"

"A coward is a person ... or in this case, a lion, who is afraid of everything, but from this moment on, he won't be scared of anything ever again and he will truly be the king of the forest."

"Dad, if you had to pick just one, what would you choose, a brain, a heart, or courage?"

He took a moment to think of the best answer to say to his youngest and most impressionable son. The three choices scattered throughout his mind, but he then confidently said "Jack, it's good to have all three, but you never want to grow up and be ... a coward.

"Is that why you're a policeman? Because you have all three, a brain, a heart and tons of courage?"

His father laughed as he responded back, "Yes Jack, but I worked very hard to become a police officer ..." and then suddenly, the delighted memory of his intimate conversation was interrupted, when he remembered the presence of his mother staggering into the living room, holding her never-empty wine glass. The whole joyous family movie experience was instantly ruined, as he watched his inebriated mom stumble across the floor, while aiming herself towards her favorite chair. She slowly sat down and then focused momentarily on the T.V screen.

"There's no place like home." She said, as she held her glass up high and then took a big long sip.

"For God sakes, do you have to drink so much ...especially in front of the children?" His father said to his her.

"I'm fine." She said, slurring her lie.

***

Jack's memory leaped a few years forward and he remembered when his mother's addiction reached its lowest point. It was the night the front doorbell rang and his very tipsy mother got up to answer it. She opened the door and was greeted by two uniformed police officers, who came to the house to deliver the unfortunate news about their father being killed in the line of duty earlier in the evening. His next memory relived the traumatic moment of watching his mother suddenly collapse and the vision of her wine glass shattering, as they both hit the floor simultaneously.

He then recalled an image of himself, dressed in a little dark blue suit and standing beside her. He remembered he was covering both of his ears, trying to muffle the powerful sound from the honorary gun salute at his father's funeral.

***

The loud imaginary gunshots jolted Jack's brain and quickly snapped him back to reality. He shook his head a few times, trying to clear his distressing memories and then he turned his attention on the sharp knife he still held in his hand. He gripped it tightly one more time and then aggressively said, "I'm gonna slit your fucking throat, old man," before he closed the blade and slipped it into his back pocket.

He then turned and once again began his trek back to the gang's apartment. With every step he took, he felt the mental frustration over the cowardly move he made. His head ached, as he replayed the ending of the back alley fight over and over again. He walked with tight clenched fists, trying to relieve some of his pent-up anger, but he knew deep down he couldn't get over the fact that he actually ran away from the homeless man.

"That old bastard ... he must be at least sixty, maybe even seventy ... and he was kicking my ass!" Jack said, torturing himself.

109

"I know that worthless piece of shit would have killed me. Probably still would, if he could." Jack said with a crackle in his voice.

"Come back you coward! ...coward ...coward." NED's word echoed deep within his brain.

Jack turned the corner and walked up the block towards their place. On his way, he passed one of the usual street vendors pedaling his illegal merchandise. He tried to avoid contact with the acquaintance, but the dealer immediately noticed his bloody face.

"What the fuck happened to you?" He said abruptly.

Jack turned his head, trying to ignore him as he quietly walked past.

"Hey man, you need anything tonight? I'm running my usual sale on everything."

Jack tucked his hands into his jacket pockets and just kept walking, but then suddenly stopped. He quickly realized that the dealer could help him with some temporary relief for his discomfort. He turned around, took a few steps back and approached the man.

"What cha need, something for that?" The man said, pointing at Jack's bloody wound.

"Got anything for pain?"

The dealer reached into his coat pocket and pulled out a large vial of pills. He looked at Jack and shook the container a few times. He then removed the lid and proceeded to dump out into his hand, various examples of pharmaceutical narcotics. Jack's eyes widened as he looked down upon the vast variety of all different shapes, sizes and colors within the dealer's palm.

"The pink ones or blue ones are the ones you want."

"How much?"

"Bro, I told you I'd give you a super deal, because by the looks of that ...you're gonna need plenty of them."

"How much?!" Jack said, anxiously though clenched teeth.

"Four for twenty and I'll throw in an extra one cuz, I like to take care of my customers."

Jack reached into his coat, pulled out a short stack of bills and slapped a twenty down into the dealer's other hand. His jittery fingers then sifted through the small pile of pills and pulled five from the numerous choices. He slowly nodded his aching head, expressing his appreciation and then turned and walked away.

"Hey bro, see ya real soon!" Shouted the happy salesman.

Jack walked a quarter of the way down the block, before he entered through the threshold of an old apartment building. The lobby reeked of its usual foul stench, as he made his way towards the stairway. He held the banister as he struggled to climb the stairs, until he finally reached his floor. He walked down the dimly lit hall and then stood quietly in front of his door. He took a moment to catch his breath and let his mind contemplate his next actions. He didn't know what to expect, as he grabbed the knob and slowly turned it. He entered the familiar dwelling and suddenly stopped short, as he saw Slugger lying flat on the couch and Spaz lying back in the recliner. He recognized immediately that they looked bloodied and bruised, but his unforgiving mind couldn't care less.

He stood silent at the open doorway. He could feel his veins popping throughout his body from the adrenaline rush he was getting from his anger. He took another deep breath, then reached back and grabbed the edge of the big thick door. Then on the count of one, Jack violently slammed it shut. The initial sound was so loud, that it instantly woke up and startled the two injured thugs.

"Thanks a lot, you fucking worthless pussies!" Jack shouted at his henchmen.

"You're alive?" Spaz responded.

"We thought you were dead for sure," Slugger said, as he lifted his head and strained to open his eyes.

"Dead, I might as well be fucking dead if I ever had to depend on you two again."

Jack looked at both of the injured young men with disgust, as he grinded his teeth, trying to hold back his short temper. He then turned his attention to the living room's coffee table, where he noticed the Jack Daniels still sitting in the middle of the dirty dishes from earlier. He reached down, grabbed the bottle of bourbon and brought up it to his eyes. He looked between the labels, noticed it was still half full and then proceeded to twist off the cap. He reached into his pocket and grabbed two of the five pills. He looked down at his open palm and saw he had pulled one of each of the painkillers, but at that point he could care less. He made a loud slurping sound, as he took a big swig from the whisky bottle in order to wash down the drugs.

"Fuck you guys." Jack said, as he held up his middle finger towards the two, then turned and headed towards the bathroom. With bottle in hand, he made his way down the hall, until he flipped the switch and closed the door. He took another swig off the bottle, then placed it on top of the toilet seat.

He paused for a second, trying to muster up the nerve to actually get a good look at himself in the well-lit bathroom mirror. He slowly wiped his hand across his face and then looked down at his palm. He

111

panicked at the sight of his blood drenched fingers and quickly reached for the bottle again. Jack took one more sip before he turned towards the mirror and bravely faced himself. It took some time and a few more sips as he began, and got through the grueling process of cleaning himself up and attending to the injury on the side of his head.

"What the fuck did that old man have?" Jack said to himself.

"Looked like some golden award of some shit … fucking son of a bitch hurt like a motherfucker."

He looked at his face with concern and then disgust, knowing the old homeless man definitely got the best of him. He reached down and grabbed the towel off the rack. He wet it and proceeded to wipe the dried blood from his face, before tending to his oozing open wound. Despite patting it with a delicate touch, the bloody gash still stung immensely.

"Motherfucker!" He cried out, trying to relieve some of the edge behind his pain.

Jack stared at the reflection of his clean face, then watched as a fresh trail of blood began to drip down from his head once again. He opened a cabinet drawer and spotted a black bandanna. He reached down, grabbed it and then carefully wrapped it around his head, trying to stop the bleeding and also conceal the seeping wound.

After securing the bandanna, Jack once again reached back and retrieved his switchblade from his back pocket. As he held it in his hand, he slid his thumb back and forth across the tarnished silver release button. His eyes then studied the shape of the worn black handle before he gripped it tightly. The feeling of the intimate object wrapped around his fingers triggered a memory that he could never, ever forget …

***

"What happened?" Jeffrey asked his crying brother.

"It's that bully again…you know … the big kid down the block."

"What happened?"

"He won't leave me alone and today he asked me for money, and when I told him I didn't have any, he hit me in the face."

"He needs to pick on someone his own age and size," Jeffrey said, after seeing his brother's bruised, swollen cheek.

"He's older, and also bigger, than you!" Jack said as he began to cry once again.

"Yeah, well like dad always said, the bigger they are the harder they fall. Wait here, I'll be right back," said Jeffrey, before he disappeared into his bedroom and then returned with something hidden in his hand.

"What's that?"

"Promise you won't tell mom."

"I promise ... what is it?"

"It's called a switchblade." Jeffrey said.

"Yeah but what is it?"

"Step back and watch this."

Jeffrey held his new object up in front of him then pressed the release button on the handle. Instantly surprised was his younger brother, as the blade swished through the air and locked securely into its rightful place.

"Wow!"

"Wait here, I'll be right back." Jeffrey said to Jack.

"Now where are you going?"

"To put an end to all this bully bullshit. Nobody is going to hit my kid brother in the face and get away with it, besides, dad always said don't grow up and be a coward. Remember when he said that to us?"

Both kids nodded at the memory of their fallen father's sacred words. Jeffrey unlocked the blade and slowly closed it back into its casing. He then reached behind him and slipped it into his back pocket.

"I'll be right back ... promise you won't tell mom," Jeffrey said as he patted his younger brother on the head.

"I promise," Jack swore as he crossed his heart before he watched his brother leave through the front door.

To Jack, the minutes seemed like hours as he waited impatiently for his brother's return but after what seemed like infinity, his curiosity finally got the best of him and he quickly jumped off the couch. He walked quietly through the apartment, trying not to disturb his bedroom-ridden mother, before he darted out the front door.

He ran down the block towards the direction he saw the bully earlier, but what he saw was a bunch of kids gathered on the corner. As he got closer, he saw a figure lying on the ground and he anxiously quickened his speed. He arrived and shoved himself through the older and taller kids, but then was completely devastated when he saw Jeffrey lying face down on the sidewalk. He noticed instantly he wasn't moving and was also bleeding badly from what looked like a severely punched face. He ran over, put his arms around him and held his unconscious brother. He began to panic, causing his body to shake and his eyes to cry, over flowing with tears. He shouted Jeffrey's name several times but his older brother remained unresponsive. Then through blurred eyes, he looked up and saw the big, bad bully walking away.

113

He quickly looked down at his brother's body, hoping to see his new shiny knife somewhere but it was nowhere in sight. Confused, he then looked at his brother's hands and they both came up empty. He instantly knew where the item was and he hesitated at first, but eventually reached down and put his hand into his brother's back pocket. His fumbling fingers touched the hard plastic handle for a few seconds and he remembered an uneasy feeling he initially got, but then he also remembered the excitement he felt when he quickly pulled it free and held it in his hand.

Jack recalled feeling an immediate sense of strength from the unopened knife. He remembered running his finger across the shiny release button, and then trying to grip it to the best of his ability. The bulky item weighed his hand down a bit, but he raised the knife up with dignity and pride, and then yelled out to fleeing bully. "Hey you, come back here!"

The big kid heard the command loud and clear and immediately stopped. He then turned around to see who delivered the abrupt order. He looked back and stared at each of the kids still standing on the corner, but then his eyes focused downward and what he saw was a little kid, standing right next to the guy he just badly beat up.

"Come back here, you …you … you fucking coward!" Jack shouted at the top of his lungs, while trying to hold back his unstoppable tears.

He then pointed the unopened knife up towards the clear blue sky and confidently pushed the release button. The sharp blade did its fast dance across the air, and then quickly locked itself into place. The new shiny steel caught the bright summertime sun, and the switchblade instantly glimmered with deadly power.

The bully began to laugh at the bizarre sight of an eight year old boy holding a knife and threatening him, but at the same time, he was also appalled. He stared at the familiar young kid as he closed both his large fists and began walking back towards him, but then he suddenly stopped, because he heard the sound of sirens coming towards him from all the nearby streets.

Jack watched as the bully turned and stared at him for a few more moments, but then turned back around and quickly ran off down the block. He continued to hold the sharp open blade firmly and directly in front of him until the bully was completely out of his sight. He then, with an exhausted hand, cautiously closed the knife back into its black plastic casing. He looked down at his brother, and then his eyes pivoted back to the brand new switchblade one more time, before he secretly tucked it into his back pocket.

The police, the ambulance and Jack's mother soon arrived on the bright, sunny corner. He recalled they let him ride up front with the driver, to avoid seeing the sight of the paramedics working and trying to save his brother's life. He remembered listening to the sirens while sitting there and feeling the bulge from the switchblade in his back pocket. He felt instant gratification, knowing that he now had protection against any bully. His mind then recalled the memory of hearing his mother scream from inside the ambulance, and he knew that something really bad had just happened.

***

Jack stared silently into space until his brain finally settled and he once again returned to reality, but only this time around, the combination of the pills and whiskey began to take its toll. With slightly distorted vision, he looked down at the knife and gripped it a bit tighter. He then conjured up several images of his older brother, his heroic father … and then his intoxicated mother.

His numbing mind remained fixated on the vision of the broken woman, as he recalled a harvest of portraits ranging across the last two decades. Each image he saw showed the progressive tale of his mother's slowly declining life due to her alcoholism. He took a brief moment and tried to remember the last time he actually saw her sober, but he couldn't pinpoint an exact time, or place.

"Drunk bitch," he said, shaking his head in shame.

He frowned as he looked down at the switchblade one last time before tucking it away in his back pocket. He then reached for the bottle of bourbon and took another swig. His head was starting to feel some relief from the medication, causing his tormented mind to finally settle down. He felt both physically and mentally exhausted as he turned and sat down on the toilet seat. He took a deep breath then closed his eyes, hoping to erase the image of his mother but she stayed front and center.

His frown remained as he reached into his coat pocket and grabbed his phone. He went to last numbers dialed and saw her name from yesterday's failed attempt. He hesitated, like he always did, but his thumb eventually pushed her number. The phone rang four or five times, before he suddenly heard the slurring sound of his mother's voice.

"H …he …. helllloooo."

Jack listened carefully, while battling his heartbroken emotions.

"Who is this … and why do you keep calling me?!" The woman

115

yelled into her silent phone.

"Ma … ma ….ma." Jack stuttered an unheard whisper.

"Whoever you are, why don't you leave me alone and just let me be!" The woman continued hollering at her unknown caller.

Jack heard his mother's plea, and responded by just hanging up the phone like always. He sat there and blamed her at first, and then himself for their estranged dysfunctional relationship, but he knew at this point, he just didn't have much to say to his mother anyway.

"Sorry mom, just making sure you're still alive," he said sarcastically to his phone.

He stood up and placed his phone back in his jacket, then reached for the whiskey bottle again. He noticed there was about two or three sips left, before he took another. He stood in front of the mirror once again, and through sad and muddled eyes, began to stare at his pathetic self.

"You are a coward … a fucking coward."

He provoked himself several more times before he pushed his brain into a mental frenzy, where he swore a personal vendetta against the old, homeless man. He reached into his coat pocket and quickly popped another pill. He chased it down with one more swig, causing the toxic combination to suddenly flare his temper. His mind began erupting with hatred and vengeance as he turned, and with bottle in hand, exited the bathroom towards the front door. As he scuttled down the hall, the sound of his trudging footsteps awoke the two thugs again.

"Where the fuck are you going?" Spaz asked.

"To find that fucking homeless man …are you two coming with me?"

"You're fucking crazy, that motherfucker almost killed us," said Spaz.

"Yeah, you should thank God that you got out of there alive," said Slugger.

Jack looked down at the two motionless young men, and reacted by downing the rest of the bourbon and then throwing the empty bottle against the wall. The thick glass shattered everywhere, causing the two injured thugs to flinch in order to protect their faces.

"I should thank God? … I don't put much trust in something I can't see. I depend on myself and after tonight… more than ever. You should pray to God …that I don't fucking kill the both of you for deserting me."

"That man would have killed us!" Spaz said again.

"It was three against one!" Jack argued.

"You saw him, he was …fucking humongous!" Slugger shouted.

116

"We had weapons!" Jack shouted back.

"So did he, look at us." Spaz said.

"We're lucky we got away …let it go," said Slugger, as he raised his hand and held his aching head.

Jack's bloodshot eye's pivoted back and forth, as he shouted his harsh statement at Spaz and Slugger "You two aren't worthless pussies …you're worse … you're both fucking cowards!"

"Let it go," Slugger said, trying to calm his gang leader down.

"Go fuck yourselves …fucking cowards!" Jack shouted while holding up his middle finger.

He then turned, grabbed the door knob and quietly walked out, but made damn sure he slammed the thick apartment door shut.

Chapter 10

The big man slowly lowered Vince's dead body and laid it upon the snow. He stared down at the corpse, and knew he couldn't just leave it lying on the sidewalk. He looked around, trying to figure out a place to hide it, but the area just consisted of parked cars and closed store fronts. The only option that quickly came to mind was to hide Vince's body under the vehicle from which he arrived in.

As he lifted the body off the sidewalk, the evening's snow began to fall even harder, quickly covering up the bloody evidence that was left behind. The man walked over to the car and kicked the passenger door shut, before placing Vince upon the curb. He then crouched down and started to slowly shove his lifeless body under Trent's car, making it temporarily disappear.

***

As Shane and Beth walked out of the club, Shane looked up and said, "Oh my God, can you believe how hard it's snowing now? Don't tell me we're in for a fucking blizzard."

"I hope not, that's the last thing I want is to get stuck down here," Beth said.

"We could always crash at Trent's place."

"I'd rather not. I'd like to go home sometime tonight."

"Yeah, me too. Alright bundle up and let's go see where Vince is," Shane said, as he zipped up his leather jacket then grabbed Beth's hand.

As they started to walk down the block towards Trent's car, their conversation continued.

"Do you think that the homeless man might have followed us?" Beth asked.

"No, Trent took off and besides, he couldn't run that fast to actually catch us."

"Well then, what do you think happened to Vince?"

"I'm sure that fucking stoner just smoked himself into oblivion and passed out, that's all." Shane said as they approached the corner.

**

The man heard faint voices approaching him from around the block. He quickly got up and swiftly moved back against the wall, blending into the darkened shadows. As the voices grew louder, he dragged himself along the flush brick exterior until he came upon a vacant store front, just a few yards past Trent's car. He ducked inside the pitch black space, and then with piercing eyes, he observed. He waited patiently to see who the unexpected people were, and what direction they might be going. Within a minute, two figures came into his view and based upon their appearances, they seemed to be a man and a woman who walked right over to the liable car. The man now knew that the arriving couple was associated with the leather jacket gang and those responsible for his tragic accident.

**

"Damn it, he's not here," said Shane, looking into Trent's car.

"Well then, where do you think he went?" Beth asked.

"I don't know, maybe he got confused and walked the wrong way and got lost."

"Really? Does that sound logical to you?"

Shane, trying to get a good look into the car, cupped his hands around his eyes and pressed his face close to the cold window. He was looking for anything that might seem out of the ordinary, but everything looked just as they had they left it.

"I don't see his drumsticks lying on the seat, so I know he took them."

"Well what do you want to do? We can't just stand here and wait for him, I'm freezing," Beth said.

Shane grabbed the handle on the passenger door and pulled on it. To his surprise, it opened.

"Stoned son of a bitch forgot to lock the door, but actually that works in our favor, come on get in," said Shane to his girlfriend.

"For what? Let's just go."

"Hold on, I've got a little surprise for you."

"What kind of surprise?"

"Well it's snowing out here and it could be snowing in there too,

120

if you know what I mean."

Beth smiled at her boyfriend, because she knew exactly what Shane meant. Unlike Vince and his marijuana habit, the couple's drug of choice was cocaine.

"Are you going to let me in on the other side?" Beth asked.

"No, just climb over the middle console and sit in Trent's seat."

Beth went into the car head first and then did exactly what Shane suggested, before planting herself in the driver's seat. Shane sat down in the passenger's seat, then pulled the door shut.

"See, this is a lot better, and it's actually still warm in here," he said, as he reached into his leather jacket and pulled out a small vial of the white, powdery narcotic. The couple exchanged smiles as Shane opened up the vial and inserted the edge of one of his keys into it. He scooped up a tiny white pile and brought it up to his left nostril, then repeated the process for the other. He slowly titled his head back and then snorted hard, forcing the powdery substance further up his nose, trying to get the full effect of the drug. The initial burning sensation made his eyes water, but the instant euphoric feeling soon triumphed.

He turned towards his girlfriend and handed her all the necessities for her to achieve the same joyous feeling. With a grin on her face, she happily accepted Shane's offer as she reached out and grabbed both items. She wasn't naïve to the procedure as she mimicked Shane's precise actions, before she flung her head back too. They giggled at one another as they repeated the process several more times, until their needs were fulfilled and their bodies tingled.

Shane, now buzzing with extreme energy and feeling somewhat frisky, leaned over and kissed Beth's pretty face. She smiled at her boyfriend as she returned his affection with a passionate embrace. Shane reached over and began to fondle her voluptuous body through her clothing, causing her to squirm about in the driver's seat.

"Hey, let's not start something we can't finish," said Beth.

"We've got plenty of time; the other band is probably playing right at this very moment.

"I'm not going to get naked in this car and besides, what happens if Vince shows up or if someone else sees us in here?"

"I bet he's already back at the club and look, the windows are practically covered from all the snow. Nobody can see us in here, and besides we still have some time."

"Time for what?" Beth asked.

"Well I gave you a little blow, maybe you can return the favor," Shane answered with a grin.

121

As usual, the powdery drug had a charming effect on Beth, as she smiled back at her boyfriend and gazed deep into his lustful eyes. The look on Shane's face was overjoyed, as she slowly lowered her head into his lap.

***

The man secretly watched as the two people had a small conversation outside the car before getting in. He noticed that the male figure was wearing a black leather jacket, indicating he was affiliated with his previous adversary. His curiosity heightened as he stared past the snow-ridden windows, trying to see what the couple was doing inside. He noticed them interacting for several minutes, before they moved closer to one another and began to passionately kiss.

Like a perverted voyeur, he watched the couple embracing in their affection. The intense sexual image triggered a flashback, as a portrait of his wife appeared within his mind. He closed his eyes as he began to conjure up memories of her beautiful face. Then his recollections commenced to run rapid as he remembered their first date, their wedding night, and then the day she gave birth to Scotty. He recalled the joyous look on her gorgeous face, and the delightful look in her eyes as she held him in her arms.

The images of Thanksgiving dinners, Christmas mornings and summertime picnics passed vividly through his brain, bringing a slight smile to his harsh, frozen face. But his cheerful expression was soon erased, as he dreaded the return of the most horrific memory.

He began to relive the moment when he came home from work early one evening. He remembered walking through the front door and calling out her name, but there was no answer. He continued to holler for her as he walked through their apartment, but the place remained silent. He began to panic and quickly moved from room to room, until he got to their bedroom. There, he found her body lying perfectly still on their bed, with an empty prescription bottle in one hand and a hand-written note in the other.

"Marcia!" He screamed over and over again, as he shook her unconscious body, trying to revive her but failing to succeed.

As the man mentally crawled back to reality, he reached up and wiped away the tears that had fallen from reliving the haunting memory. His hand once again automatically reached into his inner pocket, searching for the one thing that has always soothed this deep mental pain, but both feelings instantaneously came up empty.

His mind began to restore the hatred he had towards the punks responsible for everything that had occurred today. The images of all the leather jacket gang members reappeared, causing him to squeeze both his fists tightly, as his fury for revenge returned.

With anger in his heart, he slowly emerged from the blackened store front and advanced towards the parked car. With each creeping step, a subtle crunching sound was made from his large boots compressing the snow beneath them. As he got closer, his eyes leered deep into the frozen window, focusing on his prey and preparing for yet another strike.

***

With their eyes closed and enthralled in the moment, Shane and Beth were oblivious to the deranged predator lurking outside their safe haven. Their heightened passion secluded any outside interferences, as Shane's low, pleasured moans hid the sound of the man's arrival.

On the parked vehicle, a dark shadow slowly increased as the homeless man once again approached the passenger side door. His monstrous stature appeared like a brick wall, as he now stood outside the car and stared at the engaging young couple inside.

Without his child's voice to ease his flaring temper, the man's mind was set on vengeance as he grabbed the handle, and then forcibly pulled open the unlocked door. The surprising sound made Shane and Beth immediately open their eyes in utter shock, as they both saw the vision of the angry homeless man, bending down within the open doorway. The hideous sight of his long hair blowing wildly in the cold wind, and the evil they witness within his eyes made them gasp. The unprepared couple instantly panicked as the big man reached in, and with his powerful grip, grabbed Shane's leather jacket and quickly extracted him from the car. Beth screamed loud and continuously as she immediately flung herself back against the driver's door, watching her boyfriend being viciously attacked.

Using both of his hands, the man lifted Shane high into the air and stared deep into his eyes, as he held him up to the falling snow. It wasn't until then, that Shane had a moment to recognize who his enemy actually was. He opened his mouth and tried to scream, but nothing except a small gasping sound was heard, before he was violently thrown down to the ground.

He landed on his stomach, knocking the wind out of him. His face lay sideways, and pressed in the snow as he once again gasped, trying to refill his lungs with air. He teetered in and out of consciousness, making his vision blurry, but when his eyes finally focused, he was staring at the image of Vince's body underneath Trent's car. The horrifying sight of his dead band mate brought Shane's mouth open as he made another attempt to scream, but he was still speechless. He stared at Vince's bloody face and then at the drumsticks protruding from his eye, before he felt the strong hands of the homeless man grabbing the back of his jacket and lifting him up from the sidewalk.

Beth's constant screams echoed through the street, but unfortunately, no one was around to hear her pleading cry for help. In an attempt to muffle the sound of Beth's shrieks, the man kicked the passenger car door shut, before refocusing his attention back on her boyfriend.

He spun Shane around and then pressed him firmly against the passenger door. Like an untamed animal, the big man growled as he drew back a closed fist and prepared a potentially deadly punch. Shane saw the man's giant hand coming towards his face and reacted by moving his head, causing the impact to be with the passenger window instead. The man's mighty blow caused shards of glass to shatter everywhere, including inside the car, showering Beth with cold, sharp fragments. Her frantic, high-pitched scream pierced the ears of the man, refueling his frenzy upon Shane. He reached out, grabbed his face and forcibly pushed him down towards the broken glass of the window's pane. The sharp, jagged points sliced into Shane's skin as the man dragged his neck along the solid frame. Blood spewed from the cutting of Shane's arteries, causing him to grab hold of the door, trying to fight back but within seconds, the last few beats of his heart pumped down to none.

Beth began to scream uncontrollably as she stared at her beloved boyfriend's head, lying lifeless along the edge of the broken window. She went into a state of panic, as she watched Shane's blood pour vigorously down inside the car. She reached over and franticly tried to open the driver's side door but it was locked.

With rage in his eyes, the man leered inside the vehicle and saw Beth trying desperately to get away. He yanked Shane's impaled head off the window's pane, then threw his body back to the ground. He then reached into the car, grabbed Beth's coat and began pulling her towards him. She punched and slapped his menacing arm, trying to free herself from the man's strong grip, but his powerful strength dragged her over the middle console. With her eyes filled with tears, she continued to fight until her coat ripped, releasing the man's grasp. She quickly pushed herself back over into the driver's seat, and tried once again to open the locked door. Her jittery hands fumbled with the door handle and on the

124

lock, as she continued to hysterically scream for help.

The homeless man kicked Shane's body out of the way, before he reached down and reopened the passenger door. Now with no obstacles between them, the man lunged into the car, grabbing Beth once again. She franticly kicked at the face of the big man as she continued to fumble, trying to open the door. Her hand finally lifted the lock and then she quickly grabbed the door handle, causing her to suddenly fall backwards onto the icy street. The big man extended his arms, as he made one last thrust over the middle console towards her. He was lucky to grab one of her ankles and proceeded to pull her half way back into the car, but she dug her finger nails deep into the snow, stopping him. She then used her free leg and once again kicked the man in the face, causing him to suddenly release his deadly grip.

Now freed, but still panicking, Beth dragged herself along the street until she was able to get to her feet. She then turned and looked back through the car's windshield and saw the man crawling back out of the car. She screamed as the big man finally escaped and stood there, staring at her. His warm breath colliding with the cold air made him look more evil than ever, as his face was surrounded by a white smoky mist. She heard him growl, as he once again made an attempt to pursue her. He swiftly moved down the icy sidewalk, trying to block her way, but Beth went into a feverish sprint towards the corner. Her feet continued to slip until she finally reached the curb, allowing her to make a clean getaway. She ran furiously back down the block towards the club, with her screams echoing into the night. The man stood on the corner and watched as Beth got further away. He thought about chasing her, but in his mind, he knew she wasn't one of the gang members.

He quickly moved from the corner, because he realized it would be just a matter of time before someone would come and investigate what she would tell them. He also knew that the revenge for his loss was not yet complete. He walked back over to Trent's car, and began to come up with a solution to hide the two dead bodies. The image of the trophy falling into the sewer came to mind as he looked over at the corner. He stared at the black gated hole, and knew that the bodies would not fit into the dark opening. His brain started retrieving moments from his past, as he remembered using the man holes to enter and exit the sewer during the times he had lived down there. His eyes quickly located the round circular opening in the middle of the street. He walked over to it, and kicked some of the snow off the black steel lid. He then bent down, inserted his fingers into the little open holes and began trying to pull it upwards. After several hard yanks, he was able to break the seal of the untouched lid, by prying it off the street and exposing the darkness below.

Without a minute to spare, he quickly moved back towards Trent's car and grabbed Shane's body off the sidewalk. He then walked around to the driver's side, and pulled Vince from underneath the vehicle. With a corpse in each hand, he dragged both of them over to the pitch black opening and then, one by one, tossed them down into the underground tunnel. He then bent down and placed the steel covering back into its place, before he faded back into the shadows, where he contemplated his next move.

Chapter 11

Beth remained in a state of panic, as she ran crying and screaming back towards the club. Her tearful eyes focused on the bright lights as she tried to run as fast she could, fearful the monstrous man was still behind her. Her feet slipped upon the icy sidewalk but within seconds, her jittery hands grabbed the front door handle, and finally gave her the safety she had hoped and prayed for.

She bolted into the place, screaming hysterically, but her voice was unheard over the loud music coming from the stage. Even her sudden presence went unnoticed, as everyone's attention was focused on the band playing. She remembered where Trent and Allison were standing, and she began pushing her way through the small crowd to get to them.

Out of the corner of her eye, Allison saw a commotion amongst the small crowd, with people moving out of the way. She quickly grabbed Trent's arm and directed his attention to the distraction. They both watched with concern and finally saw what was causing the ruckus. It was Beth.

She immediately ran over, grabbed Trent by his leather jacket and shook him uncontrollably, trying desperately to tell him about the murder, but between the loud music and her hysterics, her voice was virtually impossible to hear. Both Trent and Allison saw the tears in her eyes and the distraught look on her face. They leant in trying to listen to what she was yelling about.

"He's dead!" She screamed over and over at them.

"Who's dead? Where's Shane?" Trent asked.

"He's dead; the homeless man killed him."

"What? Where?" Trent shouted back at her.

"At your car, the homeless man, he killed Shane!" Beth continued to scream.

Without thinking, Trent ran quickly through the crowd and out the front door, as Allison grabbed Beth and held onto her. Mike, the owner immediately walked over upon seeing Beth pushing furiously through the crowd, and wanted an explanation.

Trent ran like a madman down the block towards his car. As he was running, he began to think if he was possibly making a foolish mistake, by not calling the police over the sudden news from Beth. His mind raced with indecisive anxiety, but his inner will kept his feet going in a forward motion. He reached the corner, stopped and stood within the falling snow, as his parked car came into view. He stared at his vehicle and saw no signs of either bandmate. Now completely stunned and concerned, he cautiously looked around the darkened avenue for any unforeseen surprises. Before proceeding forward, he looked back over his shoulder towards the club to see if anyone had hopefully followed him, but the sidewalk was bare. He once again pondered if maybe he should have brought someone with him, like Mike or even the club's bouncer, but at this point, he knew it was too late and he was all alone.

A cold chill traveled down his spine as he took his first step forward and noticed the broken passenger window on his vehicle. He began to get a bad feeling, not knowing what he was about to see. He thought if Shane, or even Vince, were dead, they would be lying inside the automobile. His steps decreased to a mere crawl, as he slowly approached the shattered window. He looked down and instantly saw traces of blood upon the snow-covered curb. He then carefully laid his hands upon the cold door, as he slowly and cautiously inserted his head inside. He immediately noticed the shattered glass all over the driver's seat, along with the purse that Beth blindly left behind. Trent knew, after seeing all the obvious evidence, that something horrible had happened and his band mates were nowhere to be found.

***

The homeless man watched again from the dark, vacant store front as another young man wearing a leather jacket suddenly came from around the corner. He stood silently still as he observed the individual, slowly and cautiously moving towards the car. He knew the newcomer was also affiliated with the rest of the gang, based on his garment of choice and the vehicle being the reason for his sudden presence. The big man thought this individual was probably investigating the story told by the girl who'd gotten away.

He reached down and held his side, as the never-ending pain from the knife wound prevailed. Trying to escape the agony, he closed his eyes and tried to bring forth Scotty's voice, but his mind remained blank. A wave of fear came over the man's mental stability, knowing his dead child's inner voice was now lost forever, without the golden trophy in his possession. He patiently waited to see exactly what the young punk's motive was, but the anticipation also brought forth the returning feelings of hatred and revenge, as his large foot slowly advanced from the darkness.

***

Trent's mind instantly went into a panic after seeing the gruesome site that covered the inside of his car. He quickly pulled his head out of the vehicle, as a feeling of nausea came over him. Bending down and lowering his head, he vomited on the sidewalk, as the vision of both Vince and Shane being slaughtered came to mind. His lungs began to hyperventilate and his heart began to beat faster, causing him to fall to one knee from his whirling emotions. Frightened and stunned, Trent slowly stood up and began to hopelessly call out for his band mates.

"Vince, Shane!" He cried out into the night.

"Where are you?"

He waited impatiently for the answer he knew he wasn't going to get. He called out their names several more times, but nothing except the sound of the cold wind howling down the avenue was all he heard. The silence set off an uncontrollable feeling of anger as his temper flared, causing him to suddenly strike the hood of his car. He stood there, closed his eyes and then recalled Allison's voice saying, "Aren't you going to go back and help him?"

***

As the homeless man slowly progressed towards Trent, he watched the young man losing his mind over the reality of his sudden loss. He felt a sense of immortal gratitude, knowing the individual was feeling the same amount of anguish that he had inflicted upon him. He continued to stay hidden in the shadows, as he carefully slid against the wall of the building. With every step he took, he focused on the face of the individual, and soon identified him as the driver of the car. His unstable mind began to race, as he stared directly at the person who was responsible for the tragedy that eliminated Scotty's voice, the person who had destroyed what little he had left, and the person he'd been waiting for.

129

He clenched both of his fists, and deep feelings of malice suddenly overwhelmed him. He wanted to charge the young man and tear him to shreds, but just then, the image of the golden trophy flashed within his mind, and he decided that he had a different plan for this particular gang member.

***

Trent, trapped in his own emotional state, was so busy trying desperately to sort out his feelings of hopelessness and despair, that he was oblivious to the big man creeping up behind him. As he stood there helpless, he knew he had to do something about the murderous situation he was responsible for. He began to unzip his leather jacket in order to retrieve his cell phone, when he suddenly felt the presence of somebody standing behind him. He quickly turned around and was instantly shocked to see the giant homeless man. His jaw dropped immediately upon seeing NED's hideous face staring down at him. His body froze as he looked up into the angry man's eyes, and instantly saw the sign of death festering deep within them.

Panicking and scared for his life, he made an attempt to run, but the big man quickly shoved him against his car. He felt the hard impact, as he lay there with his back sprawled across the hood. Trent began to scream for help, hoping someone would hear him, but the avenue remained desolate. The homeless man reached out and grabbed Trent by his leather jacket and yanked him off the car. He lifted him slightly off the ground, as he brought him up and close to his face. Trent could smell the man's harsh, rotting breath as their faces where now just inches apart from each other.

"You … you are the one that's responsible for taking my golden boy away from me," said the homeless man.

"What? What are you talking about?" Trent stuttered with confusion.

"You and the rest of your gang have taken away the only thing that I had left, the only thing that keeps me alive. The only thing that I still love."

"Gang? Thing? What the fuck are you talking about?"

"My golden boy! It was you!" The man yelled in Trent's face.

"I don't know what you're talking about, but whatever it is, I'm sorry." Trent pleaded.

"You and the rest of your gang have pushed me too far, and now you will all pay for it. I have nothing left to live for, and it's all because of you."

Trent suddenly heard Allison's voice repeating her phrase one more time, before he saw the large right hand of the man coming towards his face. He turned his head and flinched, but a second later he saw stars. The man dropped Trent's semi-conscious body down upon the sidewalk, then bent down and grabbed his long, black hair. He pulled him off the curb and into the street, as he began to drag him towards the round steel lid of the manhole.

Trent shook his head back and forth as his mind slowly began to clear from the man's punch, when he realized he was being dragged across the avenue. He reached back and tried to free himself by pulling on the man's hand, but was overpowered by his strength and determination. He tried stopping the angry man by desperately digging his heels into the snow, but that just made him pull even harder.

"Please, stop, I'm sorry, I'm sorry!" Trent screamed up towards the man, when suddenly they stopped. The man looked down at Trent and removed the grip from his hair, only to replace it around his throat. He held Trent's head firmly against the street as he began to struggle, trying to lift up the manhole cover with his free hand. Trent reached up and tried once again to escape, but that made the man just tighten his grip even more. As he lay there now gasping for air, his blurry eyes looked over, and noticed that the man's attention was mainly focused on trying to lift off the avenue's manhole cover. He then heard the loud grinding sound of the steel heavy lid being removed from its resting place, and then the screech of it sliding across the icy, blackened tar.

Trent felt a burst of hot steam rising up from the bowels of the city, as the man dragged his head over the open, circular hole. His nostrils deeply inhaled the putrid scent that lingered throughout the underground, as his face was momentarily suspended across the avenue's cavity of darkness.

As the homeless man continued to push him further into the hole, Trent's hands gripped the round metal edge, trying to combat the strength behind the uncontrollable anger. He held on for as long as he could, until the big man overpowered his resistance and pushed him head first, down into the bitter blackness.

He let out a howling yell as his body quickly plunged towards the bottom of the sewer. Trying to avoid breaking his neck, he twisted his torso, hoping for a safer landing. Within seconds, he reached the base of the tunnel, but his perilous fall was broken upon hitting an unexpected softer ground, which caused him to fling backwards and hit his head hard against the sewer wall.

As he lay there, his blurred vision focused on the only light that shined down, coming from the round opening above. His eyes soon adjusted, and he was able to faintly see what he'd landed on that broke the majority of his fall. He crawled over to what resembled a pile of clothes, reached out and grabbed the top article. Yanking on what just looked like a leather jacket, produced an arm that came swinging around, hitting him in the face. He jumped back in dismay as his eyes focused, and he was now staring directly at Shane's face, and at the bloody slice across his throat.

"Shane!" he screamed, as he reached out and shook his band mate who didn't respond.

He quickly pulled him off the pile, where he then saw Vince's face with his drumsticks imbedded within his head. He screamed once again and jumped back against the sewer wall. His body began to shiver from the horror he was witnessing, as he stared at the faces of both his dead friends. His eyes then looked up and saw the large boot of the homeless man appear, as he placed it upon the first rung of the old, steel ladder and then he fearfully watched, as the bottom of the other boot soon followed.

***

Between her hysterics and the loud music, Mike could not hear what Beth was trying to tell him. He leaned forward and brought his ear close to her mouth, in an attempt to carefully listen to what she was screaming about, but he still couldn't clearly comprehend. He then asked both her and Allison to come back to his office, so he could understand the reason why she was crying uncontrollably. They both agreed and closely followed Mike, as he escorted them through the crowd. Allison kept her arm around Beth, trying to comfort her from her tragic experience, as they made their way down the hall to Mike's private office. He opened the door, turned on the lights and then asked them to sit down in one of his empty chairs. They both declined the offer and remained standing.

"Alright, would someone please tell me what happened?" Mike asked the girls.

"He killed him!" Beth screamed.

"Who killed who?"

"The homeless man, he killed my boyfriend!"

"What homeless man and where did this happen?"

"Around the block, at the car… He killed Shane!" Beth screamed as she continued to cry.

"Do you know what she's talking about?" Mike asked Allison.

"On our way here, we accidently ran into a homeless man."

"You ran him over?"

"No. Trent ran into his shopping cart with his car and knocked it over, but he was alright, I personally looked out the back window and saw that he was moving."

"He followed us … he killed Shane and probably killed Vince too! You need to call the police!" Beth screamed at Mike.

"Vince …now who's Vince?"

"He's the drummer of the band, he was the guy that they were waiting for earlier," said Allison.

"Well, where's Trent?" Mike asked.

"When he heard what happened from Beth he ran out of the club. He probably went to his car."

"To his car….what, all by himself?" Mike asked, stunned.

"Please call the police; he's probably in danger if he's not already dead too!" Beth continued to scream.

Mike looked at Beth, then at Allison. He nodded his head as he picked up his office phone and dialed.

"New York Police Department 9th Precinct how may I help you?" The voice on the other end asked.

"Hello, this is Mike Powers, I'm the owner of The Cave, the rock club on Sullivan Street, and I have a young lady here who is telling me she witnessed a murder. Can I please have a couple of officers come down here and check it out?"

"Yes Sir, I will dispatch two officers to your location immediately, they will be there shortly."

"Thank you very much."

"You're welcome Sir."

Mike hung up his phone and said, "They will here shortly."

"Yes, but what about Trent? He went back to his car alone, you need to go see if he's alright." Allison said.

"The police will be here shortly, they will look into it."

"You don't understand, we don't have time, Trent could be in danger, or worse, dead!" Beth screamed at Mike.

"Listen ladies, I know you're freaking out over this, but I cannot just leave my club and go investigate a possible murder that you said happened around the block."

"It's not a possible murder, I watched the giant homeless man kill my boyfriend and he's probably killing Trent right now. You have to

133

go and help him!" Beth said, becoming hysterical once again.

Mike stared at both of the girls, trying to bide his time, hoping the police would show up in the next few minutes. He knew he was stuck between a rock and a hard place over this situation, and he honestly didn't know what to do. If time was of the essence, then he knew he was wasting it when maybe he could possibly save his friend's son's life.

"Can you tell me what kind of car Trent drives?" He asked.

"It's a green Mustang. It's parked right around the corner," Allison answered.

"The homeless man broke the fucking window; it's the car with the broken fucking window!" Beth yelled.

"Alright, I'll get Joey my bouncer to take a walk with me, and I'll go check it out," Mike said as he stood up and grabbed his coat. He then opened his desk drawer and grabbed his hand gun.

"I'd advise you two to stay here, but come up to the front so you can meet the police when they arrive. I didn't mention a certain location, so they'll be coming directly to the club."

Both Allison and Beth agreed, as the three of them walked out of the office and back to the entrance. Mike opened the front door and looked outside, hoping to see the police, but they still hadn't arrived yet.

"Damn it," he said to himself.

He then walked over to Joey and started to explain the situation. Being the warrior that he is, Joey, without any hesitation, immediately went behind the cashier to get his coat. Anxious, Mike opened the front door and peeked out once again, hoping to see the police, but his results were still the same. Allison looked around the club for Trent, hoping to see that he had returned, but he was nowhere to be found. She then turned to Mike and said, "I don't see Trent, so he must still be at his car, please hurry."

"I'm ready when you are boss," said Joey buttoning up his coat.

"Alright, let's go check it out," he said to his bouncer.

He then turned to the girls and said, "We'll be right back, stay up here and wait for the police. They should be here any minute and I need you to tell them where we went, so they can meet us there."

"Thanks so much," said Allison.

"Hurry up! You're wasting fucking time!" Beth yelled at both men, as her non-stop tears continued to fall.

Joey grabbed the front door handle and held it open for Mike, as they both quickly exited the club and hurried to the corner.

Chapter 12

The tunnel suddenly went completely black, as the big man came down through the manhole, blocking out the glow from the street lights. Trent knew his fate was destined with every step the big man took downward, his eyes going back to his band mates. The dead, horrified expressions on both their silent faces made him tremble. He stared at them until his mind was interrupted, by the loud scraping sound of the large steel cover being dragged across the street above. He looked up and tensely watched the tunnel's light decrease to nearly none, as the big man carefully set the lid back in place.

Within the tainted darkness, Trent could barely see the large descending figure, but he heard each and every one of his chilling footsteps getting closer. He tried to get back to his feet, until he heard the loud splash of the homeless man reaching the bottom. He pressed himself tightly against the concrete wall, as he heard the sound of splashing advancing towards him but then suddenly stopped.

Trent held his breath as he fearfully waited. The seconds dragged, then out of the darkness came a large, thrusting hand that reached down and grabbed the front of his leather jacket. He was then lifted off the sewer's floor, where the big man then pulled him up towards his angered face, looked him in the eye and said, "You took away my little golden boy."

"W-w-what?" Trent stuttered.

"And I want him back!" The homeless man yelled so loud it sent an echo barreling throughout the underground tunnels.

"I don't know what you're talking about; I didn't take anything from you."

"You took away the only thing that was left of my heart."

"What are you talking about?" Trent panicked.

The man stared at Trent while he kept his hate-filled grip firmly upon him. He knew he wanted revenge on the leather jacket gang members, but besides Jack, he especially wanted the driver of the car responsible for his tragic loss.

"That way." The homeless man said, as he raised his hand and pointed at the dark, straight path in front of them.

***

As Mike and Joey reached the corner, they stopped, not knowing what to expect, or who might be waiting for them around the bend. Mike lightly brushed the snow off his face, then reached into his pocket and pulled out his gun. He found it extremely difficult, trying to hold it firmly in his trembling hand. Joey looked down at the shaking pistol, and knew his boss was really scared.

Mike took a deep breath, trying to find the courage to turn the corner, as he looked at Joey and said, "Are you ready?"

"Ready when you are, boss."

They stepped past the building and quickly scanned all four corners of the intersection for the homeless man, or even one of the boys, but the street appeared desolate.

"Look, that's Trent's car." Mike said, as he recognized the vehicle from Alison's and Beth's description. He and Joey approached the automobile, where they immediately noticed the broken passenger window, and then the trails of blood that dripped down the door.

"Damn, the girl wasn't lying; it definitely looks like somebody got killed here," Mike said.

"Yeah, but where are the bodies, and where the fuck is this homeless man?" Joey responded, as he quickly turned his head and looked around.

"I don't know, but I came down here to find my friend's son and he's nowhere to be found. I'm beginning to worry."

"It seems impossible for a killer to dispose of so many bodies within a matter of minutes, so he's gotta be around here, somewhere." Joey said, as he now stared at the car.

"Trent!" Mike hollered out into the cold dark night.

They stood there, silently hoping to hear the young man's response, but the sound of the howling wind was all that was heard. He shouted his name several more times, as he walked around the perimeter of the vehicle.

***

As NED and Trent began their walk down the cold, dark path, the big man kept a tight grip upon the back of the leather jacket.

136

"Where are we going? Where are you taking me?" Trent asked.

"We're going back."

"Back where?"

"To my lost little golden boy."

Trent suddenly stopped, as he thought he heard his voice being called out from the street above.

"Trent!" Mike yelled as he walked back and forth across the icy sidewalk.

Trent clearly heard his name again and reacted instantly by blurting out "Hey, Hey, I'm down here, Help!"

The big man quickly responded by cupping his filthy hand around Trent's mouth, in order to silence him.

"Did you hear that?" Mike asked Joey.

"Hear what?"

"I thought I heard someone calling for help."

"I didn't hear anything, maybe it was just the wind again," Joey said, shaking his head.

"No, it sounded like a voice and it came from over there by the corner."

Still holding his gun about chest high, Mike stepped up onto the sidewalk that was located directly above the black sewer grate. He carefully looked around the intersection and once again shouted out, "Trent!"

"Like I said before, I didn't hear anything?" Joey said, as he walked over and stood next to Mike.

"Maybe you're right, but I swore I heard someone calling out for help."

They both carefully listened, but the night remained still thereafter.

***

Trent, along with the homeless man, clearly heard Mike's voice from the street this time. He began to struggle trying to break free of his restraint, but the man's incredible strength just pulled him backwards. Trent's anxious eyes helplessly looked up at the shadows that stood outside the sewer's opening, calling out his name.

"If you make a single sound, I will snap your fucking neck, punk." The big man whispered in Trent's ear.

Trent then felt his body being dragged as NED began pulling him in reverse, trying to negate any possibility of help from the strangers above. They managed to get a few yards down the tunnel, when Trent mustered up enough will to suddenly break free. He quickly lunged back towards Mike's calling voice as his feet stumbled forward.

"Help! Help! I'm down here" Trent screamed out as his last hope of being heard.

***

"I definitely heard that. It came from down here." Mike said as he pointed at the opening of the sewer.

"Help! I'm down here! Help, he's going to kill me." Trent screamed out once again.

"Trent, is that you?" Mike knelt down and yelled passed the sewer grate.

"Yes! Please hurry!"

"How did you get down there?"

"Through the manhole, you have to open the manhole."

"He said open the manhole," Mike said, looking up at Joey.

Joey quickly ran to the middle of the street and located the circular lid. He bent down and brushed off the excess snow, before positioning his fingers into the small holes. He gave the cover a couple of strong yanks, before he was able to lift it up and lay it onto the street.

***

NED charged forward, grabbing Trent from behind and pushing him up against the tunnel's hard concrete interior. He then held him tightly against the wall, as he heard the sound of the manhole cover above them being altered. He looked up and watched, as the steel lid shifted a couple of times, and then was slowly pulled off. The dark tunnel immediately lit up, as the lights from the street instantly shined down into the hole.

"Trent!" Mike shouted over Joey's shoulder.

Trent tried to yell, causing the homeless man to quickly react. He grabbed the young man's head and slammed it against the tunnels wall, hard enough to knock him momentarily unconscious. He fell flat to the floor, where the big man then placed a heavy foot upon his body, confining him. Now, with his eyes glued to the bright circular opening, NED patiently waited for the threat that might follow.

***

138

"I don't hear him down there," said Joey.

"I know you heard what I heard; we know he's down there," said Mike.

Joey cautiously leaned forward and slowly stuck his head into the sewer's circular opening. The homeless man stood still until he saw Joey's head appear through the round hole. Then, like a hunter to its prey, he aimed for his mark and immediately lunged towards it. Joey didn't expect or see the two enormous hands, as they suddenly surged out from the sewer's darkness and latched onto his head. Mike watched in horror, as Joey immediately grabbed the steel edge of the manhole, trying desperately to stop from being pulled in. Mike quickly pointed his shaky gun towards the opening, but was unable to see where the violent perpetrator was. The muscular man screamed, as he tried to battle against the deadly tension from NED's tightly secured hands. He struggled to hold himself, but the weight of the big man prevailed, snapping Joey's neck within seconds. His hands suddenly went limp and instantly released their opposing grips, allowing the homeless man to quickly pull the lifeless body down into the darkness. Mike stood staring into the manhole in complete shock from what had just happened. He then nervously leaned forward, and began to call out for Joey and Trent.

***

Hearing his name once again, Trent opened his eyes and tried to blurt out a few words, as he began to regain consciousness. Mike once again heard Trent's voice and bent down closer, towards the round opening.

"Joey, Trent can you hear me?" Mike yelled.

He then looked down into the dimly lit sewer, where his vision was limited to seeing only an iron ladder descending downwards into the still darkness. As he leaned even further towards the opening, he thought he heard a faint rustling sound coming from the bottom. He looked down and was suddenly startled, when out of the sewers gloom appeared Joey.

"Joey, Joey, are you alright?" Mike shouted down at him.

He waited for an answer from the bouncer but there was none. He stared at his silent employee, until he noticed that his head began to slowly wobble back and forth. His eyes then focused on his face until Joey's lifeless head suddenly fell forward, revealing the hideous vision of NED standing right behind him. The horrifying sight of the old homeless man startled Mike, causing him to fall backwards. As he hit the icy street,

139

his hand lost the grip he had on his gun. The weapon flew out of his hand, and quickly slid just out of his reach upon the snow. He turned over onto his belly and extended his arm as far as it could go, trying to regain possession of his weapon. His fingertips touched the cold imbedded item, but at the same time, he didn't realize that his feet were suspended directly over the open manhole.

***

The big man looked up, saw Mike's two feet dangling over the edge and immediately dropped Joey's dead body to the floor. He repositioned himself underneath the round opening, before taking a giant leap up towards his swaying targets.

***

Mike slid his body slightly forward and was able to grab hold of his gun. He instantly felt relief with his firearm back in his hand. He gripped the handle and placed his finger upon the cold, steel trigger as he mentally prepared himself on how to deal with the situation, when suddenly from out of the manhole, came two large hands grabbing his ankles. Surprised and scared, Mike screamed, as he immediately dug the butt of the gun and his fingers into the icy street, trying to stop from being pulled down into the sewer, but the excessive weight of the big man prevailed.

Quickly and violently, Mike's body came crashing downwards into the dark hole. He hit the bottom hard, but his fall was broken as he landed on the pile of dead bodies on the sewer's floor. His gun-toting hand hit the old iron ladder on the way down, causing his weapon to escape his tight grip. His desperate eyes tried to follow the direction the gun had ricocheted, but it just quickly disappeared into the darkness. His mind began to panic as he lay, quietly trying to figure out some strategic move, and then the intense pain hit him. He rolled onto his back and then reached down and grabbed his ankle.

"Fuuuuuuck!" Mike shouted, as his hands felt an exposed, fractured bone protruding out of his skin.

Grinding his teeth to bear the agony, Mike looked up at the bright circular opening and knew that even with a broken ankle; going back up the ladder was his only way out. Utilizing his one good leg, he pushed himself close enough where he was able to reach out, and grabbed the first rusty rung. Once again, he cried out in pain as he pulled himself across the bulky mound of what he had initially landed on. With his eyes and mind focused on the street lights above, he was completely oblivious to what he was actually perched on, until he took a moment and looked down.

His mouth fell open as his eyes quickly pivoted back and forth between the three faces of the dead men lying beneath him. He began to shake with fear as he first focused on his employee, Joey. He noticed that his neck had turned a purplish black from where it had been broken. Next, he looked at Shane, and particularly at the deep slice across his neck. His attention then shifted to Vince, and the sight of his drum sticks sticking out of his eye socket sent the final chill down his spine that made him franticly grab the higher rungs, in a desperate attempt to pull himself up.

"Help me." Trent cried out from within the darkness.

Mike heard Trent's voice and stopped his personal struggle momentarily, to turn his head towards the direction of the sound. His eyes squinted as he looked deeply into the cold black, but saw nothing.

"Trent, is that you?"

"Yes, please help me; he's going to kill me ... he's going to kill me and then you." Trent said, as he stumbled out from the sewer's gloom and into the sparse light.

"We have to get out of here right now!" Mike said, as he began to panic.

"But the only way out is back up the ladder," said Trent.

"I have a broken ankle, so I'm going to need your help."

"He's down here and he's going to kill us just like he did to them," Trent said, also in a panic as he pointed down at the three dead bodies.

"The police have been called and they're on the way, but if we want to get out of here alive, we need to help each other. Listen, I had a gun but it got knocked out of my hand when I hit the bottom, but you …you can find it, it's somewhere around there," Mike said, pointing to a certain area right before NED's large, terrifying hand pierced the darkness and grabbed him by his neck.

Trent screamed as he stumbled backwards, and fell to the floor from the abrupt shock. He then watched in horror, as the hideous sight of the big man came into the light, while mercilessly holding onto Mike's throat. Then with his powerful and relentless grip, NED pressed Mike's face tightly against the cold iron ladder.

"Sorry, but there's no such thing as heroes." NED said to Mike, right before he began his vicious assault. He initially pressed Mike's face firmly against one of the cold iron rungs, then proceeded to slam his head repeatedly into the sturdy steel. Mike felt the first blow shatter his nose, the second break his jaw and then nothing after that, as the homeless man unleashed a display of unstoppable brutality. Trent looked away, but mentally counted how many times he heard Mike's head hit the old ladder. Three, six, then up to ten times is what he mentally counted, while he tried to crawl away from the murderous scene. As his body slithered slowly down the cold icy path, in the distance, he heard, and then felt, the rumble of a subway train. He thought to himself that the station must be somewhere close as he pushed himself up, trying desperately to get to his feet but despite his effort, to one knee was the best he could do. He then thought about going back and trying to find Mike's gun, but that also sounded suicidal.

Mike's freshly dead body fell neatly upon the other victims, as the big man finally released his ravishing grip from his bloody head. He then took a moment and looked down at all four of his victims. He stared at each of their silent faces, until he heard the subtle sound of a police siren coming from the street above. He knew he had to climb back up the ladder and put the manhole cover back in its place, or else he'd risk the chance of never getting back his golden possession.

With no regard or remorse, NED stepped upon the four dead bodies to reach the first few rungs of the old rusty ladder. He quickly alternated his feet up the iron until he was back at the top. He slowly lifted his head out of the manhole and up to his eye level, where he saw the flashing red and blue lights of a police car, parked in front of the club. He knew his time was limited before they would be down here investigating, so he quickly grabbed the manhole cover and pulled it back over his head.

The tunnel went back to black, as the heavy steel lid was once again placed securely back in its spot. The big man descended down the ladder until he reached the bottom, where he stopped and stared into the tunnels darkness in search for Trent. He carefully listened and heard him just a few yards away, splashing through the sewer's shallow puddles. He nodded his head confidently, as he slowly stepped off the ladder and onto the remains of the four dead bodies, in pursuit of his own personal justice.

***

Allison wrapped a warm, comforting arm tightly around Beth, as the punishing toll of her traumatic experience continued to mentally

142

torture her. Even inside the safety of the club, Beth's unstoppable tears continued to fall, while her body shook uncontrollably with fear and anxiety.

"Where are they? Why aren't they back by now?" Beth shouted.

"The police should be here any minute."

"But if they were alright, they would have been back by now. The homeless man must have killed them too!" Beth cried out.

Allison remained speechless, as the thought of Beth's accusation really frightened her. She held Beth just a little bit tighter but this time, it was for herself. Then suddenly, a strong gust of cold wind hit their faces, as they turned to see who opened the club's front door. Standing before them were two police officers. The relieving sight of the two men brought a glimmer of hope to Allison, as she stood up and introduced herself.

Chapter 13

"Hello, I'm Officer Tom Phillips and this is my partner, Officer John Martinez. We were dispatched here on the account that someone would like to report a homicide."

"Yes that's correct, this girl's boyfriend was killed and she witnessed it," Allison said, pointing to Beth, who was still hysterically crying.

"Where? Here at this club?"

"No, around the block, at the car we drove here in. I would tell you more, but you have to go quick and help the club owner and his bouncer."

"The owner? Who, Mike? Is he here?"

"No, he and the bouncer went to find the guy I came here with, his name is Trent, he owns the car. About thirty minutes ago, Beth ran into the club, crying and saying that her boyfriend was killed. Trent immediately ran out of here and when he didn't return, we told Mike. Then he and the bouncer went to go get him, but they haven't returned either. Please hurry, they might all be in danger."

"You said they went around the block? What, on the avenue?"

"Yes."

"What kind of car is it?"

"It's an older Mustang. It's parked right around the corner."

"It's the one with the broken window!" Beth shouted.

"Please hurry!"

"Alright, but you two have to stay here until we come back so we can get more information, understand?"

"Yes sir, we'll be here."

"Thank you. Alright one more time, old Mustang, broken window, parked just around the corner?" asked Officer Phillips, as he pulled out a pen and jotted down the details on a small notepad.

"Yes sir, please hurry!" Allison insisted.

"We'll be right back." Officer Phillips said to the girls, as he and his partner quickly exited the club.

Allison put her arm back around Beth and held her tightly. In her mind, she ran through the whole scenario of what had happened in the car. She remembered everybody screaming at the poor homeless man that was standing in the middle of the street, and then she recalled Trent actually knowing him and calling him by name. She closed her eyes and said to herself, "NED, NED, NED." Then the image of the man's horrifying face staring at her through the windshield appeared in her mind, causing her to shiver with fear.

The two police officers got into their vehicle and brushed the loose snow off their uniformed coats. Officer Martinez turned the key, revved the engine and then put the car in gear. He looked at his partner and said, "Should we call for back-up?"

"Absolutely, I'll call it in, but we should still go down the block and check it out."

Officer Martinez nodded his head as he pressed his foot down on the gas pedal. With lights flashing and the siren screeching, the cruiser sped down the street towards the corner.

***

Trent gazed into the path's unknown darkness, and reacted by pushing back against the man with some resistance. Once again the man grabbed the back of his leather jacket and brutally shoved him forward, as they advanced closer to the lost trophy.

"Where are we going? Where are you taking me? Trent asked as they continued.

"Back."

"Back where?"

"Back to my little golden boy."

Trent remained confused and scared, as the man's answers made absolutely no sense to him. The images of all the dead victims flashed within his mind, reminding him the level of unstableness that the homeless man now possessed.

"I want you, the driver of the car, to find my little golden boy."

"Golden boy? What are you talking about?"

"You and your gang should have just left an old homeless man alone. But you, your leader, and all the rest of you leather jacket punks have pushed me too far."

"Leader? What the fuck are you talking about, I don't have any leader."

"Jack, the leader of your gang, the one that sent you to get me."

146

"I don't know what you're talking about! I don't know any Jack! And I'm not in any gang! I swear to God!" Trent screamed.

As they continued forward, the excitement of soon having his son's golden trophy back in his hand made the homeless man shove Trent a little harder down the tunnel's path. Step by stumbling step they walked, until they finally reached the location that the accident had occurred on the avenue above.

The man's piercing eyes looked down at the large, icy puddle that was located directly below the sewer grate above him. He was hoping to see the shiny golden item revealing itself, but it was completely submerged. Dismayed, the big man violently pushed Trent down into the dark shallow pool.

"My little golden boy is somewhere in there, find it."

Trent, down on all fours, began franticly crawling around. His hands instantly felt a numbing pain as they plunged beneath the ice cold water, in search for something he had absolutely no clue of. His fingers scraped the sewer floor as he started to pull articles of debris to the surface. He retrieved a hair brush first, then an old beer can. He held both items up, hoping for the man's approval, but the pieces were quickly denied.

"What the fuck am I looking for?" Trent yelled in desperation.

"My little golden boy."

"What the fuck is that?"

"You'll know it when you find it, keep looking!" The homeless man demanded.

Trent continued his blind search, as his hands sifted through the large cold puddle, until he touched a hard metal object. Underwater, his tingling fingers lightly examined the item before he grabbed it and brought it to the surface. The sight of a gold child's baseball trophy was what Trent saw within his hand. He lifted it up and held it within the lighting that shined downwards, past the sewer grate. A small flickering glare ricocheted around the dark tunnel as he began to twirl the trophy around, trying to get a better look at it. Trent, feeling a sign of relief, took a deep breath of the pungent air and then slowly exhaled, because he knew he had hit the jackpot.

"Is this what you're looking for?" Trent asked as he stood up, turned around and presented the golden trophy to the man.

Like a child, the big man lunged clumsily towards Trent, quickly snatching the lost item from his hand. He felt a warm rush of blood immediately soften his darkened heart, as he held the golden trophy up into the light upon their reunion. The bright brilliance of the object

147

blinded his eyes for a moment, as he too found it irresistible not to spin it around within the downward glow.

He held the golden trophy tightly within his hand, as his fingers began to caress the familiar frame of the small, metal object. His eyes followed his subtle touch as they both moved up the tarnished item, until they reached beyond the shoulders of the little bat boy. His finger scraped across the rough edge of the place where the small head of the golden boy once appeared.

The big man suddenly opened his eyes widely to examine the trophy's new flaw closer. He stared directly at the sharp jagged spot, as his finger continued to touch the top of the decapitation. He couldn't believe that the little precious face that he has always kissed in order to rekindle his memories of his dead child was gone. He closed his eyes and began to speak to the golden object like he had a thousand times before.

"Scotty, it's me, daddy. Are you there?"

The man waited for his cerebral answer, but there was only silence within his head.

"Scotty, its daddy, we're back together again. Please talk to me." The man pleaded desperately, as he continued to run his finger across the top of the damaged area.

Trent stood there and watched as the homeless man began talking to the obscure found object. He was confused, seeing the behavior of the man who was trying to personally interact with the small, golden item. The sound of the man's voice trying to conjure up something began to horrify Trent, as he stared at the closed-eyed face of the mumbling man. He could tell that he was deeply engrossed within his thoughts and saw this as an opportunity to possibly escape. He turned and slowly began to step back towards the dark tunnel. His feet moved cautiously as they waded through the murky water, trying desperately not to make a sound that could possibly cause the big man to break his hypnotic trance.

The man repeated his mental solicitations to the trophy, begging for his son's voice to return to him, but his head remained quiet. He tightly squeezed his adored item as he opened his eyes and saw Trent trying to get away. With his free hand he reached out, grabbed the back of Trent's leather jacket and forcibly pulled him back towards him. Trent turned his head, looked the homeless man in his eyes, and shivered as he saw the return of madness behind them. The hate-filled stare and the tension of the man's grip indicated that something was still wrong.

"Let me go, I found what you wanted, let me go!"

The man continued to stare at Trent as he began to growl under his long gray beard. His adrenaline soared as his resentment towards the young man returned. His hands started to shake as the maniac known as NED began to resurface.

"It's broken!" The big man screamed out loud.

"What's broken?"

"My little golden boy, it doesn't talk anymore!"

"Talk? It's a fucking statue; it's not supposed to talk."

The homeless man knew he didn't owe Trent an explanation. He just knew the voice of his dead son didn't return upon his touch like it always had, and the driver of the car was responsible for it.

"You broke it!" He screamed once again.

Trent, fearing for his life, remembered a discussion in one of his Sociology classes, on what to do if you were ever in a homicidal situation. He recalled the professor saying that you must try to reason with the killer by somehow bringing his mind back to reality. In a soft and calming voice, he began to speak to the man. "Listen, my name is Trent, I go to college, I play guitar, I live with my father, and I've seen you sitting on the corner of the avenue for months, just around the block from where I live. You know me, I've given you money on numerous occasions, like I did earlier today.

The man closed his eyes, trying to comprehend all of what Trent was saying to him, but his deranged mind remained disoriented. He squeezed the trophy one more time and said to himself, "Scotty, it's daddy, please come back, please talk to me." But his son's voice no longer existed.

Trent stared at the mumbling man, hoping his words would jog his memory and bring back the quiet, homeless man he once knew from the avenue, but when the man's eyes reopened, all he saw was bitterness and hatred.

"For God sakes, my name is Trent and I ...." He cried out before he was quickly interrupted.

"My name is NED ......and you're dead!"

The big man lifted the broken golden object above both of their heads, and swiftly brought it down upon Trent's skull. Then, like a relentless killing machine, he hit him once, twice and then three times with the sharp edge of the marble base. As the blood began to spew out of the top of Trent's head, he released the grip he had upon his leather jacket and watched him fall to the sewer's floor. Trent began to slowly crawl back along the dark puddled path, trying to get away. His mind began to repeat the phrase that Allison had said to him in the car one more time, "Aren't you going to go back and help him?"

He slithered a couple of feet, before the big man reached down,

149

grabbed a handful of his long black hair and pulled him back. He turned him over to get one last look at the person, who in his mind, re-murdered Scotty. He held Trent's head tightly, as he repositioned the trophy within his hand and then with brute force, he plunged the top of the object down into his face. Like a knife, the small bat held by the gold headless player pierced Trent's flesh first, which forged the gruesome, bloody path for the rest of the trophy to follow. Fragments of shattered bone and torn facial tissue quickly covered the headless golden boy, as NED uncontrollably ravaged his adversary over and over again. He then pushed and held his prize possession deep into the head of his enemy, as he stared Trent directly into his dying eyes until they permanently closed.

With his heart still racing and out of pure hatred, NED forced the trophy deeper into Trent's head one last time before he yanked it out. The man then raised his bloody weapon up into the light, and watched as the thick, red substance subsided onto his hand. The bright, mesmerizing sparkle returned as Trent's blood slowly dripped off of the golden object. He then bent down and submerged the trophy into the shallow puddle, to cleanse the remains from his ungodly act.

Now mentally and physically exhausted, the big man leaned back against the sewer wall and tried one more time to summon Scotty's voice, but just like the underground tunnel he was standing in, his brain was silent.

As his malevolent mind and scattered emotions began to regain their composure, he stared off into the cold darkness. He grinded his teeth as he held his broken little golden boy in one hand, and reached down and held his side with the other, as the intense pain from Jack's knife wound returned. A small tear descended down his cheek, as a sense of hopelessness returned, leaving him saddened with loneliness and dismay. He held the broken trophy tighter than ever as he momentarily closed his eyes, fearing his future existence.

Chapter 14

As the police car pulled up to the corner curb, both officers prepared themselves by unfastening their holsters and pulling out their weapons. They exited the warm vehicle and into the night's persistent snow fall, in pursuit of their call of duty. With their fingers on their triggers, they began to visually examine the potential crime scene. They immediately noticed Trent's green Mustang and the broken passenger window. Officer Phillips walked cautiously towards the vehicle, as officer Martinez kept a watchful eye on the avenue's intersection. Phillips pulled his flashlight from his belt and shined it directly at the shattered window. The beam of light followed the jagged edge, and then proceeded downwards, along the frozen trail of blood upon the passenger door.

He moved closer to the damaged car, as his eyes began to investigate the gruesome scene. With his gun aimed and ready to shoot, he shined his flashlight into the parked vehicle. He took a quick glance at the backseat, assuring him that the car was indeed vacant, then directed the beam towards the front, where he discovered the blood-drenched passenger seat.

"Do you see anything?" Officer Martinez shouted.

"Definitely a murder scene, the inside is covered in blood, but I don't see a body anywhere."

With his guard still up, Martinez walked over to Trent's car to also see the murderous evidence. He peeked inside the car to confirm Phillip's statement, and witnessed the same bloody sight. Phillips pointed the flashlight at the door to show his partner the trail of blood, then bent down and flashed the light underneath the car, where he discovered the reddish mixture upon the frozen street.

"I see a pool of blood. I think that the girl's boyfriend was probably hidden under here at one point."

"Yeah, but I don't see a single soul, not even Mike the club owner, who the girls told us to meet down here."

"It seems like there's a group of people missing now." Phillips said with regret.

Both officers began to quickly scan the snow-covered intersection, looking for the killer, or even the bodies of his victims. Phillips flashed his beam up and down the sidewalk, and then underneath all the parked cars, but saw nothing. Martinez also grabbed his flashlight and accompanied his partner in search of all the missing people. They shined their flashlights all around the quiet intersection, but there was still no sign of anybody. They stood in the middle of the avenue and looked at each other as they both shrugged their shoulders. Their minds were completely confused, because they had no idea how to solve this mystery, or where to even begin.

***

The homeless man stared at Trent's dead body, as he ran his thumb back and forth across the coarse edge of the decapitated trophy. He felt no remorse for any of the horrendous acts he executed this evening, knowing it was all done on the account of revenge. He held his side as the image of the blonde leader Jack flashed into his mind. Under his long grey beard, he made a faint growl with the realization that his battle with him and the leather jacket gang wasn't over yet.

As his mind and his body grew weaker, he closed his tired eyes, trying to get a moment of relief, but flashbacks from of all the evenings altercations began to race through his brain. The faces of all the people he had come in contact with appeared, first in their living state, followed by the images of how he had left them all gruesomely murdered. These recent, bitter memories made the big man squeeze his broken possession tighter, as he felt a true feeling of loneliness without his son's voice to comfort him.

As he leaned his head against the cold concrete wall, scenes from his tragic past began to invade his mind, as he pictured himself many years ago, sitting in his employers' office. His head was hung low as he sat there and listened to his boss giving him his termination.

"This isn't personal, this is just business. But you haven't sold a single thing in months, and I can no longer continue having you on my payroll," Rodney said.

"Just like that, after all these years. My wife and my son died less than a year ago, and now you're firing me?"

"This isn't personal, this is just business."

"Yes, that's right, it's just business. It's always business with you. It's all about your money! If I didn't have to work on that Saturday, my son would still be alive and so would my wife, but because of your money, your god damn money, they're dead."

"Here, I gave you a three month severance," Mr. Turner said, ignoring what the big man had just said to him, in order to move the termination process along quicker.

"They're fucking dead!" The man shouted, as he began to stand up from his chair.

Rodney's head tilted backwards, as it followed the rise of the big man from his desk. He sat there and looked up at his ex-employee, and tried to calm the situation back down by saying, "I think you should take the money and get away, leave the city, go someplace else …start over."

"Three months, I've been here for over ten years."

"Like I said before, this isn't personal, this is just business. Please, just take the money and leave," Rodney said as he pushed an envelope containing the man's final pay.

"I'd rather be homeless than take another penny from such a heartless piece of shit like you!" The big man shouted, as he hit the desk with his large closed fist.

The employer jumped in his seat, as he flinched from the loud sound and the initial threat. He quickly reached forward, pushed his finger on his intercom and said, "Jane, can you send security to my office immediately."

***

He reopened his bloodshot eyes and stared into the tunnel's darkness, as hopeless thoughts of suicide emerged. The idea of going through the rest of his pathetic life without Scotty's soothing and guiding voice seemed worthless. After years of numerous hardships, the only thing left that had any value to his existence was broken. He stared back down at Trent's lifeless body, and tried one last time to mentally bring forth his dead child's voice. He held the golden trophy with both hands and then slowly shifted his eyes upwards, as he began to pray to the Lord for help.

"Our Father, Who art in Heaven, Hallowed be Thy Name…"

He repeated the prayer and any others that he could remember, as he desperately tried to summon Scotty from beyond, but his efforts were of no avail.

His evil eyes fell back upon Trent, as he stepped forward and then lifted his large boot over his head.

"You son of a bitch!" He shouted, as he plunged his heavy foot down with hardened revenge.

***

The sound of the approaching siren brought a brief sign of relief to officers Phillips and Martinez, as they stood on the corner and waited for their back up to arrive. Within minutes, a flashing squad car pulled up, followed by an unmarked vehicle. Two more uniformed officers, along with Detective Glenn Houston, a short stubby middle aged man, exited their vehicles and met Phillips and Martinez on the corner. Officer Phillips began to give the new arrivals all the explicit details of the crime scene, and any inside story he might have been told by the young ladies.

Upon hearing the gruesome facts, the other two officers, along with Detective Houston, immediately pulled their guns from their holsters and began to comb the snow-covered area. The two officers accompanied Officer Martinez, as all three men cautiously walked along the avenue, looking for signs of the homeless suspect. Officer Phillips escorted Detective Houston over to Trent's car so he could begin his in-depth investigation. He shined his flashlight again at the damaged vehicle, and then underneath it, as he pointed out all the areas that were covered in blood.

"So you said there are several people missing?" Houston asked.

"Yes, the club owner, his bouncer, the owner of the car and a young woman's boyfriend, who she claims was murdered. I'm going to assume that the blood inside the car is his, according to her story."

"So then, where the hell is everybody?"

"Officer Martinez and I have been trying to figure that out since we first arrived."

"Hey, any of you guys see anything?" Detective Houston shouted out to the other officers.

"Not a damn thing. Except for the car, the area looks clean," responded Martinez, as he unknowingly walked across the intersection's manhole cover.

"I'm going to call this in and get a crime scene unit down here, to start taking some prints off the vehicle. I suggest you go back to the club and talk to the girlfriend of the victim. Maybe we can find out exactly what happened here tonight."

"Sure thing," said Phillips.

"I'll meet you back at the club in about fifteen minutes, until then, the officers and I will continue to search around for any possible clues."

Officer Phillips nodded his head as he holstered his weapon. He then turned and walked over to his car to retrieve all the paper work that needed to be filled out for his report. As he began walking back up the block, his mind raced, trying to piece together some of the information about the present crime. He recalled the young lady telling him a homeless man had murdered the other young woman's boyfriend. His memory then flashed back to the man sitting on the corner with the long, gray hair and beard. He remembered him being calm, peaceful and unthreatening.

As he walked up to the club, Phillips took off his hat and tapped it against his leg, knocking off the loose snow before he grabbed the handle of the door. He pulled it opened and saw the two young ladies, still sitting by the cashier. Allison stood up to greet Officer Phillips once again.

"Where is everyone?" Allison asked.

"I'm not sure," said Phillips, as he bowed his head with disappointment.

"What do you mean you're not sure?"

"We saw the car but there wasn't anybody around."

"You didn't meet the owner of the club and his bouncer?"

"No, they weren't there."

"They're dead too! They're all dead!" Beth suddenly shouted.

Allison and Phillips both stared at Beth, knowing what she said might be true. Phillips raised his folder and pulled out the standard police form, as he began to ask his questions. Allison began to tell her side of the story first, because Beth was still too emotional. He jotted down detail after detail, until she mentioned the name of the homeless man and location of the incident.

"NED? Do you know this man personally?"

"No, that was the name Trent called him when he was standing in front of the car."

Officer Phillips memory instantly recalled the gray-haired man sitting on the corner again, and his mind tried to remember the few details of their brief encounter, and what name the man had mumbled under his long beard. He closed his eyes, concentrated and recollected the vivid image of the homeless man's face, and then his mind heard him say the name …NED. Officer Phillips nodded his head as he reopened his eyes, knowing an important clue of the crime was just unveiled.

"And you're also telling me that all this happened just a few blocks from here?"

"Yes, it wasn't far. I think just a couple of avenues over and a few blocks down."

155

"Did the homeless man have long grey hair and a beard?"

"Yes, he was also a very large man, over six feet and he was pushing a shopping cart."

Officer Phillips memory went back to the man and his mind tried to picture the corner scene. He focused on the man's surroundings and recalled seeing a shoebox containing some money, the sign he was holding and then … the shopping cart against the wall.

"I think I know who you're talking about. I believe I met him earlier this evening, but he was just sitting on a corner."

"Well he was definitely going somewhere when Trent accidently hit his shopping cart and knocked it over. I told him to go back and help him, but they were already running late. They were supposed to play here tonight."

"Well we have several people on the case already, and we'll find out where everybody went in no time."

Just then, the front door opened and in walked Detective Houston. He greeted Phillips again, and then introduced himself to both of the young ladies as he held up a purse. Beth quickly got up and snatched her possession out of the detective's hand and then sat back down. She opened it up and began to rummage through it. She pulled out her wallet, unfastened it and then began to cry, as she stared at a picture of her and Shane together.

Phillips handed Houston his report and began to tell him all of the important details. When the number five came up as the number of people missing without a trace, everyone stood silent for a moment as the reality of it all set in.

"They're all dead! Just like my Shane …They're all dead!" Beth shouted, breaking the awkward silence.

NED scanned his underground dwelling, as he slowly lifted his bloody foot off of Trent's crushed head. He looked downwards at the large icy puddle, as his eyes searched for more of his personal belongings that might have also fallen through the sewer grate. He noticed the old baseball, floating just a few feet away. He bent down, grabbed it and held it up to the dim light. His fingers spun it a couple of times, before he inserted it into his coat's side pocket. He slowly paced around the small area as his fast-beating heartrate began to decrease. His eyes fell back upon Trent, as he took one last look at the person who in his mind, re-murdered his son Scotty. His hand tightly squeezed the broken trophy one more time, before he carefully tucked it back inside his coat's inner pocket.

Chapter 15

"I think I might have met this particular homeless man when Martinez and I were on patrol earlier," Phillips said to Houston as he pulled him aside.

"Really? Where?"

"Just a few blocks from here, I remember seeing him sitting across from Lorenzo's Pizzeria. He told me his name was NED. "

"Did you get his last name?"

"No, I didn't think I needed too. He wasn't breaking any laws and besides, I've seen him around."

"Approximately how long ago was this?"

"About two hours or so but by now, he could be anywhere in the city."

"Yes, but if he's our killer, he couldn't have taken five bodies along with him. I still think they all must still be somewhere in the area."

"What about the girls? I think we should take Beth to the hospital, and the other girl home," said Phillips.

"Absolutely, we've gotten all the information we needed from both of them, but I do recall hearing the other girl, Allison, saying she might have remembered the exact corner that their accident actually happened."

"Yes, she did say that."

"I'll take her home, but I'll drive down the same avenue and maybe she'll be able to see something that might lead us to the homeless man's identification."

Both gentlemen agreed upon their decisions then walked back over to the girls. They began to tell the young ladies what they had decided, and Allison was more than willing to help in any way, but Beth immediately rejected to the idea of going to the hospital alone. She insisted she wasn't going unless Allison was going along with her.

"Have you two called your parents yet?" Phillips asked.

"My parents are in Vegas and won't be back until late tomorrow, and that's why I'm not going to the hospital alone!" Beth yelled as she began to panic again.

"What about you, have you called your parents yet?" Houston asked Allison.

"No," Allison said and then mumbled, "I've been trying to avoid that all evening."

"I'm sorry, I couldn't hear you," said Houston.

"No sir, I haven't, not yet," Allison then said promptly.

"Would you like to take a few minutes and call them? Let them know what's going on?"

"Ah, yeah, sure," said Allison, as she quietly stepped away from the small circle.

She walked down the hall back towards Mike's office, digging through her purse in search for her phone. She stopped and leaned her shoulder against the wall, as she turned it on and went to her personal contacts. Her eyes focused immediately on her two choices, Mom & Dad or Meaghan. She took a deep breath, and then pushed her best friend's phone number.

It rang two times then she heard Meaghan's sarcastic voice say, "So how's your date with the rock star going?"

"You're not going to believe this," Allison said as she began to cry.

***

The big man stepped over Trent's lifeless body, as he began his solo walk within the sewer's darkness. With his mind still disillusioned and his body growing weaker, he struggled along the underground tunnel, towards the direction of the shelter. Step by stumbling step, he proceeded forward, as an abundance of visions from the past and present intertwined inside his head. Lovely images of his beautiful wife and smiling child mixed madly with the horrifying impressions of all of his victims and enemies. The haunting battle he fought within began to tear at his heart and soul, as his will to live began to diminish, but the repetitious picture of Jack's smug face gave him the strength to take another step forward.

***

Allison wiped the rest of her tears, as the conversation with Meaghan came to a close. Her best friend advised her to leave the murderous situation strictly to the police and not to put herself in harm's way, but Allison knew she was the key witness in their investigation. She

160

hung up her phone, turned and leaned against the wall, as she tried to mentally prepare herself for whatever was to come. She tucked her phone back into her purse and then walked back over to rejoin the others. She immediately put her arm back around Beth and gave her a much needed hug, before her attention was focused back on the words said by Detective Houston and Officer Phillips.

Beth became hysterical again as the thought of going to the hospital alone continued to frighten her, but Allison reminded her that in order for them to move forward, she needed to be strong, if not for herself, but for Shane and the respect of all the others still missing. Beth held Allison tightly, then released the tense hold that she had on her. They both looked at each other, as Allison tried to assure Beth that everything was going to be fine, but she knew damn well that Beth might never be able to get over the traumatic experience she had endured this evening.

A gust of cold air rushed into the club, as the front door reopened and in walked Officer Martinez. He greeted his fellow colleagues, as he gave both Phillips and Houston an update involving Trent's vehicle. He told them that several prints had been taken off the door handles of the car, and that a tow truck was in route to impound the automobile for further investigation.

Officer Phillips informed his partner on what their next procedure was going to be, and agreed to take Beth to the hospital in their patrol car, while he would ride along with Detective Houston and Allison. Their brief conversation soon ended, as the small group of people exited the club.

Officer Martinez held the back door of the police car open for Beth, as she turned and gave Allison one more extended hug.

"Remember, you have to stay strong … for yourself, for us … and for Shane." Allison said quietly into Beth's ear.

"Can you call me later?" Beth asked.

"Absolutely, let me get your number."

Both women rummaged through their purses in search of their phones, when Beth noticed droplets of Shane's blood splattered on the outside of her handbag. The sudden shock made her immediately drop her open bag, scattering her items across the ground. Both Allison and Officer Martinez immediately bent down and began picking up the articles which included Beth's phone. Allison stood up, added her contact information into the phone, then handed it back to her and said, "Here you go, call me later."

Officer Martinez handed Beth her purse after picking up the rest of items from the ground. He then went back and held the door open again for his troubled passenger. With her tears still flowing, she sat down in the back of the police car and tried to make herself somewhat comfortable, before Martinez shut the door. Beth then looked out the window at Allison, as they exchanged goodbyes and the car drove away.

"Are you ready, young lady?" Houston asked Allison, as he held the back door of his car open for her.

"If you don't mind, I have a small problem sitting in the back of a police car; can I sit up front instead?" Allison asked, as memories from her past gave her a small jolt of anxiety.

Both men looked at each other, and then laughed. Houston stepped back and opened the passenger door, as Phillips courteously sat down in the back of the vehicle. Allison politely thanked the detective as he shut the door behind her. Houston then walked around, and got into the car. He turned the key and revved the engine, as all three passengers sat quietly for a moment and thawed themselves, with the warm heat blowing from the vents. Houston brushed the loose snow off his coat, and then put his car in gear, causing the unmarked vehicle to slowly move down the icy street. Everybody turned their attention to the busy corner as they approached it, and the car came to a stop. Houston lowered his window to talk to one of the officers and received a quick update, with negative results keeping the unsolved mystery a confusing puzzle.

Allison stared at the commotion surrounding Trent's car. Her eyes began to tear from a rush of sudden emotions, as she watched a city tow truck jacking up the vehicle.

"Please turn your head, there's no need for you to see anything at this point," Phillips said to Allison.

Houston thanked the outside officer, and then proceeded cautiously through the intersection. Allison tried to turn away, but her curiosity drove her eyes back to the scene of the crime. Memories of all the events leading up to this moment flashed through her mind, causing her to panic and shiver in her seat. She held herself tightly, as she now stared out the front windshield, trying to refocus her attention.

Phillips gave Houston directions back to where he had seen the homeless man earlier. They kept their eyes open for the wandering suspect, as the vehicle approached the avenue that the accident had occurred.

"Keep a lookout for anyone or anything suspicious," Houston said to Phillips.

Allison knew it wasn't far, so she began to look closely at every corner they passed. Within a few blocks, she noticed the tipped over shopping cart, planted in the snow on the left side of the street.

"That's it, right there, there's the homeless man's shopping cart!" shouted Allison.

Houston turned on his spotlight as he pulled up to the desolate corner. Out of the front windshield, all three of them stared at the old rusty cart, and then at all of the man's possessions that were scattered across the snow covered corner.

"For your safety, stay here," Houston said to Allison.

"But I want to help."

"We have to make sure the area is safe before you can get out, just give us a few minutes," added Phillips.

Both men prepared themselves by pulling out their weapons. The site of the two hand guns made Allison shiver once again, as her anxiety returned.

"Ready? Let's go," said Houston, as both men cautiously exited the vehicle.

They stepped out into the cold, dark night and quickly scanned the quiet corner, but unfortunately saw nobody. They stepped up onto the curb and looked at the toppled cart first, and then down at all of the dispersed items.

The large woolen blanket, Vince's Yankee hat and the man's cardboard sign were now covered in a loose layer of fallen snow. They all lay perfectly still from where they had landed from the accident earlier. Phillips eyes were drawn to the rectangular cardboard item, and through the faint snow, he was able to still read the words, HOMELESS Need Every Dollar. His mind then immediately recalled the old man holding the exact sign on his lap earlier.

"All of these items should be gathered for evidence, and hopefully we can find something here that will have the exact same prints taken from the car," said Houston.

"Yes, I think I should call the crime scene unit and have them investigate this too," said Phillips.

Allison began to tap on the passenger window, wanting permission to exit the vehicle. Both men looked around the area one more time and then Houston said, "I think it's alright for her to get out. Let her get a good look at all these items too, maybe she could identify something."

He walked over, grabbed the handle and opened the door. Allison got out and quickly walked over to the old rusty shopping cart. The haunting vision of the homeless man trying to push it across the avenue suddenly appeared in her mind.

"It's him; I know it's him, it's NED!" Allison cried out.

"You said you got a good look at the homeless man, right?" Houston asked.

"Yes, he was standing right in front of me and at this point, I don't think I'll ever be able forget his face."

"Have you tried to call Trent since all this has happened?" Phillips asked her.

"Huh?" Allison said as she shook her head, trying to clear the horrifying image of NED from her mind.

"Have you called Trent?" Phillips asked again.

"No."

"Do you have his phone number?"

"Yes, yes I do." Allison said nervously, as she opened her purse and reached for her phone.

She pulled it out and turned it on. Her fingers fumbled around her phone's menu, trying to get to Trent's number. Finally, she was staring at her contact list and there was Trent's name. Her thumb paused as she looked up at the two gentlemen, displaying a face full of fright.

"Would you like me to do it for you?" Phillips asked.

"No, no, I got it … I got it," Allison stuttered.

She took a deep breath of the crisp air, trying to find the courage to actually push the button on her phone. She stared at Trent's name while she slowly exhaled. She looked up at both men one last time, before her cold thumb pressed his number. Her shaking hand brought the phone close to her ear, as she heard the first ring and then the second.

"Did you hear that?" Phillips asked Houston.

"Hear what?"

"I think I heard a ringing sound coming from somewhere," Phillips said.

Allison's phone continued to ring Trent's unanswered number. Her eyes began to tear as the phone rang a third and fourth time, before it went to Trent's voicemail, causing the distant ringing to suddenly stop. Phillips stood and stared into the dark silence, wondering if his mind was just playing tricks on him.

"There's no answer," Allison said as she reached up and wiped a fallen tear.

"Call him again," Phillips said.

"Why? He's not answering," Allison said as she began to cry.

"Please call him one more time."

Allison struggled to press her phone once again, but she did. She brought it back up to her ear and listened as it began to ring. Phillips immediately turned his head in the direction that the sound had returned.

"I knew I wasn't crazy, it's coming from over here," he said, as he walked over to the corner curb.

Phillips looked down at the sewer grate to confirm where the sound was coming from, as it rang out once again.

"It's coming from down here, in the sewer," Phillips said to Houston, as he grabbed his flashlight.

"I need your phone and for you to also get back in the car." Houston said to Allison.

"Why?"

"Because I'm not sure what we're about to find."

Houston took Allison's phone as he escorted her back to his car. He held the door open as she got back in the front passenger seat, before securing her inside. He then walked over to Phillips, who was now bending down in front of the open sewer, and showed him the phone.

"Go ahead and push redial one more time," Phillips said.

Houston pushed Trent's number and within a few seconds, the ringing returned, but this time, the sound was clear to both men. Phillips turned on his flashlight and Houston withdrew his gun, as both men leaned closer to the black icy grate. Phillips directed his light down into the sewer's darkness towards the sound. The strong beam of light raced around the tunnels bottom, until it stopped on Trent's lifeless body.

"Fuck," Phillips said upon his gruesome discovery.

"What do you see?"

"I'm going to assume it's ...Trent," he said with deep regret.

***

Allison pressed her head against the cold window, as she watched the two men huddling on the corner. She was oblivious to what they were looking at, or what they'd possibly found ... but she had a good idea.

Chapter 16

The big man trudged through the underground tunnel, until he reached a point where he knew he was by the shelter. He stared up at the manhole cover located directly above him, and took a deep breath of the cold air. His anxious mind began to race, knowing on the other side of the circular lid lay his salvation. With a determined will, he grabbed a rung of the old ladder, and began to pull his aching body up to the street.

With each grueling step, a relentless, torturous feeling expelled from the open knife wound, but he mentally forced his way through the pain and advanced to the top. There, he held onto the ladder, while he placed his other hand flat against the cold cover and felt for any vibrations coming from the street above. When he knew it was safe, he began to push the sealed lid from its secured resting place. He grunted as he used what little strength he had left to loosen, and then remove, the heavy cover. He slid the iron circle to the side, thus clearing his escape from the city's dark underworld.

As he slowly lifted his head out of the open hole, he felt the icy wind and the falling snow sting his face. His fatigued eyes focused on the corner building, confirming his destination. He slowly crawled out of the opening, and then pushed the heavy lid back into place. He remained on his knees as he looked up into the dark winter sky. His unstable mind repeated the words forsaken and forgiveness, as he tried to wipe the blood of his victims from his hands. He ended his spiritual conversation with an "Amen" as he struggled to his feet. His eyes were drawn back to the dimly lit corner, as he staggered across the snow-covered street, towards the front door of the shelter.

***

Phillips shined his light directly on the face of the body lying flat on the sewers' floor and saw the unbelievable. The horrifying sight of Trent's crushed head made his body jump and his eyes turn away.

"We need to get down there."

"Is he alive?"

"Not according to what I see; here take a look for yourself," Phillips said as he handed Houston his flashlight.

Detective Houston shined the bright light down into the darkness and witnessed the same gruesome sight.

"Damn, looks like his brains were bashed in...."

"It doesn't make sense, such a level of violence stemming from a knocked over shopping cart," Phillips said, as he shook his head in disbelief.

"Yeah, this homeless man is one angry bastard."

"We need to get down there," Phillips said urgently.

"What about the girl? We can't leave her alone," Houston said with concern.

"Then I'll go..."

"No, the homeless man might still be down there, and that's a good reason why you should wait for some back-up."

"We don't have time!" Phillips argued.

"At this point in my career, I have nothing but time," Houston said, as he shook his head disagreeing.

"But ..."

"Hey, you wanna know how I lasted this many years on the force? It's easy, I'm not fucking stupid," Houston said as he grabbed his phone.

Feeling helpless, Officer Phillips began to pace the snow-covered corner while Detective Houston completed his call. While his feet dug a small trench, he looked down at the scattered articles and wondered why the homeless man would bring Trent back to this exact spot, when the first murder happened by the club. Confused, he walked back over to the corner and stared into the sewer's darkness, trying to piece together a clue.

"Someone should be here in about five minutes," Houston said.

"That's fine," Phillips said, still feeling somewhat disappointed.

"Hey, if the girl wasn't here, it would be a whole different story, but you know we can't just leave her alone in the car while there's a murderer at large."

"That's true; I just saw the kid's body and ..."

"I know ... believe me I've been there ... I've just become callous over the years," Houston said cold-heartedly.

"Well I hope I never get to that point."

"If you stick around for as long as I have ... it's inevitable."

Their bleak conversation was interrupted, by a flashing cruiser

168

pulling up to the corner. Both men looked at each other in a respectful way, before they turned their attention back to the situation. Officer Phillips glanced over at Allison, and saw her face pressed against the car window. She looked curious, anxious and scared. He nodded his head, trying to give her a little reassurance, while thinking how lucky she was to be alive.

Detective Houston greeted the police officer as he exited the vehicle, and quickly filled him in on the details of what they had found. The officer agreed to guard Allison, so they could go down into the sewer to further investigate Trent's dead body. The police officer then walked over to the parked car, looked through the windshield and tipped his hat to Allison, promising her a sense of security, as he put his hand on his weapon and patiently waited.

"We'll have to go through the man hole to get down there," Phillips said, as he urgently walked to the middle of the avenue.

"Yeah, I guess there's no other way," Houston said as he followed.

Phillips bent down and brushed the caked snow off the large iron lid, uncovering the small access holes. He placed his fingers into the openings and began to pull up on the sealed cover. After a few tries, the secured circular cap was loosened and then removed. The pungent stench of the city's underground filled his nostrils as he pushed the heavy lid to the side. Houston stood armed over the dark opening, as Phillips retrieved his flashlight. He pointed it down into the black hole and turned it on.

Both men leaned over the opening, as the rusty old ladder leading downwards came into their view. Phillips waved his beam around the perimeter of the open hole, and then aimed it at bottom, confirming there weren't any more bodies in site.

"I'll flip ya for it," Houston said, as he reached into his coat pocket for a coin.

"No, I'll go first," Phillips said.

"I'll be right behind you."

"If it were up to me, I would have been down there fifteen minutes ago."

"If it were up to me, I'd be sitting on a beach in Florida, completely drunk," Houston said with a smirk.

Phillips rolled his eyes and then proceeded to step into the round opening, as Houston stood armed and ready. He shined his light throughout the darkened haze, as he slowly descended to the bottom. As his feet hit the floor, he instantly withdrew his gun. He waved both his weapon and the flashlight down the tunnel, towards the direction of

169

Trent's body. He stared at the corpse, hoping to see any movement, but the lifeless victim remained still.

"What do you see?" Houston hollered down.

"A dead body."

"Just one?"

"Fortunately and unfortunately …yes."

Houston looked over and nodded at Officer Cummings before he entered the manhole. He mumbled several profanities, as he struggled down the ladder before reaching the bottom. With their guns cocked and ready, both men began to slowly walk down the darkened tunnel toward Trent's body. Phillips kept his bright beam upon the motionless figure, as Houston turned to watch the rear. They stepped closer and closer, as the faint sound of their feet splashing along the puddled trail cut the dead silence. As he led the way, Phillips' eyes were drawn to the sewer's floor, as he noticed a morbid mixture of blood flowing within the shallow water. The color red became more prominent upon reaching the vicious crime scene, as they stood in front of the ungodly mess the homeless man had left behind.

"Long black hair, leather jacket, I'd say that fits Trent's description," Phillips said.

"Yeah, and don't forget about this," Houston said as he reached into his coat pocket, pulled out Allison's phone and pushed Trent's number one more time.

It took just a few seconds before the jacket of the lying victim began to ring. Houston and Phillips silently stared at Trent, as the eerie sound of the young man's cell phone echoed throughout the underground tunnel.

"He looks like he was bludgeoned to death, mercilessly."

"Yeah, this homeless guy is definitely pissed off," Houston said, as he turned Allison's phone off and put it back into his coat pocket.

"I can't believe the same man that I saw earlier is even capable of this sort of act."

"Look at this kid's face …that's right, there ain't one. This guy is fucking crazy and he just finally snapped. I've seen it happen many times throughout the years with the homeless," Houston replied.

Phillips shined his light directly at Trent's mangled head and said, "God, it looks like he used a fucking sledgehammer."

"I see a footprint along his shattered cheek, but I believe that came after the fact," Houston said, pointing at the dirt across Trent's face.

Phillips bent down and aimed the light directly at the bloody sight. He used his flashlight to reposition Trent's head so that it would be

170

facing upwards, and then he brought the light back down upon the subject. Both men cringed as they witnessed the horrifying sight of what appeared to be severe hatred inflected upon the victim.

"What kind of object could do this to someone's face?" Phillips asked as he shook his head in disgust.

"Do you see a weapon anywhere?" Houston asked.

Phillips waved his light around the dark underground dwelling, shining it across the puddled floor and around the concrete walls. He then quickly scanned the place one more time, with the same negative results.

"No," He said, as he placed the bright light back on Trent.

Both men stared into the hideous head wound, as Phillips waved his beam around the bloody gaping hole. As the light swiftly passed, Houston noticed several tiny sparkles that shined from within Trent's torn flesh.

"Did you see that?" He asked.

"See what?"

"Direct your light back over here," Houston said, pointing within.

Phillips brought his beam back to the area, where he too witnessed the shiny sparkles.

"What the fuck is all that?" He asked with confusion.

"I don't know but we're about to find out," Houston said, as he reached into his coat and pulled out a small kit. He opened it up and pulled out a pair of rubber gloves, and a pair of medium size tweezers. He snapped his gloves tight to his hands, then bent down over Trent's distorted face.

As Phillips held his flashlight steady upon the ghastly subject, Houston slowly inserted the tip of the tweezers into the deep fatal wound. The stainless steel instrument probed through the bloody gore, trying to select and snag a prominent piece of one of the tiny particles. With a little patience, Houston was able to extract a sliver of metal.

He held the blood-covered fragment tightly with the tip of the tweezers, as he lowered it down into the puddle and carefully rinsed it off. He raised the now cleansed item up to Phillip's light for both men to examine. Within the bright beam, the small piece glistened with a tarnished golden glow.

"What the fuck is that?" Phillips asked.

"Hell if I know, but it looks like a piece of metal with some kind of gold flake covering," Houston said, as he turned the small fragment around under the flashlight.

"What kind of weapon is gold plated?"

171

"Nothing I'm aware of."

"Well, then what the fuck did this guy use on this poor kid?"

"I don't know. I've never seen anything like this before," Houston said, as both baffled men continued to stare at the shiny little particle.

"Let me take another look around," Phillips said, as he waved his flashlight throughout the dark tunnel once again. He directed his light around their vicinity and like before, saw nothing odd standout.

"I see an old beer can, shoe, just your normal everyday sewer shit."

He pointed the bright beam back down to the puddled floor, and began to slowly scan the bottom. As the light skimmed across the shallow water, Phillips saw a small flash coming from beneath the surface. He stopped and held his flashlight directly on the item, as he slowly walked towards it. He looked down at the submerged shiny piece, but he wasn't able to identify it. He bent down and stuck his fingers into the cold water and retrieved the foreign object. He held it up to his flashlight and mumbled, "It's a tiny broken head."

As he looked closer at the item, he noticed that the small piece had the same golden tone as the metal sliver Houston had extracted from Trent's face.

"This is odd," Phillips said to Houston.

"Did you find something?"

"Maybe… check this out," Phillips said as he walked back over to Houston.

He held the tiny object up to his flashlight for the detective to observe. Within the tips of his fingers, the little golden piece shined like a diamond.

"It looks like a head from a trophy of some sorts," said Houston.

"Yes, but look closely, especially at the color of it."

Houston noticed the same resemblance, as he brought his tweezers up to join the golden head under the light. He held the tiny metal sliver close to the little face and began comparing the two items. Tiny sparkles appeared simultaneously from both pieces, as the light reflected off their similar gold plated colorings.

"They definitely look related in some way," Houston said.

"Well that explains why the kid's face looks like that… he was bludgeoned to death with a metal trophy."

"Do you see the rest of it lying anywhere around?"

Again, Phillips waved his flashlight throughout the underground tunnel, and again saw nothing.

"No." He replied.

"That means what we've found actually makes a little sense…" Houston said, nodding his head.

"Yeah, the killer must still have the rest of the trophy in his possession." Phillips said with a glimmer of hope.

"Now all we just have to do is find a crazy homeless man wandering around the city, holding a bloody trophy in his hand," Houston said sarcastically.

"Well, it's a start," Phillips said in a positive manner.

"It's a speculation and a long shot," Houston replied.

"So which way do you think he went?" Phillips asked, as he pointed his flashlight down both of the tunnel passages.

"The club is back that way, so it just makes sense that he would keep moving in a forward direction."

"The club… Hmm, something just dawned on me; I bet all the rest of the missing people are somewhere down here, that's why we couldn't find anyone."

"That makes sense," Houston agreed.

"Which way should we go? Back to help the other victims, or forward to find the homeless man?" Phillips said as he unfastened his gun.

"Neither… we, need to get the hell out of here."

"But they might still be alive … or the man, he might still be down here."

"If you want to walk around these pitch black sewers looking for a homicidal killer, be my guest. I'm going back to my car and getting all the right people involved. I'm not a hero; I'm a detective that wants to retire soon."

Phillips again felt disappointed, but saw the logic behind the detective's decision and half heartily agreed.

"I'll have the Medical Examiner pull all the rest of these metal slivers from the kids head, and we'll see if all the pieces match," He said, as he tucked the tweezers back in his kit.

"Here, do you want this?" Phillips asked, as he offered the detective the little golden head.

"Thanks," Houston said, grabbing the tiny object and slipping it into his coat pocket.

"We're just going to leave him here?" Phillips asked.

"You're more than welcome to stay down here and keep him company, but I'm going back to my nice warm car and make some phone calls."

Phillips aimed his flashlight at Trent's barely recognizable face one more time, and then bowed his head in a respectful way.

"I'll do my best to find the person who did this to you," he said softly.

He then turned the light at the tunnel ahead one more time and stared into the dark haze, personally seeking and wishing for something, or someone that wasn't there.

"Let's go," Houston said breaking Phillips' trance.

Both men turned and cautiously walked back towards the downward glow of the open manhole. Phillips kept watch while Houston went up the ladder first. He kept his hand on his weapon, while his eyes continued to stare into the infinite darkness. He smirked as he heard the subtle sounds of Houston cursing as he struggled upwards. He waited until he saw Houston climb safely out onto the avenue, before he reached out and grabbed a cold rung. Phillips looked up and focused on the black winter sky, as he began his ascending climb.

As he reached the top, he was greeted by Houston offering him a helping hand. He grabbed a hold of the detectives grip and pulled himself out from the sewer.

"Thanks man."

"No problem."

"How's the girl?" Phillips asked, as he looked over at Allison sitting inside the car.

"She's alive … unlike her date."

"Would you like me to break the news to her?"

"If you want to … just remember to give her the basic facts without all the gory details," Houston said.

***

The man grabbed the shelter's front door handle and pulled it open. He instantly felt the warm trapped air caress his cold face as he stood in the entryway. His eyes became fixated on the woman sitting behind the front desk, as he began to slowly stumble towards her. The large, approaching man immediately caught the attention of the woman, as she lifted her head and said, "I'm sorry sir, but we're full tonight."

He continued forward until he stopped in front of her desk. The woman's eyes were stunned as she got a good look at the hideous homeless man standing before her. She reacted by pushing her chair backwards and finally standing up, to draw some distance between her and the stranger.

"I-I-I'm, s-s-sorry sir, but were f-f- full tonight," She repeated again, but this time with a scared stutter, due to her noticing the blood upon the man's hands.

The big man stared at the lady as he reached into his coat's inner pocket. His fingers touched and gripped the broken trophy as his hand continued to dig deeper. The woman became alarmed and grabbed her phone, not knowing what to expect from this sudden confrontation. The man's fingers continued to shuffle around internally, until they finally found what they were searching for. Then he slowly extracted his hand from his coat, and politely presented the fearful woman with Officer Phillips' card, before he collapsed to the floor.

Chapter 17

The two men walked back over to the Houston's car, to update Officer Cummings on what they had discovered. The detective kept his description short and to the point, as Phillips opened the passenger door to break the bad news to Allison. She could tell by the look on his face that whatever they saw down in the sewer wasn't good.

"I'm sorry to tell you ... but we've ..."

"You don't have to tell me anything ... your facial expression says it all," Allison said, as another tear rolled down her cheek.

Phillips bowed his head in a sympathetic way then said, "We need to call the C.S.I. team over here too; I will have Officer Cummings bring you home as soon as we get this situation organized."

"Is he going to drive me home in his car?"

"Yes, if that's okay with you?"

"I'll just wait till you and Detective Houston can drive me home ... or I can take a cab or the subway."

"How come?" Phillips asked.

"Because this car looks ordinary and that's an actual police car ... my father will flip out if I get dropped off in front of the building in that."

"Your father?"

"Yeah, he's a ... well, he calls himself a high profile attorney, and he's constantly worried about his reputation in this city."

"I'm going to assume you didn't call your parents earlier?"

"No ... my parents were so upset before I even left. They didn't want me going out tonight; and we got into a major argument over it."

"I understand, but your parents are going to need to be informed. We might need you to come down to the station as this case evolves."

"I know, but I just wanted to wait until later ... and pulling up to the building in a police car would just cause more problems, believe me."

"I understand, let me talk to the detective and see what he says."

"Thank you," Allison said.

"Again I'm really sorry about your friend ... but remember ...

177

you're a very fortunate young lady."

"Yes … I know… I know."

Phillips slowly shut the door, securing Allison back in the warm vehicle, before joining the others. He walked in on them mid conversation, and listened as Houston finished telling Cummings the rest of the details and what they plan to do next. He then pulled Phillips aside and asked, "So, how'd she take it?"

"She's still shaken up over everything but strangely, she's more afraid of how she's going to tell her parents about what happened than the actual murder."

"That's really sad; when she told me her address, I knew she was a rich kid. I bet her old man is a real jag off."

"She told me he's some hot shot lawyer."

"Really? What's her last name again?"

"I think she said …Thompson."

"Hmmm, I wonder if her father is Walter Thompson. He's one of New York City's best, and known to be a real asshole."

"Let's give the girl a break and take her home, she's had enough stress already."

"No problem, I'll even go sit in Cummings car and take care of my business, no use in her hearing anything more than she already knows …and besides, I'm sick of standing out in this fucking snow!" Houston said, before he walked over and got into the other car.

***

As the big man lay silently on the shelter's floor, the frightened woman immediately pushed a preset emergency number on her phone and moments later, two male employees came running towards the front to her aid.

"What's going on, Shirley?" Henry asked the panicking woman.

"Down there," She said as she pointed to the floor, directing the men's attention to the unconscious homeless man. Both men looked down and were immediately stunned by his enormous size.

"This guy's a monster, how the hell are we going to move him?" Adam said.

"Be careful, he has blood on his hands," said Shirley.

Both men reached into their pockets, pulled out a pair of rubber gloves and slipped them on. They took a few awkward steps around the big man, before they bent down and attempted to roll him over. The two positioned themselves on each side of the lying man, and then, after a slow three count, they turned him over.

Shirley cautiously leaned over her desk to get a glimpse at the unconscious man as Adam and Henry stood up. All three of them stared down at his face, and then at the blood stain on the shelter's floor.

"See I told you he had blood on him, be very careful," She said.

Henry reached down and pulled the man's coat open, exposing his blood drenched shirt.

"It looks like he's been stabbed."

"I'll go get a stretcher," said Adam.

"What's that on the floor?" Shirley asked.

Henry bent down and picked up the blood stained card. He turned it over and read it aloud. "Thomas Phillips N.Y.P.D. It's a card from one of our local police officers," Henry said, as he placed it face up on her desk.

"I know Officer Phillips, and he wouldn't give his card out unless it was an emergency. Is there someplace we can put him?" Shirley said, now feeling sympathy and concern for the homeless stranger.

"I'm not sure, but I don't think there's a vacant bed in the whole place."

"He could lie on the stretcher until we're able to get him some help."

A few minutes later, Adam came from the back, pushing an old ambulance bed. He parked and locked the mobile cot next to the big man, then pushed a button alongside the frame that lowered the plastic covered mattress closer to the floor.

He walked around and positioned himself on the opposite side, then bent down to assist Henry. They gave each other a disgusted look, as the foul stench emitting off the man burned their nostrils. They turned their heads, counted to three again and then groaned, as they struggled to lift and transfer the large homeless man.

"There ya go big fella," said Adam, as he exerted the last of his strength trying to straighten the man's legs on the portable mattress.

"That's fine ...thanks guys," Shirley said with a little relief.

"I'll wheel him to the back," said Henry, as he turned the crank to lift the wounded man back to the stretchers normal locked position.

"I'll get a mop," Adam said staring down at the bloodstain floor.

"Thanks again," said Shirley, as her nerves began to settle.

"You're welcome," said Henry, as he nodded.

"Yeah, no problem," Adam responded, while displaying a fake smile.

All eyes were upon Henry and the wounded man, as he slowly

pushed the stretcher across the crowded room. The normal rowdiness from the homeless patrons became somewhat muted, as they slowly passed by the all-curious onlookers.

While transporting the stranger, Henry kept looking down at the man's face, after he thought he heard him mumbling a few words. He stared at his long gray beard, trying to comprehend what he was trying to say, but he only heard faint whispers.

"Hang in there, help will be here soon." Henry said quietly to the man, as he parked the stretcher in a dimly lit corner.

The big man fell in and out of consciousness as he lay peacefully upon the portable bed. His eyes twitched as his unsettled mind conjured up images of the evening's traumatic moments, while his hand automatically reached into his coat's inner pocket. His fingers lightly touched the broken neck of the trophy, as his mouth repeatedly whispered, "Scotty...come back, Scotty ...come back."

***

Phillips, along with Cummings, kept a watch on the quiet intersection. His eyes pivoted between the dark endless avenue, the black grate of the sewer and the open manhole. As he stood on the corner, his mind kept thinking about all the other victims that could still be alive down in the underground tunnel. He began to pace back and forth, trying to brush off his feelings of uselessness, when he suddenly had a hunch.

Houston opened the door, exited the squad car and walked back over to the corner to update the others. "They'll be here shortly, they're just finishing up over there," he said.

"Did they find the other missing people?" Phillips asked.

"No, I don't think so, or they would have mentioned it."

"Then we have to go back by the club."

"Why?"

"I have a gut feeling about something."

"We can't, we have to take the girl home."

"It'll just take a few minutes."

"Well, alright." Houston said as he shook his head.

He then turned to Officer Cummings and said, "I informed the unit on what we found down in the sewer, they're on their way, are you okay waiting here for them?"

"Yes sir," Cummings responded.

"Good, then I'll see you soon."

Houston got back into the driver's seat, while Phillips returned to the back of the vehicle. The detective immediately revved his idling engine, trying to increase the warm air flow from the vents. He sat there for a moment and thawed his chilled body, before he turned to Allison and said, "I'm really sorry about your friend." She looked over and nodded her head, thanking him in a passive way.

"We're going to swing back by where Trent's car was parked, it will only take a minute. I hope it's not an inconvenience to you."

"No, it will be okay, besides I'm really not in a rush to get home at this point," Allison said.

Phillips leaned forward and said, "Thanks, I just have to check something out; I swear it will only take a minute."

"That's fine," Allison answered, as she kept her head down.

Houston made a U-turn in the middle of the avenue and headed back to the original crime scene. The short ride seemed to take forever, and all three passengers remained silent as they drove through the desolate village streets. Houston remained focused on the icy road, while Phillips kept his eyes focused on the passing neighborhood for a possible siting of the rampant homeless man.

Within a few minutes, the unmarked car pulled back up to the crime scene. They noticed there were still a few people from the C.S.I unit investigating the possible clues left behind. They also witnessed the tow truck leaving with Trent's car on the back of it, which caused Allison to tear up once again.

"I'm sorry we brought you back here," said Houston.

"I knew it wasn't going to be easy," She said wiping the tears from her cheeks.

"Stay here, we'll be right back," Phillips said, before he and Houston exited the vehicle.

Allison lifted her head and watched, as Phillips and Houston walked to the middle of the intersection, and stared at the closed manhole.

"So why are we back here?" Houston asked.

"I just have a gut feeling about something," Phillips said, as he bent down and inserted his fingers into the little holes of the large iron lid.

Houston withdrew his gun from his holster and stood over Phillips shoulder, prepared for the unexpected. Phillips yanked on the cover several times before he was able to lift it off the steel edge. He pushed the heavy lid to the side, then grabbed his flashlight. He turned it on and then aimed it down into the dark hole.

"My hunch was right, look down here," Phillips said.

181

Houston leaned over the open hole, and saw the bloody massacre that lay on the bottom of the sewer. Phillips waved his bright beam upon all of the faces of the unfortunate victims.

"Damn just like the kid, they're all violently murdered," Houston said in disgust.

"Yeah, look at them all, it's an indescribable horror," Phillips said.

"How many do you see?" Houston asked.

Phillips shined his light on each of the corpses, one at a time. His eyes squinted and his stomach began to turn, as he witnessed the brutality behind each murder. "Four …there's four," He muttered.

"Four plus one is five … that's everybody," Houston said.

"Yeah, now all we need to do is find the person responsible for all this … the homeless man."

Just then, Phillips' phone rang. He pulled it out of his coat pocket and answered it. "This is Officer Thomas Phillips."

"Hello Officer Phillips, this is Shirley Robbins from the homeless shelter."

"Yes Shirley, what can I do for you?"

"Sorry to bother you, but I have sort of a strange situation over here tonight."

"Oh really, what's going on?"

"I just had a man walk in and he's …well, he's bleeding …looks like he's been stabbed … but the strange thing is that … he gave me a card with your name on it."

"Can you describe this man to me?"

"Well… he's tall with long, gray hair and matching beard. I'm going to assume he's homeless, but I've never seen him before and like I said, he's bleeding badly. What should I do?"

Phillips' mind immediately raced back to the encounter he had earlier with the homeless man. He remembered handing him his card, and telling him to go to the shelter to get out of the cold.

"Is he still there?"

"Yes."

"Great, I'm on my way."

"Thanks Officer."

"No, thank you Shirley, I'll see you soon."

"Okay."

Phillips tucked his phone back into his coat, then turned to Houston and said "We have to go."

"Go where?"

"That was a woman I know named Shirley, she works at a nearby homeless shelter and … I think we found our man."

"What? Where?"

"He's at the shelter, let's go."

"What about all the dead bodies down there? What about the girl?"

Phillips waved the rest of the police force over, to witness what he had discovered down in the manhole. He quickly explained the situation and the reason for his urgency to leave. The officers agreed to take care of the morbid scene, giving Phillips and Houston the opportunity to follow their lead.

"Let's go," He said again to Houston, while walking back towards the car.

"What about the girl?" Houston shouted.

"She's coming with us," Phillips said, as he opened the back door and got in.

Houston walked briskly to his vehicle and sat back in the driver's seat. He turned and looked at Allison, and saw the expression of confusion upon her face.

"What now?" She said nervously.

"We have to make one more stop," Houston said, as he dropped his car in gear and quickly pulled away.

***

The big man had a look of innocence, as he lay peacefully in the back of the crowded room. His now settling mind had replaced his nightmares with pleasant memories of his family, bringing about a calm and soothing effect over his weakened body. The conjured visions of his beautiful wife and son seem so real, he subconsciously felt their touch as they embraced him. Mentally, he had returned to a tranquil place where he once lived before.

As the man lay in his harmonious state, another patron of the shelter kept an eye on him. Known on the streets as a heartless petty thief, the grungy old man rose up from his blanket, after seeing what appeared to be easy prey. With bad intentions, he nonchalantly strolled to the back of the rowdy room towards the unconscious man.

He stood at the foot of the stretcher and gazed down. He eyed his big gray coat, wondering if he had anything of value, or even anything edible, hidden inside the pockets. He took a step closer, and his eyes were immediately drawn to the man's face, upon hearing the sounds of him

183

mumbling under his beard. He listened to the incoherent ramble as he stared at his sleeping target. He brushed his hand lightly across the front of the man's coat, and felt a round object tucked in one of the pockets. Thinking it might be an apple or an orange, the old man blindly reached in and grabbed the soggy baseball. He tried to carefully extract the unknown item, but his hand got stuck within the lining of the fabric. He momentarily took his attention off the man's face to focus on the dilemma. He slowly wiggled his hand, trying once again to steal the object, but he knew his little plan failed when he heard the sound of a gut-wrenching growl. He slowly turned his head and found himself staring into the hate-filled eyes of a monster called NED.

The surprised old man was imprisoned by his trapped hand, allowing him no chance to escape as NED reached up and grabbed his throat. With a deadly grip and the vengeance to punish him for his greed, the big man began squeezing the life out of the poor old thief. His grip was strong and merciless, as the demon inside his tortured soul returned. He held his enemy in one hand, as his other automatically reached inside his coat for the golden weapon. His hand grabbed the prized possession and quickly pulled it out. He stared into the old man's dying eyes as he began to slowly rise up from the stretcher. The criminal pleaded for forgiveness, but the anger behind NED's clenched fist proved unstoppable. Then with his loaded hand, he swung the base of the broken trophy. He hit him once …growled, and then hit him again.

***

The ride to the shelter was quiet, as Houston concentrated on the icy streets and Phillips prepared himself for the apprehension of the homeless man once they arrived. With the red light flashing, they raced through the lower east side, until Phillips pointed out the shelter's small illuminated sign.

"There it is, on the right," he said.

The detective pulled up to the corner curb and put his car in park. Phillips then leaned forward and said to Allison, "We'll be right back."

She looked out the window and read the words East End Homeless Shelter across the old broken sign, and quickly figured out the reason why they were there.

"Be careful," she said to the men.

"We'll just be a minute, stay here and remember … do not get out of the car no matter what," Houston said sternly to the young woman.

"I won't."

"Are you ready?" He asked, as he looked back at Phillips.

"Sure am."

"Then let's go get us a homeless man."

The two men quickly exited the car and walked up the sidewalk towards the front door. Houston tucked his hands into his coat pocket, where his fingers retouched the little golden head. He rubbed the surface of the face, as he imagined matching it up to the rest of the trophy upon the apprehension of the homeless man.

Phillips reached out, grabbed the door handle of the seedy establishment, and held it open for Houston to enter first. The short, plainclothes detective respectively walked in, followed by the tall officer in blue. As they approached the front desk, they first saw a young man mopping the entrance floor, then they saw Shirley, who immediately stood up from her chair upon recognizing Officer Phillips.

"Hello Shirley."

"Good evening Officer."

"This is Detective Houston."

The detective tipped his hat in a polite and courteous manner towards the woman. Shirley smiled, and then reached down and picked up the bloodstained card from her desk.

"Here, this is what the homeless gentleman gave me before he collapsed," she said, as she carefully held it up for both men to see.

Officer Phillips reached out and grabbed the card from Shirley to verify that it was indeed his. He nodded to Houston after he saw the N.Y.P.D emblem and his name in bold letters.

"You mentioned that he was bleeding?" He asked Shirley.

"Yes, under his coat, his shirt was drenched in blood. It looked like he had been stabbed."

"Did you call an ambulance?"

"No, I called you."

"By any chance, was he holding a trophy of some sorts?" Houston asked, as his fingers continued to rub the little piece of metal that lay inside his pocket.

"Not to my knowledge, all he had was this card."

"Where is this man?" Houston then asked the woman.

"Henry, who's another employee here, wheeled him somewhere to the back on a stretcher."

"I can show you where he is," said Adam.

"Please," Phillips said to the young man.

185

Chapter 18

NED brought the bloody trophy down to his side, as he held onto the throat of the unconscious petty thief. He pushed himself up and off the stretcher, as he continued to squeeze the last breath from the culprit. His eyes were morbidly pleased, as they stared at the torn flesh displayed across the head of the now dying man, but his concentration was suddenly broken, when he noticed the front door open and two men enter the building.

As he looked over the shoulder of the helpless old man, he focused in on them one at a time, and immediately recognized the blue uniform. He quickly turned and dragged the man up and onto the mattress of the stretcher. He flipped him onto his stomach, and then he slowly turned back to observe the front door once again. He noticed the men were engaged in a conversation with the lady at the desk, and took the opportunity to make his move. He stumbled across the back wall, until he came to an open doorway that led to rear of the building. He took a few steps into the back room, where he was immediately greeted by a startled older man.

"Hey, what are you doing? You're not allowed back here!" Henry shouted.

Without giving it a second thought, the big man instantly lifted the golden trophy and struck the defenseless employee across the head. Henry fell to the floor from the hardened blow, allowing his perpetrator the ability to quickly escape. NED grabbed the knob on the back door, pushed it open and staggered back into the cold winter's night.

***

Allison sat patiently and stared out of the front window at her unfamiliar surroundings. The continuous sweep from the windshield wipers gave her a clear view of the dark, depreciated area. She looked up and read the sign on the building once again, as visions of all the homeless people she came in contact with earlier, flashed within her mind. She revisited the grotesque smile on Violet's pitiful face, along with the leering stare from the man called NED. She shook her head, trying to combat her mental fears, when she suddenly saw a tall, shadowy figure stumbling from the back of the shelter. She forced her eyes to focus on the individual, and immediately recognized the figure, as it momentarily passed under a distant street light.

"Oh my God, that's him …that's NED!" She yelled to herself.

Allison turned her head and looked at the front door of the shelter, hoping to see Phillips and Houston, but unfortunately they were still inside. She became anxious and unsettled, as she watched the homeless man they came to apprehend, escaping without their knowledge.

"What should I do?" She repeated to herself, as her head pivoted back and forth between the entrance and the disappearing man.

"He's fucking getting away!" she yelled, as she turned and looked at the shelter one last time, before she grabbed the door handle.

Her body trembled in fear as she thought twice about the decision she was about to make. She looked out through the windshield, and focused again on the vanishing figure. She took a deep breath, and then pushed the passenger door open. Allison felt the sting of the winter's air, as she placed her feet onto the ground and exited Houston's vehicle. She pulled her coat firmly around her body, and then quickly slammed the door shut. The loud sound of the closing door echoed down the street like a gunshot, causing the fleeing man to stop and turn around. She could see his long hair blowing in the howling wind, as he looked back in her direction. Allison stood motionless, as the big man took a few steps forward, acknowledging her presence from afar. As he stood under the light, Allison had a clearer vision of the tall, hideous man, thus confirming his identification. He immediately noticed the red flashing light in the windshield of the car she was standing next to. He stared at her one last time, before he quickly turned and began to stumble away. Impulsively, Allison began to briskly walk in the direction of the fleeing homeless man, leaving the safety of the car and the police behind. Her body shook as her anxiety returned, but her will not to lose sight of the wanted killer kept her pushing forward.

* * *

The homeless man turned his head and saw that he was being pursued by the person from the car. He grinded his teeth as he forced himself to move faster, away from the persistent stalker. His pace quickly got him to the end of the block where he stopped, leaned against the corner building and looked back once again. He saw within the grace of the falling snow, the gaining individual. He groaned as he forced himself to move, disappearing around the corner and temporarily out of Allison's sight.

***

Allison tried to keep up with the fleeing homeless man, but his lead was far too great. She watched as he reached the far corner, and then stopped to look back at her. She knew she was heading into danger, but something inside her couldn't let this man just get away. Her brisk walk escalated as she watched the big man vanish from her sight, but her pace deadened to a mere crawl as she approached the quiet corner. Her body began to shake once again, as she slowly and fearfully took each and every step with serve caution. She got to the edge of the building and stopped. She shivered as she hesitated to look beyond the safety of the concrete structure. She turned and looked back at the red flashing light, hoping to see Phillips and Houston returning to the car, but through the snowy haze, the far corner still looked deserted.

"Where the fuck are they?" Allison said to herself.

***

Adam escorted the two men to the back of the shelter. Both Phillips and Houston withdrew their weapons from their holsters and held them down by their sides, as they followed the young man across the large, crowded room. As they passed, the loud sounds of the chatty voices diminished, after seeing the sight of Phillips' blue uniform within their presence. He directed them towards the dimly lit corner, where they both saw a man lying on the stretcher.

"That's him over there," Adam said, as he pointed to the figure.

"Stay here," Houston said to the young man.

Both men quickly moved in on the suspect. They pointed their guns at the lying man, while Phillips shouted, "This is the police; let me see your hands."

The man remained motionless, causing Phillips to grab his shoulder and forcibly turn him over. The unconscious individual fell onto his back, causing his head to twist and exposing his bloody face to the men. They both took a step forward, to get a better look at the damage that was inflicted upon the man.

189

"What the hell happened to him?" Houston asked.

"I don't know, but it looks pretty bad," Phillips said, as he noticed the deep lacerations across the man's head.

"Is he alive?"

"If so...barely."

"We need to call an ambulance," said Houston.

Adam stepped forward, took a look at the man in custody and politely said, "That's not him."

"What do you mean that's not him?" Houston asked.

"That's not him," he repeated.

"He fits the description; long gray hair, beard and Shirley said the man was bleeding," said Phillips.

"Most homeless people fit that description, besides the other guy was big and tall, and bleeding from his side, like he was stabbed or something."

"That's right, that's what Shirley told me earlier on the phone," Phillips agreed.

"Yeah, I'm telling you, that's not the same man," Adam insisted.

"Maybe the other guy who works here, Henry, wheeled him somewhere else," said Houston.

"Maybe ...I'll go ask him, he's in the back," Adam said, as he began to walk towards the open doorway.

"Wait, we'll go with you, it could be dangerous," said Houston.

The three men cautiously walked towards the open doorway. Phillips and Houston kept their guards up and their fingers on their triggers as they approached the backroom.

"Wait, let us go first," Phillips said to Adam.

Adam stepped aside, allowing the two officers to move pass him. Both men held their weapons at a chest level as they physically and mentally prepared themselves. They looked at each other, nodded and then burst through the open threshold.

They immediately saw an older man lying on the floor, holding his head. Phillips quickly bent down and tried to assist the injured man, while Houston scanned the quiet backroom in search of the suspect.

Adam curiously peeked into the backroom and saw his coworker lying on the floor. "Henry!" he shouted, as he quickly ran over to assist Officer Phillips. He pulled Henry's hands away from his face and saw the large bloody gash across his head. Phillips suddenly grabbed the older man and carefully shook him in an attempt to revive him. Henry then let out a soft moan, as he slowly opened his eyes and recognized Adam's familiar face.

"What happened?" Phillips asked.

"The big guy …he…" Henry tried to speak, but his words were slurred and his thoughts were still disoriented.

"What big guy?" Phillips asked urgently.

"The one that showed up earlier he …he came back here and …and …that's all I remember."

"Fucking asshole!" Adam shouted.

"Is he alright?" Houston yelled over to Phillips as he continued his search.

"Yes, I think so, but we need to call an ambulance and get him and the other man to the hospital, immediately."

"I can do that," Adam said, as he stood up and dashed to the front desk.

"Damn it, we have another problem," Houston said to Phillips.

"What's that?"

"Look," Houston said, as he pointed to the open back door.

Phillips and Houston cautiously walked over and then looked out through the opening into the cold, dismal night. Their eyes searched through the falling flurries, hoping to see their suspect, but he was nowhere in sight.

"Son of a bitch!" Phillips shouted, as he took a step outside.

"He could be anywhere by now," Houston said, standing in the open doorway.

"He couldn't have gotten very far."

"Should I remind you that we promised to take the young lady home? Her safety is our responsibility, and coming to the shelter in the first place was already crossing the line," Houston said as he holstered his weapon.

"Damn it!" Phillips shouted, as he too tucked his gun back in its place.

Adam darted back into the room and made his announcement to the officers. He then knelt down next to Henry, laid his hand upon his chest and softly repeated, "The ambulance is on their way, you're going to be fine my friend."

"Thanks," Henry said, looking up with appreciation.

"We've got some other business to take care of, are you two going to be alright until the ambulance gets here?" Houston asked.

"I'll take care of him," Adam said honorably.

Phillips pulled the door shut and locked it. He looked at Houston, then down at Henry as he began to pace back and forth, trying to deal with the failure.

"Hey, we gave it our best shot, don't take it so personal."

"We were so fucking close," Phillips said clenching his fists.

Houston lowered his head as he saw the vast disappointment across the officer's face. He remembered when he too took his job that seriously, but over the years he'd come to realize that there are no happy endings.

Phillips and Houston then exited the backroom and walked towards the front door. They looked at the filthy faces of all the staring homeless patrons, as they once again crossed the crowded room and just like before, the noise level quickly diminished, as their authoritative presence intimidated the majority of the lodgers.

Phillips caught Shirley's eyes as they approached the front desk, assuring her of Henry's condition. The concerned look on her face lightened when the officer informed her that Henry was going to be alright.

"Thanks again," Shirley said, with a bit of sadness in her voice.

"You're welcome; I'll come back and check on you later," Phillips said, as he gave her a warm and friendly smile.

Houston tipped his hat respectively to the older woman, then both men exited the shelter. Phillips quickly looked up and down the quiet avenue, hoping to see the homeless man as they walked back to the car. Houston glanced into his vehicle as he bent down to unlock the door, when he suddenly discovered Allison's disappearance.

"God damn it!" He shouted loudly.

"What?"

"Look!" Houston said, pointing inside his car.

Phillips peered through the frosted window and witnessed the same empty seat.

***

The homeless man staggered down the icy sidewalk, as he tried to maintain his forward momentum in order to keep his lead. At an attempt to cross the avenue, he stumbled between two parked cars and immediately fell to his knees. The sudden stop felt relieving, and he decided to stay in the secluded spot for a moment. The man caught his breath, then slowly lifted his head to look back at the corner. He stared at the dark serene intersection, hoping his determined opposition had gone elsewhere.

Chapter 19

Allison peeked around the corner and gazed across the dimly lit avenue, searching for the fleeing homeless man. She felt a tinge of despair, as she slowly walked out past the safety of the building and saw no one in sight.

"Damn it, he got away," She said, disappointed.

She stood on the corner and stared down the block. Her eyes searched desperately for the man, but the desolate avenue remained still and silent.

She felt an inner feeling of failure as she slowly lowered her head. Her mind conjured up a flashback of Trent that triggered her to immediately drop a tear into the icy snow. Her body began to tremble, as she began to blame herself for the brutal slayings.

"If only I would have just stayed home, none of this would have happened. Trent and his friends would still be alive, if only I had listened to Meaghan … or my mom … even my dad."

Several more of Allison's tears descended into the snow until she lifted her head, seeking forgiveness. She felt the familiar sting from the cold gusting wind, but the immediate pain across her face felt somewhat deserving.

***

The man's peaceful moment ended abruptly as within a minute, the stranger appeared. His eyes twitched as he looked at the individual standing on the corner. He held his wounded side, groaned and then forced himself up. He knew if he had any chance of getting away, right now would be the only opportunity. He grabbed hold of the back end of the parked car, took a deep breath, and then found the strength to force himself into an awkward running frenzy across the avenue. His feet began to stumble again, but he kept his balance as his eyes kept their focus on his goal of reaching the far corner.

Allison stared hopelessly down the endless avenue. A deep feeling of sadness overwhelmed her as she began to turn around and go back to the shelter, when suddenly she saw, about halfway down the block, a large man-like figure dash out from behind the parked cars. Her eyes followed the individual as he crossed the avenue, which immediately caused her heart to race. She quickly rushed along the sidewalk, trying to catch up to the fleeing person, but there was still a considerable distance between them. Her feet tried to obtain a quick sprint, but within a few moments, she saw the homeless man turn the far corner and disappear from her sight once again.

***

The homeless man staggered frantically along the frozen sidewalk, as his eyes stared at the far end of the block. He experienced a moment of dementia, as the vision of the opposite corner seemed unattainable. Knowing his weakening body couldn't keep moving at such a pace, he began to search along the dark street for a place to hide. He got about a quarter of the way down, when he noticed an open alleyway between two boarded up buildings. His feet stumbled towards the pitch black entrance and within seconds, he slipped into its hidden shadows.

***

Allison quickly crossed the avenue and hurried towards the far corner, trying to catch up to the homeless man. Her racing feet continued to stumble upon the icy pavement, until they came to a sudden stop, as she reached the corner. She stood and looked down the long dark street, but again saw no-one.

"Now where'd he go?" She said to herself.

She stared with bewilderment into the snowy haze until she noticed a trail of large footprints leading down the block. Her gut feeling told her to go back to the shelter for the police, but her inner rebellion forced her to open her purse, grab her can of mace and take a step forward.

She followed the man-made trail down the sidewalk until she saw the deep footed impressions veer off. She stopped, turned and found herself staring into the darkness of an alleyway, nestled between two abandoned buildings.

194

The homeless man stumbled a few yards down the dark, narrow passageway, then collapsed upon the soft virgin snow. As he lay quietly, he closed his eyes and enjoyed the peaceful silence, but within a few minutes, his tranquility was disrupted when he heard the sound of approaching footsteps. He lifted his head and saw his pursuer, standing outside the alleyway's entrance, looking in.

A feeling of threat and uncertainty overcame him, as he propped himself up and stared at the individual. He noticed it wasn't one of the police officers that had come into the shelter, but he wasn't going to take a chance. He struggled back to his feet. He turned and looked deeper into the alley for a possible alternative escape route, but then quickly turned back and stared at the person waiting for him outside of the entrance. He reached into his coat's inner pocket and gripped the golden trophy, as he took a step back in their direction. He once again yearned for Scotty's imaginary voice for guidance, but his mind remained mute. He shook his head in frustration as his discontented feelings made his anger return, pushing him to take another step towards his pursuer.

***

Allison held her can of mace tightly, as stared at the trail of large footprints that led into the dark passageway. She took a small step forward, as she moved closer to the alley's invisible line that separated the street light from its darkened shadows.

"I know you're in there!" She yelled out then paused.

She stared into the alley's blackened haze, trying to listen for the hidden homeless man.

"The police are on their way!" She cried out as a last attempt to possibly convince the man into surrendering.

Allison continued to stare deep into the darkness, trying to see, or even hear, any evidence that the man was still present. She shook her head and was about to walk away, when suddenly she saw somebody walking up the block. She turned and stared at the approaching stranger, not knowing who or what to expect. For a quick moment, she thought it might be the homeless man coming towards her, but as the person drew closer, she saw the individual was wearing a black motorcycle jacket identical to the kind Trent wore this evening. For a second, she imagined it was him, but was instantly brought back to reality upon the arrival, and her initial meeting, with the maniacal gang leader Jack.

"What's a nice girl like you doing in a place like this?" He asked the old cliché arrogantly.

Allison immediately stepped back, looking at the face of the stranger and spotting a trail of blood dripping down from his head. She quickly turned to walk away, but Jack reached out, grabbed her shoulder and said, "Hey, where ya going, pretty girl?"

"Get the fuck away from me, asshole!" Allison said, reaching up and pulling his hand off her.

"Oh, a bad bitch. That's okay; I like my girls to be a little rough and tough," Jack said with a flirtatious but sinister smile.

"I said get the fuck away from me!" Allison yelled, as she turned and aimed her can of mace at the eyes of her aggressor.

"Listen bitch, this is my neighborhood, and nobody tells me what to do around here," He said, reaching into his back pocket.

Jack stared into Allison's eyes, as he pulled out his weapon and proudly displayed it to her. She looked at him as she nervously held her can of mace directly at his face. Jack produced an evil grin, before his finger pushed the release mechanism on his switchblade. The screeching sound, and then the appearance of the sharp, gleaming knife, made Allison instantly jump back. Jack started to laugh, as he began his lunatic ritual of waving the blade through the air, trying to intimidate his victim.

"Leave me the fuck alone or I swear I will…" Allison screamed.

"Swear? … Swear you'll do what?" Jack asked, as he stopped and pointed the shiny weapon directly at her pretty face.

***

The homeless man wrapped his fist around the precious broken object and slowly withdrew it from the inside of his coat. He held it tightly in his grip, as his unsettled mind prepared its defense against the threat that stood outside of the alleyway. He dragged his feet within the deep snow as he began his small trek back down the narrow path. His eyes focused on the light that illuminated the entrance, and the dark silhouette of his enemy that stood within it. He stumbled along as the distance between him and his pursuer shortened, but he suddenly stopped when he saw another person come into view.

He hesitated for a moment as he observed the two individuals, and noticed that the new arrival was a lot taller than the one who had been following him. He inched closer in order to get a better look at what he now considered to be two adversaries. He watched as the two people conversed for a moment, and then to his astonishment the meeting turned into a sudden altercation.

His eyes became fixated on the situation happening before him, but when he saw the taller individual suddenly retrieve an item from his back pocket, the scenario seemed all too familiar. He took a few steps closer towards the two arguing people, and immediately noticed that the taller one was wearing a black leather jacket.

He stared long and hard at the individual, trying to determine if it was the person he thought it was, and in reality, hoped for. But when he saw the bright, blinding gleam reflecting off the knife now displayed in his hand, his thoughts confirmed his accusations.

"Jack," he said angrily to himself.

His teeth grinded underneath his long gray beard, as his adrenaline ignited and his mind raced with revenge. He kept his eyes on Jack as he walked to the middle of the dark alleyway, opened his coat and carefully placed the broken trophy back into the inner pocket. He then reached around and pulled out the old, soggy baseball from his coat's side pocket.

His mind recalled the feeling of stepping up to a pitcher's mound, as he held it tightly in his hand. His scattered brain imagined a large crowd cheering him on, as his body automatically remembered the old routine. He first prepared himself by digging both of his feet into the snow for traction, and then he placed two fingers properly around the worn leather ball. His heart raced, but he took his time as he focused directly on the target in front of him.

***

Houston looked at Phillips and shook his head in profound disappointment.

"I told her not to get out of the fucking car, what part of that didn't she understand?" Houston shouted angrily.

"Maybe she got a cab or walked to the subway?"

"Really? Is that what you really think happened to her?" Houston asked with a brazen look upon his face.

"No," Phillips said, lowering his head.

"God damn it!" Houston hollered into the night.

"We have to find her! We have to find her now!" Phillips said, as he began to panic, thinking about the young woman's safety.

"Get in and we'll drive around."

"No, you go ahead and I'll go back and search around the

shelter."

"Keep your radio on and call me the moment you find her, and I'll do the same," Houston said.

"Yes sir," Phillips responded.

"We'll find her, she couldn't have gotten far. Hell, maybe we'll get lucky and accidently run into the homeless man too."

"We should be so lucky," Phillip said.

"Alright, we're wasting precious time, stay in contact," Houston said, as he got back into his car, shut the door and slowly drove away.

Phillips turned and ran back towards the entrance of the shelter. He grabbed the door handle and hurried inside. His sudden burst into the building startled Shirley, whose nerves where already on edge from all the previous commotion.

"Officer Phillips ...you startled me!" The frazzled woman said.

"Did a young woman with long blonde hair come in here?"

"No officer, no one's been here since you left."

"Thanks Shirley, sorry I scared you."

"That's alright Officer ... is everything okay?"

Officer Phillips politely nodded his head towards the older woman, and then quickly exited the shelter. He ran out and stood into the middle of the avenue, but saw no sign of Allison.

"Where'd the fuck did you go?" Phillips said, as he contemplated which way to begin his search.

He brushed the loose snow off his hat's visor, unfastened his weapon, and then quickly proceeded down the avenue towards the next block.

***

Jack took a step closer to Allison, as he held the sharp glistening blade closer to her face. Allison began to panic as her feet retreated backwards across the icy sidewalk. She then began to scream as she frantically waved her can of mace at Jack.

"Go ahead! Spray me with your can of bullshit. I'm still gonna cut you up into little fucking pieces!"

Allison stared into Jack's eyes and by the cold, hard look she received, she knew he wasn't joking. She screamed louder as her feet continued to move backwards, causing her to eventually fall down to the ground. When her body hit the concrete, her hand automatically released her only defense. The small can of mace rolled out in front of Jack,

198

causing him to immediately kick it away from both of them. Allison tried to get back to her feet, but they just kept sliding across the slippery snow. She laid there helpless, as she stared at the sharp blade of the knife, and then up at Jack with tearful eyes.

"Now what are you going to do, my pretty little thing?"

All Allison could do was scream, and so she did, as loud as she could.

***

The homeless man stared directly at the haunting face of his true enemy, as he went into his windup. His mind conjured up wonderful memories of his youth to accompany this eventful moment, as his fingers gripped the old baseball tightly. And then with a loud grunt, he released his grand fastball pitch one more time. He imagined hearing the rip roar of the crowd, as his eyes watched the ball sail from his hand in a slow-motion type fashion, but in reality, it traveled swiftly through the alley's dark haze and directly towards its target.

***

Jack began to laugh. He began to laugh even louder than Allison's screams, until out of nowhere, he was hit with an unknown object. He fell to the ground and immediately grabbed his head, as he began to shout out in intense pain. Allison was suddenly shocked as to what just happened, causing her eyes to pivot between Jack and the pitch black alleyway. She then looked down at the dirty baseball, and then at Jack's knife lying next to him. She was confused on what action to take first, until she saw the vision of the tall homeless man emerge from within the alley's darkness. She became instantly petrified as she looked up at the giant man standing before her. She dug her fists into the snow and pushed herself back along the icy curb, trying desperately to get away, but there was nowhere to go.

She looked hard at his face and recognized him as the same man in the middle of the street, pushing the shopping cart earlier. The same man the police were looking for; the man that most likely killed Trent and his friends. She looked into his eyes and saw both hatred and sympathy deep within them. She tried to scream but was speechless.

"NED." She mumbled to herself.

The homeless man looked down at Allison as he took a few steps forward. She shivered as the big man drew closer, but to her surprise, he

199

suddenly stopped. He stared at her with his bloodshot eyes and then slowly raised his weakening arm, pointed to the end of the block and told her to go.Allison began to cry in a demented form of happiness, as she quickly scrambled to her feet and began running as fast as she could back towards the shelter. The big man stood there and listened, as her hysterical screams diminishing as she ran further and further away him. He kept a watchful eye on her until she safely turned the corner, and then he turned his complete attention back to Jack.

He looked down at the young punk and felt a sense of enjoyment watching him squirm in the snow. His eyes were then drawn to the sight of the sharp, familiar object lying next to his enemy. He immediately grabbed his bloody side and intentionally squeezed the deep wound, to bring forth the pain as a reminder of what this particular individual had done to him.

Then, with hatred from his bitter soul, he slowly reached into his overcoat to retrieve his weapon. He gripped the cold metal item tightly and pulled it from its hidden home. The tarnished trophy sparkled under the streetlights as the man held it up in front of his face. He rubbed his thumb across the jagged neck of the damaged golden player, only to intensify his already fueled anger.

Jack looked up and in spite of his blurry vision, he knew exactly who was standing before him. The presence of the large figure both terrified, and ignited, his rattled brain. He shook his head then took a deep breath, preparing himself for the fight of his life. Fearless thoughts began to ravaged his mind because he knew he was now placed in a do or die situation.

His eyes eventually focused and were immediately drawn to the golden glare reflecting from the object within the big man's hand. He stared at the shiny item and then down at the marble base. He then brought his hand up to his head and lightly touched his bloody bandanna, recalling their initial meeting.

"Get up, you fucking coward!" The homeless man ordered Jack.

Jack looked up and stared the big man dead in the eyes. He tried not to flinch as saw the deep anger boiling from behind his blackened pupils, but then his body froze as he heard the big man growl like a suffering beast.

"This is it. This is how it's all going down," he thought to himself.

Deep within his stubborn mind, Jack had just as much hatred for the homeless man. Their earlier altercation was the only street fight that he didn't walk away victorious from, and here was his only chance to regain his reputation, and redeem any self-worth that he might have left for himself.

He then dropped his vision to the icy sidewalk, and saw his trusty steel friend lying right beside him. He reached out, grabbed the knife and immediately swung it awkwardly through the air. The big man just stood there and prepared himself by gripping his precious trophy tighter.

"Get up and fight like a man ...you   ... you fucking piece of shit," the homeless man said, as he returned the same vulgar insult to who initially said it to him.

Jack fumbled but eventually stood up. His legs wobbled as he looked at the towering man with both intimidating fear and sweet revenge. He felt a slight sense of security having his switchblade back in his hand, but he knew more blood would be spilled before this confrontation was over.

"I'm going to kill you!" Jack screamed with a vengeance.

The big man snarled at the idea as he stood his ground. He watched and listened as the gang leader poised his threats, while waving his shiny blade through the cold air.

"And then I'm going to take your fucking trophy, and shove it up your fucking ass!"

The big man's knuckles became white; he squeezed the golden piece with extreme intensity and anger. He gave Jack one more deadly stare, and then like an untamed animal, he charged the young punk. With pure hatred spewing from his heart, he swung his loaded fist directly towards his opponents head. Jack swerved out of the way, just in time to avoid the big man's unexpected assault.

"I'm gonna slice you up!" He shouted, as he held his knife up in front of him.

The big man was amped and took no heed to his adversaries warning. Jack stepped cautiously upon the icy sidewalk, awaiting the man's next move, which abruptly came following his menacing statement. Again, the big man swung his prize procession at the face of his despised enemy, but once again with no success.

"Come on mother fucker!" Jack screamed up at the man.

Jack could see the thick condensation expelling from the homeless man's flaring nostrils, and the impatience growing deep within his eyes. He continued to wave his knife through the air, as he took a few steps closer to the big man, trying to get into a striking position. The sharp blade feverishly danced just inches from the homeless man's face, but he just retaliated by gripping the trophy tighter and swinging it back around once again.

201

Jack saw the man's golden weapon coming from beyond his shoulder, but he had foolishly gotten too close to avoid it this time. In his only defense he plunged his knife forward and was able to stab into the big man's stomach, before he felt the dull corner of the marble base connect with his head once again.

The man instantly felt the sharp steel pierce his flesh. He stumbled backwards and immediately grabbed his abdomen, while he watched his opponent fall to his knees. He grinded his teeth from the grueling pain, then gripped the golden trophy tighter and proceeded back over to Jack.

Jack saw the dark, enormous shadow coming towards him and he immediately moved out of the way. He could hear the sound of the big man's arm swinging the object viciously, which caused him to quickly roll onto his back, and then point the knife straight up into the air as his only defense. The marble base and the steel blade clashed once and then twice, causing Jack to suddenly relinquish the grip on his weapon. He felt an immediate rush of genuine fear as he stared up at the dominating homeless man, and looked him dead in the eyes with a plea for mercy, knowing he had just lost his only hope.

The big man leered down at his helpless foe and relished in the moment, as he focused on the blood trickling down Jack's pitiful face. He took a slow deep breath, exhaled, and then graciously took two steps backwards.

"Get up coward," He badgered his enemy.

Jack located his switchblade, and he quickly slithered across the icy sidewalk towards it. His cold, numbing hand grabbed the base of the knife, and then he slowly propped himself back to his feet. He held the sharp blade up once again, as he tried to prepare himself for the big man's forthcoming attack.

The homeless man followed the shiny knife as it began to dance through the cold air once again. His spine twitched as he witnessed his own blood covering the pointy gleaming blade. He groaned beneath his beard, trying to withstand the pain, as he stood tall and proud, awaiting Jack's next move.

Jack was silent and admittedly scared. For a second, the thought of turning and running from the battle seemed rational, but he knew his ego couldn't carry the weight of the word coward upon his shoulders for the rest of his life. He looked at his opponent a final time, before he scraped up his last ounce of bravery and then, with a wielding knife, charged the man.

The big man swung his packed fist, as he saw Jack suddenly

202

lunge towards him. The marble base once again united with his opponent's head, but Jack's burst of adrenaline kept his determination pertinent. He felt the rock-hard corner crack his skull, but his body's forward momentum kept its persistence and was able to get close to the big man. He reached out and grabbed the man's coat tightly with his left hand, as he raised his right arm up into the air and quickly plunged the knife down into his chest.

The homeless man felt the blade slice into him, causing him to immediately drop his weapon. He looked down at Jack's bloody face, and loathed the evil grin he saw so proudly displayed. He quickly reached out and gripped the young punk's leather jacket and lifted him up off the ground. Jack held onto both the man's coat and his weapon for dear life.

"Die motherfucker!" He screamed into the face of the big man, as he pushed his dagger even deeper into his chest.

The big man felt Jack's warm breath upon his face as he stared into the possessed eyes of his aggressor. He grinded his teeth immensely as he growled with severe pain. And then with conjured force, he pulled Jack off him and viciously threw him down to the ground.

Jack's hands were suddenly ripped free of both the man's coat and his weapon. From the sidewalk he looked up at his dying foe and screamed once again, "Die motherfucker, die!" Then a vision of his older brother Jeffrey appeared in his mind, saying, "The bigger they are the harder they'll fall."

The homeless man stumbled backwards but miraculously remained standing. He looked at Jack lying upon the ground, and then at the knife lodged within his chest. He reached up and grabbed the black metal handle and began to slowly pull it out. He groaned like a suffering beast until he finally extracted the steel blade from his wound, and then focused his attention back on Jack.

"Fall motherfucker …Fall!" Jack screamed.

He held the bloody blade in his right hand and snarled down at the young punk. Jack immediately panicked and tried to get to his feet, but he was unable to find the traction needed and remained trapped within the man's presence. He dug his hands into the snow and tried to push himself further away, as the big man took a fumbling step forward. He could see the blood gushing from the open gash he inflicted, but that wasn't stopping the restitution the homeless man had within his heart and soul. He stared up at the wounded giant, and then directly at his hand holding the lost sharp possession. Jack held his breath, anticipating his proverbial fate, as the big man took another step closer to him.

Chapter 20

Officer Phillips hastily searched the bleak remote area, calling out Allison's name constantly along the way. He reached the adjacent corner and stood helplessly in the middle of the cold, desolate intersection. His eyes strained against the winter's wind, as they tried to scour the darkness that dominated the downtown district.

In the distance, he heard the faint sound of the approaching ambulance, but then he thought he also heard a high-pitched scream intertwining with the noise of the siren. He turned his head, trying to distinguish between the two projecting sounds and which direction they were possibly coming from, but as the emergency vehicle drew nearer, its roaring volume overpowered his auditory perception.

***

Allison turned the corner and continued running desperately towards the shelter. Her feet slid madly on the icy pavement, as her mind fought with terrorizing thoughts of the homeless man, Jack and her miraculous deliverance from death. Her frenzied scream continued to pierce the silence, as she stumbled across the avenue and ultimately reached the far corner. She rounded the bend and immediately saw a pair of headlights in the close distance, which caused her to run into the middle of the street and begin waving her arms frantically in the air.

***

"What the fuck?" Houston said to himself, as he saw up ahead, the vision of a person dart out into the middle of the street.

He quickly flashed on his high beams to identify the stranger, and was startled, and then overjoyed, to see Allison running towards him.

"I'll be damned," he said, as he pulled up and immediately got out of his car. He instantly saw the look of horror imbedded on her face as he quickly approached her.

"Are you alright? Where'd you go? Why'd you get out of the car? Don't you know you could've been killed?" He said consecutively, as he put his arm around her shoulder.

Allison began to shake uncontrollably under Houston's protective arm. She tried to speak, but couldn't.

"You're okay. You're safe now," Houston said, trying to comfort Allison's sudden trauma.

"Let's get out of the cold," he said, leading her to the passenger door of his car.

He grabbed the handle, opened the door then slowly helped her into the vehicle. He took caution as he securely seated her and then closed the door. He hurried back around the car then got inside. He sat quietly for a moment and stared out of the front windshield. He took a deep breath and then looked over at Allison. Her body was still convulsing as she tearfully stared out the side window.

"Are you hurt in any way?"

Allison remained silent, but shook her head in a negative motion.

"You're gonna be alright. Try to calm down and tell me what happened."

Allison tried to speak, but her voice was gone from screaming.

"Did you see the homeless man?"

Allison heard Houston's question and responded by mumbling something.

"Yes? You saw him? Where?"

"He saved me," Allison whispered.

"What? ...What did you say?"

Allison turned her head, looked Houston in the eyes and with a sore, raspy voice, she repeated the words, "He saved me."

***

The big man dragged his feet across the snow as he closed in on his enemy. He held Jack's knife with a vengeance as he hovered over the slithering punk. He slowly raised the sharp blade, and then proposed a lethal threat to his opposition.

Jack wallowed upon the ground, trying to avoid the impending peril from the unstoppable homeless man. His eyes became fixated on the intimidating steel object being pointed directly at him. He felt a true feeling of fear and cowardice, as his hands and feet continued to franticly backtrack upon the icy sidewalk.

The big man felt a deep pain within his body, but it didn't

compare to the hatred he held within his heart. He next mustered up every last bit of pride and determination he had left, and began swinging the relinquished item erratically at his rival.

Jack immediately rolled onto his side, trying to avoid the unleashed onslaught of terror behind the wielding blade. He panicked as he tried to get to his feet, but they continued to slip underneath him. He remained on the ground and stared up at the unstoppable villain he had created, before he saw a bright brilliant glare whisk past his face. Within seconds, Jack felt the repercussion, as he grimaced from the intense sting that suddenly embraced his newly lacerated cheek. He held his breath as his eyes continued to follow the sharp blade, as it reached its highest point over the big man's shoulder, before it made its rapid return on the anticipated down swing.

He quickly lunged forward, trying to avoid the next deadly strike and possibly tackle the homeless man, but the big man's stubborn feet remained firmly planted. He grasped and then pitifully held onto the man's legs as he began to cry, awaiting his final moment and the restitution for his sins. He stared down at the red-splattered snow that surrounded him and his foe, while thoughts of what Slugger said filled his mind, and he began to pray to a God. He got lost in his momentary sanction, until his thoughts were abruptly halted by the acute grip of the big man's hand grabbing the back of his leather jacket.

The homeless man grew weaker by the minute, but he swore to himself he wasn't going out alone. He reached down, grabbed Jack and yanked him up. He quickly spun him around, and then brought him close to his chest. He held him as tight as he could, as he slid the sharp knife under his chin and then against his throat.

His hand began to shake as he began to recall all of the disputes he had with Jack earlier. Memories of them by the park started to intertwine with the fight behind the restaurant, to what was going on right then and there. His intense thoughts continued to fuel his anger, as his murderous dark side returned with fatal intent. His enraged mind was momentarily content; he suddenly heard Jack's bloody screams, as he pressed the sharp edge of the switchblade firmly into the flesh of his sworn enemy.

The knife's shiny steel began to slowly disappear, as it dug deeper and deeper into Jack's throat. It began to neatly carve its way through the muscle, cartilage and arteries of the young man as it made its way to the center of his neck. Jack continued to scream, as he felt every agonizing slice from his lifelong friend cutting into his skin. His feet slid madly upon the once white snow, as his body jerked uncontrollably within the dominance of the big man's hold.

An overwhelming feeling of sadistic gratitude showered the big man's consciousness, as his ruthless hand continued its remorseless deed. The sharp, sturdy weapon maliciously slashed its immoral trench with fury, until it collided with a hardened bone. The merciless man felt the blade suddenly stop as it reached the middle of Jack's severed neck. He paused, retightened his grip, and then pressed the sharp knife harder and deeper into the solid obstacle, but the edge refused to penetrate the stubborn matter. Disappointed and still unsatisfied with his hell-bent revenge, he withdrew the switchblade from his victims' neck and threw it to the blood-covered ground. He then repositioned his large hand to the side of his enemy's head and began to violently push.

Jack's dying eyes looked up at the fading street light and mentally caressed its luminous glow. He stared directly into the bulb, as his vision and mind conjured up images of his family. He saw a jumbled collage of mental pictures that included his dad, his older brother and then his mother. He saw her through the eyes of a very small child being held by a young, sweet and sober parent. He stared hopelessly at her joyous smile, causing his soothing thoughts to momentarily ease away his torturous pain, until he felt one last excruciating snap, and that came from his neck as he instantly entered into the realm of death.

The deranged mind of the homeless man experienced another personal heroic moment, as he felt Jack's life end directly under the strength of his own hand. He released his grip and leered down at his enemy's lifeless head swaying back and forth. He held his body proudly within his arms, as his mind recalled more childhood memories accompanied by a rip roaring crowd. Mentally, he imagined hearing loud, boisterous ovations from devoted fans applauding him for his good deed, but then his head began to rattle as the fictitious cheers grew louder, because the fans wanted more action, more violence ...and most of all, more blood.

He released his strenuous hold upon Jack's deceased body and watched it fall, face first onto the red slushy ground. He then placed his large boot securely across the back of his enemy's body as he bent down and grabbed hold of his long blonde ponytail. His hand gripped Jack's hair tightly, as he slowly raised his head up and looked into the dark sky. He imagined seeing all the faces of the screaming fans as they cheered him on for the grand finale. His unstable mind absorbed all the erratic encouragement and then, with a heartless soul, and a handful of Jack's mane, the big man proceeded to slowly yank upwards.

He growled as his muscles strained against the remaining

unscathed flesh and tendons, but eventually the forceful tension ripped it all apart. Blood gushed from the top of the lifeless body, as the big man sadistically pulled Jack's head from his shoulders. He stumbled slightly backwards upon the blasphemous decapitation, but he regained his composure and stood proud, as he held up his new trophy for all of his imaginary fans to see.

He looked at Jack's bloody face, and began to remember all the threats and insults the now headless gang leader said to him earlier. His scattered mind suddenly created a handful of memories, but it abruptly stopped on the recollection of Jack asking him his name. He stared long and hard at Jack's pitiful face, and then in a low husky voice said, "I'm NED ... and you're dead."

In his mind, the crowd went completely crazy once again; they couldn't get enough of the mayhem. He pictured them all beginning to chant his name, NED ...NED ...NED!!! He held Jack's bloody head up into the air like a gladiator one last time, before he under-handedly tossed it into the cold winter sky.

The homeless man watched as Jack's head spun clockwise, as it rose to its highest peak and then quickly descended downwards. Upon impact, the severed item made a loud thump as it landed directly in the middle of the street. The sudden, blustering sound of Jack's head hitting the ground snapped the homeless man out of his trance-like state and immediately back to reality, where the sound of the fictitious roaring crowd was instantly replaced by a distant, but real siren.

He looked down the block in the direction of the wailing sound and then down at himself. He saw his blood still seeping rapidly out of his chest, and then felt the return of his agonizing pain, which finalized his dying state.

Like second nature, he automatically stuck his hand into his coat's inner pocket and was instantly startled to find it empty. He began to panic, as his blurry eyes searched blindly around for the trophy, but he was quickly relieved upon seeing the golden glare nestled within the white and red snow. He limped over, reached down and grabbed his prized possession from the ground. He held it securely in his hand, as he brought it up to his face and once again stared at the empty space that once occupied the golden smile. He felt his heart ache again, as he rubbed his blood stained thumb across the jagged neck, wishing to hear Scotty's humbling voice one last time. The big man shook his head with utter disappointment, and then shifted his attention to the serene darkness that engulfed the narrow alleyway. He stared deep into its hidden shadows as his stumbling feet reentered back into the familiar gloom. He managed to get about two yards in, before his weakened body collapsed upon the soft snow.

He groaned as he laid there helpless, suffering, and ultimately dying. He struggled through the intense pain and was able to roll himself over onto his back. With his head now in a flush and comfortable position, he stared up into the dark winter sky. His agony was momentarily subsided as he lost his mind within the black, endless beauty, along with the twinging feeling of an occasional snowflake landing upon his face. He tried to cherish these final moments, as he began to reminisce of all the wonderful memories he had over his lifetime. Joyous flashbacks of his parents and close family members, to best friends and lovers enticed his fading mind, but his rambling memory suddenly stopped, as impressions of his wife Marcia and son Scotty were recalled.

He quickly closed his eyes and tried to permanently capture the stunning images he saw before him. He felt a warm feeling overwhelm his body, as his mind replayed scenes of him kissing his beautiful wife on their wedding day, and then shifting over to him throwing the baseball with his little boy in the park. His memory was so surreal that it caused him to grip the trophy tighter, as he brought it up and rested it upon his bleeding chest. He began to pray, in hope of hearing his son's voice accompany the glorious picture, but his tormented mind kept a bitter silence. A tear rolled down the side of his face as he clung desperately to the golden object, and began his long mental walk down his darkest path.

Chapter 21

Houston tried to comprehend what Allison had just said to him, but it didn't make any sense. The homeless man he was looking for was a deranged maniac.

"What do you mean he saved you?" He anxiously asked.

"There was this guy, and he had a knife, and then all of a sudden ... he was there."

"The homeless man had a knife?"

"No, another guy did, and then the homeless man came out of the alleyway...and ... and...saved me."

Houston looked at Allison and could clearly see the peculiar feeling of sympathy she now had for her unsung hero, but he still had to uphold the law and try to capture the wanted killer.

"Can you tell me exactly where all this took place?" Houston asked.

"Just around the corner."

Houston pressed down on the accelerator and quickly drove to the end of the block. He reached the stop sign and then asked Allison, "Which way?"

Her fear-ridden hand shook as it pointed to the left. Houston turned his head and looked down the avenue, and then turned and looked back at Allison.

"I thought I told you to stay in the car!" He said in a stern manner.

Allison looked up at the detective and said, "I'm sorry, but I suddenly saw a man running out from the back of the shelter, and he looked like the homeless man I saw earlier and he ...well, he was getting away. So I tried to follow him."

"Why? You were almost killed!" Houston raised his voice.

"I did it for Trent ...and his friends. I didn't want the man who killed them to get away. I'm sorry," She said as she began to cry once again.

Houston looked at Allison and couldn't help but respect her, despite the insane move she attempted. He lowered his head in order to calm himself down, and then in a much softer voice said, "I'm sorry too."

There was a brief and awkward moment of silence, before Houston turned his car down the avenue. He drove slowly along the icy black top as Allison directed him again by saying, "Turn right at the corner, he's down there."

Houston sped to the next intersection and then made his turn. He flashed on his high beams to get a brighter view, and immediately saw the severed head lying in the middle of the street.

"Oh my God," Houston said as Allison screamed.

Houston was stunned as he slowly pulled up to Jack's head. He put his car in park and sat there for a moment, as he tried to prepare himself. He unfastened his gun, grabbed his flashlight, and then looked over at Allison.

"That's him!" she screamed.

"That's who?"

"Jack, the man with the knife, the guy who wanted to kill me."

"You're telling me he's the bad guy?" Houston said, pointing to the bloody head.

"Yes, the homeless man must have done that to him."

"Okay, I'm going to get out and take a look, promise me you will stay in the car no matter what!"

Allison nodded her head respectively and then lowered it back down.

"I'm serious; I will be right outside. I'm just going to check on … Jack," Houston said, as he grabbed the handle and slowly got out if his vehicle. He shut the door and walked around to the front of the car to begin his investigation on the new gory scene. He quickly grabbed his radio and contacted Phillips, as he peered downwards at the bloody object by his feet. His eyes stared directly at the frozen expression left on the screaming face of the victim, as he waited for Phillips to answer.

"Did you find her?" Phillips voice said suddenly on the radio.

"Yes …she's fine. She's sitting in my car, but we have another victim."

"Another?"

"Yes, you'll see when you get here."

"Where are you?" Phillips asked.

"Like, a block and a half away from the shelter."

"I'll be right there …by the way, what about the homeless man?"

"There's no sign of him yet." Houston said, as he quickly turned and looked around his vicinity.

"At this point, he's considered real dangerous. Wait for me and we'll search for him together."

"Okay, but hurry," Houston said.

He tucked away his radio and withdrew his weapon. He walked over to the curb and quickly spotted the rest of Jack's remains, lying in a pool of blood upon the icy sidewalk. He held his gun in a ready form, as he slowly walked over and stared down at the headless corpse.

"What the fuck is going on around here tonight?" Houston said out loud, as his eyes focused upon the hideous sight.

He shook his head with disgust then turned his attention over to the dark peacefulness of the alleyway before him. He stared deep into its calming gloom, until he remembered Allison saying that the homeless man appeared from the alleyway. His eyes quickly shifted to the snow-covered ground, where he saw a row of large footprints and a trail of splattered blood leading into the black, bitter darkness.

He reached down and grabbed his flashlight with his left hand, turned it on and pointed it into the alleyway. The bright beam instantly illuminated the narrow passage, leading the man-made trail right to the grounded figure, just a few yards ahead. Houston held the light directly on the still suspect, as he slowly and cautiously walked up to the entrance of the alley. He stopped and shined the light across the motionless body for his own mental identification purposes.

"I'll be damned …that must be the homeless man."

He took a small step into the alleyway as his curiosity began to increase. He waved the beam across the body again and with every passing stroke, he noticed a tiny golden sparkle reflecting back at him. He took a few more steps towards the man and the shiny object, until he was close enough to identify what was causing the mesmerizing glare. His heart skipped a beat as he looked at the lying man, and saw him holding a gold baseball trophy across his bloody chest.

"Holy shit," Houston said, as he held the bright light steadily upon the man's possession.

He then slowly moved the beam up to his grim face, where he observed no movement from the suspect. He took another step closer and brought the aim of his flashlight back down upon the golden trophy.

"I'll be damned," Houston said, as he zeroed in on the shiny object peering out from within the grip of the lifeless man. His eyes traveled from the square marble base to the tarnished bat protruding out from the top of his large hand, but then his eyes were shocked when they suddenly focused down upon the broken part of the trophy.

Houston stared directly at the jagged neck of the golden player, as his mind suddenly recalled the tiny object Phillips had found and had given him down in the sewer. The correlation between the two pieces made him anxious, because he knew there was only one way to confirm the identity of the dead man lying before him. He brought the bright light back to the man's face to reassure himself of his previous assumption and just like before, the suspect remained motionless. Houston took a deep breath, as his right hand slowly holstered his weapon and then reached into his pocket to retrieve the tiny object. His fingertips fumbled upon the item, before he pulled it out and held it within his palm.

"Unfuckingbelievable," Houston said, as he brought the bright light's attention upon the little golden head.

He reexamined its tarnished color and then it's jagged neck. He ran his thumb across the rough surface as he stood amazed by the bizarre, accidental reunion between the two separated pieces.

He turned his head and looked back at Allison sitting in the car. He waved his flashlight in her direction, assuring his safety, and then waved it back down at the homeless man, only to be immediately startled by his unexpected opened eyes, and the unavoidable marble base coming right towards his head.

***

The homeless man momentarily pulled himself from his mental grave and suddenly opened his eyes. He was stunned to see a hovering stranger, and reacted instinctively by swinging his golden weapon. The trophy connected with the unknown culprit and instantly knocked him out, causing him to fall down next to the big man.

Despite his agonizing pain, the homeless man forced himself to sit upright. His head spun with disorientation, as he tried to focus on the contentious situation. He looked down and saw the bright beam from the dropped flashlight aiming directly at the face of the motionless stranger. He slowly raised the golden trophy above his unconscious adversary for yet another bludgeoning strike, when suddenly he saw a tiny golden glare within the flashlight's luminosity.

His mind was bewildered as he stared down at the obscure sparkle that lay just outside the open hand of the fallen victim. He quickly closed his eyes, thinking it was just a strange illusion, but upon reopening, he suddenly gasped with utter amazement as he focused on the details that graced the small item. His head spun with delirious emotions, as he slowly extended his left hand towards the shiny piece. He hesitated at first, allowing just his fingertips to softly touch the object, but when he finally grabbed it and held it in his palm, he felt a warm, overwhelming feeling from their joyous reunion.

A tear instantly fell from the big man's eye when he suddenly realized his dream just became a reality. Both of his hands began to tremble from anxiety and fear, as he speculated the glorious outcome by possibly reconnecting the two items. He took a short and painful breath, trying to calm his emotions enough to successfully complete his challenge.

His right hand gripped the body of the trophy and held it securely upon his lap, while his left hand raised his newfound object up to his eyes for a positive confirmation. He stared at the familiar face of the little baseball player, as he rolled it around between his bloody fingertips. He then brought the golden head up to his mouth and kissed it like he had a thousand times before.

He cherished the unimaginable moment, but the divine result was what he'd been anticipating. His left hand began to jitter as he guided the missing piece back down to its rightful spot and began trying to connect them. The tarnished metal rubbed and scraped against each other as the homeless man struggled, but eventually was able hold the two items back together again.

The big man suddenly felt a comforting feeling of peace throughout his dying body, as he simultaneously heard the miraculous return of Scotty's child-liked voice within his deranged mind.

"I missed you daddy," the imaginary youngster said with sincerity.

***

Officer Phillips began running towards the destination Houston had given him on his radio. He reached the corner of the avenue and quickly turned down the sidewalk en route to the next block. As his feet moved along quickly, so did his mind. His head was filled with emotions, from feeling relieved that Allison was once again safe, to the apprehension of the homeless man in honor of all of the brutally murdered victims.

He advanced to the next corner, rounded the bend and immediately saw Houston's car parked in the middle of the street. He ran quickly down the icy walkway, until he came within a few yards away from Jack's headless body. He stopped, withdrew his firearm, and then slowly approached the horrific crime scene.His hand held his gun with great tension, as his eyes looked down at the slaughtered individual and its blood soaked surroundings.

"Damn another fucking bloodbath," he said out loud to himself.

He turned his head away from the vile scene and turned his attention towards Houston's parked car. He saw Allison sitting up in the front seat, waving her hands and pounding on the passenger window. He motioned over to her with a slight tilt of his head as he cautiously stepped passed Jack's headless body. He kept his attention on the young woman, until his eyes looked deeper in the car and he noticed the empty driver's seat.

Phillips turned his head and quickly scanned the area, as he shouted out the detective's name. He waited for a response, but he only heard the sounds of the brash, gusty wind and Allison's fists hitting the car's window. He called his name out once again, but this time he heard a sound coming from behind him. He quickly turned around and was initially shocked, as his startled eyes looked blindly into the dark alleyway.

He pointed his gun into the darkness as he slowly stepped across the bloodstained snow, towards the entrance. He called out the detective's name a final time and then listened closely. Within a few seconds, he heard another suffering sound coming from within the dark alley. As he progressed even closer to the opening he could see up ahead, a small beam of light from a dropped flashlight lying on the pavement. He then heard another moan, and his eyes were able to focus on the one shadowy figure lying on the alley's snow-covered ground.

Phillips reached down, grabbed his flashlight from his belt and turned it on, but his motions were abruptly interrupted when he suddenly heard Allison's voice. He turned his head towards the parked car, and saw her standing behind a slightly open passenger door.

"Don't go in there!" She cried out desperately to the naïve officer.

He heard her warning, but he suddenly heard something directly behind him. He quickly turned his head back towards the dark alleyway, just in time to see a close-up view of the gray marble base, and the large right hand fist of the man administering the unexpected blow. The solid bottom of the headless trophy was merciless as it plunged out of the darkness, aiming right for Phillips. His hat fell towards the ground, a second before the dull hardened corner hit his head and ripped into his flesh.

Phillips felt the powerful force behind the sudden impact and fell instantly to the icy sidewalk. He began to squirm upon the blood-drenched snow, from the pain and the initial shock from the surprise

216

assault. He reached up and touched his open wound, while he heard the sound of Allison's screams fading in and out from somewhere behind him. His tearing eyes blindly looked back towards her loud voice, but his vision was distorted. He then pulled his hand off his head and gasped as he stared at his bloody fingers. He then gasped again when he looked straight up and saw the large, malevolent figure towering over him.

The dim streetlights kept the face of the attacker a dark blur to his eyes, but Phillips could see the man's long gray hair blowing in the snowy wind, and the shiny weapon he held within his hand. He then watched the rise of the glimmering object as the big man proceeded to lift it up and over his head. The stunned police officer stared at the hazy glow, as it rested momentarily against the cold, dark sky, but then he quickly panicked upon seeing the rapid descent of the golden trophy coming down towards him again.

Phillips dug his palms into the cold red snow and franticly pushed himself backwards, trying to escape another vicious, and possibly deadly, blow. His body slid across the slippery sidewalk, as the loaded fist of the homeless man came plunging down, but luckily missed his face by just inches. He dug his hands deeper into the snow and pushed himself back once again, but this time, his trembling body was suddenly stopped short as he collided with what was already lying stiff on the icy sidewalk.

He laid still for a second and kept one eye on the homeless man, while his other tried to see what was blocking his way. He slowly turn his head and saw the black leather jacket first, but then his eyes traveled upwards and he realized that he was lying next to Jack's headless body. His mind went into a state of hysteria as he focused directly at all the jagged cuts around the victims neck, and then at a grotesque combination of sliced arteries, severed tissues and a broken neck bone.

He tried to scream, but his voice was stolen from utter fear. His brain was delirious and also oblivious to the corner of the marble base, as it came sweeping back down towards his face, determined to repeat its last grisly act. A new bloodstain graced the bottom of the trophy after it collided perfectly with the police officer. Phillips flinched then immediately saw stars, as the hard carved stone came sweeping down and hit him directly across his nose. Two streams of blood shot out from both of his nostrils simultaneously, and splattered across his cold rosy cheeks as his mouth silently screamed. The powerful hit made him instantly disorientated, and in an attempt to ward off the relentless assault, he began waving his hands mercilessly in the air, begging for the beating to stop. He then dug his heels into the patchy snow and tried desperately to push himself away from the violent homeless man, but

Jack's headless corpse blocked his escape. As he lay helplessly on his back, his right hand began fumbling for his holstered gun, knowing it was his only chance to save his life.

***

The homeless man raised his loaded right fist up once again, while his left hand kept a closed solid grip on his newly found and important item. He squeezed the tiny golden head just enough to reinsure its safety, before he continued his brutal assault. He snarled under his long gray beard, as he took another step closer to the injured officer, preparing himself for his victim's fatal blow. His bloodshot eyes focused directly down at their target, as his anxious right hand began to shake with anticipation and deadly desire. The homeless man saw red as his lethal hand began its final descent towards Philips, when his focus was suddenly interrupted due to hearing a loud and desperate scream of …"NED!"

***

Allison, who was now panic-stricken, screamed the name of the homeless man so loud, as she watched him take another step towards the already injured officer and raise his golden weapon in a deadly manner. She didn't know what else to do to stop the killer from carrying out his murderous deed but yell at him.

"Stop! … NED! …Stop!" Allison cried, as she screamed over and over again.

***

The homeless man suddenly halted his lethal attack when he suddenly heard the high-pitched tone of a loud, feminine voice call out his alter-ego name. He turned his attention towards the boisterous distraction, and his angry eyes instantly felt a warm, soothing sensation upon seeing the vision of Allison once again. He found her angelic and mesmerizing, as he stared at her long, swaying blonde hair and her young, wholesome face. He imagined she was sent here from heaven, to take him away from his miserable life. His unstable mind began to drift, when he suddenly heard two loud gun shots come from behind him. It took about a second before he felt the first, and then the second, blistering bullet enter his body through his back.

218

He fought the pain at first as he kept his eyes on Allison, but eventually, he fell to his knees upon the bloody snow. He lifted his head and looked up into the winter's sky for some inner strength, as another tear rolled down his face. He then looked down and opened both of his hands. He gripped the broken trophy tightly in his right hand, as his left hand moved the little golden head to his fingertips. His blurry eyes struggled to see, but his hands once again quickly rejoined in unison, with a specific mission to accomplish. His fingers fumbled, as he began trying desperately to reconnect the two broken pieces back together. It took several tries, but eventually the old, dying man was able to hold the dual objects back in their proper aligned place. Within seconds, his brain was instantly filled with his son's glorious imaginary voice once again.

"I love you daddy," Scotty said softly, within his fragile and twisted mind.

The homeless man slowly closed his eyes and began a fictitious conversation with his deceased son. He conjured up a mental image of himself and the young boy, playing catch on a sunny spring day.

"I've been waiting for you daddy … and Mommy's here too," The boy's pleasant voice said, comforting the man's dying pain.

"It's okay dear, you don't have to run anymore. We're here for you now," said Marcia in a soft harmonious voice.

The homeless man immediately summoned up an image of his wife. He then had a celestial vision of both Marcia and Scotty, standing side by side while extending their open arms to him. Mentally, he reached out and grabbed both of their hands, but in the real world, he physically kept the two golden pieces tightly together.

His reunion with his family was beyond belief, as he imagined kissing Marcia's beautiful face, and then bending down and picking up Scotty. He envisioned them all smiling and laughing as a true, happy family, but their joyous reunion was extremely short-lived as he heard another loud gunshot come from behind him, and within less than a second, his mind went completely blank.

***

The barrel on Houston's gun was still smoking after he finally took aim and ended the evening's mayhem, by putting a bullet right in the back of the head of the homeless man.

***

Phillips heard the fatal gunshot ring out from the dark alleyway, before his eyes witnessed the homeless man falling down dead, right beside him.

***

Allison screamed as she heard the sound of another loud gunshot, and then a second later, saw the homeless man known as NED …fall lifeless onto the winter snow.

The End

Made in the USA
Charleston, SC
31 July 2016